"I'm guessing you ☑ **P9-DLZ-295 to meet with you,"** she said and smiled. He smiled back, looking at her as though they'd already sealed the deal.

"You need my help," he said, sounding confident. Assured. Not the least bit egotistical, though how he managed that she didn't know. He had a lot to be proud of. He sounded...willing to help.

"Yes," she said, opening Bill Heber's file.

"You want me to join the High Risk Team, and I have to tell you, I'm intrigued..."

"No!" She hadn't meant to blurt out the word. But there was no way she wanted to work with the man on a regular basis. "I'm sorry," she said, glancing at the file that would right her brain instantly. "I need your help with a case."

She couldn't lose Suzie Heber. She just couldn't. And it was in his power to help her make certain that didn't happen.

* * *

Dear Reader,

I was invited to a reader event as I was writing this book. After an unfortunate night, I was sitting at a table feeling as though I wasn't contributing when a reader sat down, immediately filling the space with calm. With a sense of kindness. She happened to be carrying some lavender oil—my go-to when I'm stressed—and offered it to me. I was rejuvenated, as much by her kindness to a stranger as by the oil.

This angel, an avid romance reader, was also a probation officer, just like my hero, Jayden. One who believed successful rehabilitation was possible and tried to help her clients achieve their second chances—again, just like the hero I was writing. This woman graciously answered my many questions over the next weeks, via messaging, to bring Jayden most completely and accurately to life. All good things about Jayden's work come through her. Any mistakes in the representation are mine.

Beth Maeder, thank you. For Jayden. For the lavender oil. But mostly for the heart and kindness you bring to the world. Your clients, your fellow officers and the citizens you help protect are very lucky to have you.

Tara Taylor

SHIELDED IN THE SHADOWS

Tara Taylor Quinn

HARLEQUIN

ROMANTIC
SUSPENSE

HARLEQUIN®
ROMANTIC SUSPENSE™

Recycling programs
for this product may
not exist in your area.

ISBN-13: 978-1-335-62659-2

Shielded in the Shadows

Copyright © 2020 by TTQ Books LLC

This edition published by arrangement with Harlequin Books S.A.

For questions and comments about the quality of this book,
please contact us at CustomerService@Harlequin.com.

Harlequin Enterprises ULC
22 Adelaide St. West, 40th Floor
Toronto, Ontario M5H 4E3, Canada
www.Harlequin.com

Printed in U.S.A.

Having written over ninety novels, **Tara Taylor Quinn** is a *USA TODAY* bestselling author with more than seven million copies sold. She is known for delivering intense, emotional fiction. Tara is a past president of Romance Writers of America and a seven-time RITA® Award finalist. She has also appeared on TV across the country, including *CBS Sunday Morning*. She supports the National Domestic Violence Hotline. If you need help, please contact 1-800-799-7233.

Books by Tara Taylor Quinn

Harlequin Romantic Suspense

Where Secrets are Safe

Her Detective's Secret Intent
Shielded in the Shadows

The Coltons of Mustang Valley

Colton's Lethal Reunion

Harlequin Special Edition

The Parent Portal

Having the Soldier's Baby
A Baby Affair
Her Motherhood Wish

The Daycare Chronicles

Her Lost and Found Baby
An Unexpected Christmas Baby
The Baby Arrangement

The Fortunes of Texas

Fortune's Christmas Baby

Visit the Author Profile page at
Harlequin.com for more titles.

For Adam Stoddard, another officer who made a tough choice, stood by it and won my respect even before he met my daughter and became a member of my family.

Chapter 1

Shots rang out. At first, Jayden Powell had thought a car had backfired. Ducking behind a tree by instinct, he identified the source as gunfire seconds before the sound came again and he fell backward with the force to his chest. Upper left. The only part not shielded by the trunk he'd been using for cover.

Lying still, in agony, his head turned to the side on the unevenly cut lawn, Jayden played dead, figuring that's what the perp wanted: him dead. Praying that it was enough. That the guy wouldn't shoot again, just for spite. Or kicks.

A long blade of grass stuck up his nose. Tickling. Irritating. Damn. If he sneezed, he'd be dead. Killed again—by a sneeze. Did his breathing show? Should he try to hold his breath?

Why wasn't he hearing sirens?

They were in Santa Raquel, California. It was an oceanside town with full police protection—not some burg where they had to wait on County, like some of the other places he served.

His nose twitched. Had to be two blades of grass. One up inside trying to crawl back into his throat. One poking at the edge of his nostril. Maybe if his chest burned a little more, he wouldn't notice. Maybe if someone mowed once in a while, a guy could play dead in the front yard without fear of exposure.

Where in the hell was Jasper? His sometime partner and fellow probation officer, Leon Jasper, had waited in the car on this one, just as Jayden, the senior of the two, had insisted. Harold Wallace was Jayden's offender. His newest client. He preferred first meets to be one-on-one.

Good thing, too, or Leon would be lying right next to him—and the guy had a wife with a kid on the way. A boy. No…maybe a girl. Had he actually heard yet?

Jayden was going to sneeze. If he took another breath, he'd be dead for sure. Maybe just a small inhalation through the mouth. Slow and long and easy, just like he'd been doing. Right?

Shouldn't have let his mouth fall open. Now he had grass there, too. It tasted like sour bugs and…

Sirens blared in the distance. An unmistakable sound. Thank God.

Prosecutor Emma Martin was having a chicken salad sandwich in her office when a paralegal stopped to tell her that there'd been a shooting and an officer was down. Immediately concerned, she could hardly get the bite in her mouth past her dry throat.

"Is he alive?" she asked Kenny, the best paralegal

she'd ever worked with. Married with three kids, Kenny was an integral part of the mechanism that kept the district attorney's office running smoothly. At the moment, Emma wanted to run out and help gather every detail that would put a cop-shooting perpetrator behind bars for good.

"Yeah, he was wearing his vest, thank God," Kenny told her, his balding head bobbing up and down a couple of times to punctuate his words. Something so intrinsically him, the bob had become a "Kenny" trademark. "He's at the hospital but insisted on going in his own car."

"He drove himself?"

"I heard his partner took him."

Ready to leave her lunch behind and get on the case, to be ready to help obtain warrants and find the culprit as soon as possible, if she was assigned the case, she asked, "Who was it?"

"Powell."

Her jaw dropped. The man she'd been thinking about while eating lunch?

"Jayden Powell?" she asked, heart thudding for no valid reason. She already knew the probation officer was okay.

And it wasn't like she knew him personally.

Or even wanted to.

She'd been planning to call him, though. To request a sit-down. This morning, one of his client's names had come up at the meeting of the High Risk team—a group comprised of professionals from the fields of education, medicine, law, counseling, domestic violence shelter workers and law enforcement who came together with the sole purpose of preventing domestic violence deaths.

Had Bill Heber, the offender she'd needed to speak with Powell about, been involved in the morning's shooting?

"Is the shooter in custody?" If it was Bill, that would be great news.

"Yeah. Shame, too. It was the thirteen-year-old son of the offender. Powell had set up a first meet at the guy's home." A "first meet." The offender was newly out on parole if Powell was seeing him on the outside for the first time.

"Was his partner hit, too?"

"No, Powell insisted the guy wait in the car."

Powell had been doing a first meet at the home of an offender who was already armed just two days after getting out? Reading the guy's record, in prison and before, should have given Powell some indication that he might want to schedule that meet in a more protected setting...

Reckless.

And fitting, too, from what she'd heard about Powell. He went all out for the job, which was good, but he was also known as a bit of risk-taker.

Those were the types of men she usually went for. Which was why she'd been thinking about him over lunch. Worrying over the call she had to make. She wasn't going to let herself be at all sidetracked by desires that had never served her well.

"I'm assuming they brought the offender in, too?" A newly released parolee wasn't permitted on any premises with guns. Possible charges, degrees of same, popped into her brain.

"They held him for questioning, but no, they aren't keeping him. He's the one who disarmed the shooter, his own son. Wasn't Wallace's gun. And he had no idea it was on the premises. Turns out," he continued, "when the kid heard his dad tell his girlfriend some officer was coming to the house, the kid stole the gun from a friend's brother and backtracked to the house instead of going to school. His dad didn't even know he was there. Kid's filled with a boatload of anger. Blames all law enforcement for the fact that his father was put away to begin with. I have a feeling some bad stuff is going to be coming out there—things that happened to the kid while the dad was locked up."

Wow. Okay, then. Possibility off her desk. Minors were not in her area of responsibility.

And the offender wasn't Bill Heber, either—an offender she'd never forget. The forty-two-year-old abuser and his twenty-eight-year-old wife, Suzie, didn't have any children.

Not since the night, four years before, when Bill had beaten his pregnant bride so badly she'd lost the baby she was carrying.

Emma had caught that case. Charged him with attempted murder for Suzie, and second-degree murder for the almost-four-month gestational-aged fetus. And had failed to get the conviction. If she'd gone for lesser abuse charges, she probably would have won. Bill would have been sentenced to four years, served two, and been out. She'd been trying to put the bastard away for life. To protect Suzie for life.

As it turned out, Heber had landed his ass in jail anyway, for breaking and entering. Not her case. But she'd heard he'd been convicted, sentenced to five years and served two. He'd been out for three months and, according to Suzie's physician at the High Risk team meeting that morning, the woman was badly bruised again.

Thank God for the creation of the High Risk team, whose members were legally permitted to report suspected abuse and who, on coming together, were able to get a more complete picture of a victim's circumstances. Sara Havens Edwin, lead counselor at The Lemonade Stand—the unique, resort-like women's shelter in Santa Raquel that had led to the formation of the High Risk team—was charged by the team with keeping in contact with Suzie. Something she'd been doing anyway.

Emma's planned move had been to meet with Bill's current PO: Jayden Powell. A man who was dangerous to her in a completely nonabusive way. His bad-boy way of going beyond protocol, his sexy body—they called to Emma's lesser being. The shadow side of the hardworking, caring, responsible woman she'd always thought herself to be.

That hidden, foolish woman who consistently went for the wrong guys and had the deep burns to prove it.

If it had been left up to him, Jayden would have gone back to the office that afternoon. He could have pushed the point, but figured he'd get more done from home where he could move judiciously and cringe now and then without someone harping at him to rest or take a pill.

No paid meds for him. Or alcohol, either, if he could help it. He didn't have an addictive personality, thank God, or any sign of alcohol dependency. He just didn't like anything messing with his brain.

Or his ability to make decisions. Alcohol contributed to foolish choices—sometimes life-changing ones—and a man was accountable to those choices when he sobered up.

Had to live with the ramifications forever.

He'd learned that lesson the hard way—and his self-imposed penance was the solitary life he lived.

Looking at the massive bruising around his left ribs, he figured he'd gotten off lightly that day. No cracks or breaks. And no blunt force trauma to internal organs. Just discomfort and bruising.

That, he could live with.

His nose had quit itching, too. Thank God. The damned grass had driven him nuts.

In his softest, oldest, hole-spattered T-shirt, a left-over from the police academy, and a pair of gray running shorts, he wandered barefoot out to the kitchen. He looked at the unopened six-pack on the bottom shelf of his refrigerator—the only alcohol in the house—and opted for a fruit-flavored sports drink.

Maybe he'd have a beer with dinner. Or before bed. Lying down wasn't going to be all that pleasant, according to what the emergency room doc had said in his release instructions.

Moving into the extra bedroom, he sat at the desk, flipped on the 70-inch flat-screen TV hung on the opposite wall, and picked up the phone. Every time he left the office, he had his calls forwarded to the home line. Or to his cell if he was going to be away overnight. The message light was blinking on the answering machine. He'd get to those.

Opening the file he'd dropped on his desk when he'd come in, he dialed.

"Pick up, Wallace," he said aloud, reminding himself to feed the goldfish he'd purchased when he'd realized he was talking to himself too much. And then he remembered the feral cat he'd taken in had eaten the fish. He was not caregiver material.

He'd fed the cat that morning. That was a plus.

Three rings and then four. The man had been released and told to go home. If he—

"Yeah?"

"It's Jayden Powell." *Officer Powell* would have been better.

"Yeah."

"What's up with your kid?"

"Yeah."

"Whose gun was it?"

"Some gangbanger brother of a kid I coached in T-ball, for Christ's sake." At one time Wallace had been Joe Dad, a banker climbing the ranks and doing well for himself and his family. And then he'd had an affair and gotten hooked on meth, which had derailed his life. He'd gone to prison for fraud, but on a plea deal.

His wife had died while he was in prison. Though he'd tried to get the courts to let his girlfriend take his son, the boy had ended up in the foster care system—until two days before when Wallace had been released early on good behavior.

"You still clean?" Jayden asked, though he knew if the guy wasn't, he wouldn't get a straight answer.

"I am. I peed for the cops today, just to prove it, too."

Good man, Jayden had thought after he'd read the man's file and watched a tape of his parole hearing. "I gave you the benefit of the doubt, meeting at your home, alone, as you asked," he said.

"Yeah."

"You owe me some good behavior."

"I owe myself and my son good behavior. I don't

know what the hell I owe you. More than that, I'm sure. My kid shot you today."

And that was the crux of the matter, as far as Jayden was concerned. He needed his client to succeed at re-acclimating to the outside. A son in jail and facing charges, his offender blaming himself, wasn't a promising start.

"What about Bettina? Where's she at with all this?" Jayden asked about the woman Wallace'd had the affair with, the woman he was still with. The one who'd turned him on to meth. And, ironically enough, Bettina was the reason the courts had let Wallace's son leave foster care. She had no criminal record and had already been in the process of petitioning for his care.

"Telling me not to blame myself. Yeah, right."

"Is she clean?"

"She never was hooked," Wallace told him. "Only tried it a couple of times. I let her down, too, when I got hooked. But she stuck by me."

"And now?"

"She says Tyler needs me, she needs me, and I better keep my stuff straight."

"I'll help any way I can. I know a lot of people. Can try to smooth things for the kid." What the kid had done was wrong. But he'd done it out of panic and love for his father. To defend his father. There was still a chance for him to turn his life around. And doing that was the best shot Jayden had at getting his client successfully reentered into society.

"He shot you, man!"

"From what they told me today, he had it rough in the system. Heard you talking to Bettina about my visit, was afraid I was taking you back... Why don't you let people show you what they can do before you automatically assume they'll disappoint you?" He'd said the same to Bill Heber in his most recent conversation. That parolee was one he knew better, one who'd passed every single one of Jayden's tests, being where he was supposed to be, doing what he was supposed to be doing, on every surprise visit. And Heber's response had been pretty much the same as Wallace's was then. Complete silence.

"I'll be by in the morning," Jayden said. "Same time. You going to be there?"

"Yeah."

It wasn't any kind of assurance that life would go well for Wallace. Or that he'd manage to not join the statistics of repeat offenders. But it was a start.

Jayden was all about new starts.

Chapter 2

Jayden studied the beer in the refrigerator as he contemplated dinner. Opted for store-bought cookies and milk instead. Mostly he went for the cookies because it was one bend, a grab, and he could take a seat.

He'd listened to his messages—tended to the one call that had come directly from a client. A parolee who wanted to visit his daughter in another county over the weekend. Unfortunately, he'd been unable to allow Luke Lincoln to leave the area and hoped his refusal didn't have adverse effects on the man's progress.

When he'd made a couple of calls to check the man's story, he'd found that the little girl wasn't actually in the hospital, nor had her mother given permission for her father to see her. She'd said something about apparently needing to take out another restraining order against him.

Jayden called for an extra drive-by on Lincoln's house that night, penciling in a time in the morning to make a surprise work visit. And he called police in the county where the mother and daughter resided, alerting them to the possibility that one of his clients might break parole. There was nothing more he could do. Not until the guy actually did something wrong. In the end, everyone had the right to make their own choices. Even bad ones. And if he didn't believe in second chances, he might as well be dead. The system he believed in, and worked for, had a process by which a man was given a second chance. He could help some, but in the end, he had to let that system work, or fail, according to the parolee's individual choice.

That brought him to the return phone call he'd been putting off. He had to make it. Just didn't trust himself not to answer any other types of signals the beautiful prosecutor might put out while they talked business. She never crossed a line or did anything overtly flirtatious. He never would, either. But the tension between them simmered there, ready to ignite if either of them gave it a chance.

According to his take, anyway. And when it came to women, and matters of consensual sex, or even consensual attraction, he could pretty much rely on his take. The one thing he'd always gotten right.

Even when he'd done everything else wrong.

Emma Martin… He hardly knew her. Had only had a few brief conversations with her. And she turned him on like none other.

Weird.

He didn't like it when things—even spontaneous

attraction—happened out of the ordinary. When he didn't completely recognize what was happening.

Too hard to control things like romantic connections.

But he made the call. His job required it, and one thing was absolutely certain. Jayden was all about the job. Because it was his own second chance.

He was still hot.

Maybe hotter.

Shut up!

Emma's internal monologue didn't bode for a good meeting as she strode toward the probation officer standing in the reception area of the newly established Santa Raquel County prosecutor's office.

She'd been out with friends when he'd called the night before. She'd also been halfway through a glass of iced tea at a wine bar and defending herself against their constant barrage in her ongoing fight against giving in and getting a cat. She'd mentioned one night over wine that she hated going home sometimes because there was nothing there but furniture and things. She'd been trying to confide in them about something hugely personal. They'd been certain her solution was a self-sufficient pet.

Growing her family was already in her plans—but not with a cat. Because of her friend's earlier reaction, she wasn't yet sharing that tender and fragile news with anyone. Her friends also had no idea she was prone to thinking that the man in front of her in jeans and a light-colored polo shirt, with a weapon on his hip, was Hunk of the Month material. And good for all twelve months.

"Officer Powell."

"Call me Jayden."

She met his gaze because it would be churlish not to. Took his hand, started to shake it and stopped when he gave a little start. His ribs…he'd told her the night before he was fine, just a bit of bruising, but she figured he'd been making light of his injury.

"How did you sleep?" she asked, trying to ignore the shot of awareness that burst through her as the warmth of his palm connected with hers. And even resisted the urge to wipe her hand down the hip of her slim-fitting black pants—anything to stop the tingling as she stood there next to him.

"In my recliner," he said with a slight chuckle. "Once I got settled, I was fine."

She'd had bruised ribs once—in high school when the male component of her dance partnership failed a lift—and she'd had trouble lying down, and then sitting up, for nearly a month.

He seemed fine. Better than fine. Showing him back to her office, she tried not think of him lying asleep. Didn't want to know what he slept in. His dark hair had always been a little long anytime she'd had a glimpse of him in and out of court or the prosecutor's office, but she'd never noticed before that it curled on the edges where his neck met his shoulders.

He entered the office. She shut the door. Pulled at the bottom of the short, black-and-white suit jacket she was wearing, and half tripped when her pump hit the leg of her desk as she rounded it.

Reaching her chair was almost a feat. She sat with a bit of a thud. She'd done it. Made it.

"Thanks for seeing me on such short notice," she said, indicating with a nod of her head that he should take a seat on the chair in front of her desk.

He sat, a little slowly, but with no obvious pain showing. Hands on his thighs, he looked at her respectfully.
Ready. Completely unaware of her as a woman, she
was sure.

She'd heard he was as much of a workaholic as she
was. Did that mean he was also like her, in that he didn't
allow himself to entertain non-work-related feelings?
How did he manage that? She worked all the time because she honestly loved what she did and wanted to
work all the time. But she'd never managed to find a
way to shut up that shadow side that lurked inside her.
Ready to strike.

Temptation was an evil beast.

If he had found a way to shut down outside of work,
maybe that was something he could pass on to her during their brief association.

"Have you ever heard of the Santa Raquel High Risk
team?" she asked, forcing her romantic thoughts back
into the dark corner of her mind where she usually stayed
without any fuss—where she was mostly glad to hide
out.

Until someone like Jayden Powell came around and
coaxed her out.

"They deal with domestic violence victims, right?"

"They—" She stopped and started again. "*We* were
formed for one purpose only. To prevent domestic violence deaths," she told him. "We're comprised of professionals from any fields that involve working with
victims."

He nodded politely, giving zero indication to his
opinions, which put her on edge.

"The current team consists of a couple of police officers, a pediatrician or his assistant, a charge nurse from

the children's hospital, a couple of adult physicians who take reports from any of their peers to bring to us…" She paused to see if he had any reaction, to see if perhaps he knew of a reason to suspect that Suzie Heber's physician might make a report. But didn't see any indication that the mention of a doctor meant anything to him. And so she continued. "We also have victim counselors, a psychiatrist, me, and representatives from each of Santa Raquel's schools, and most recently a private detective joined the team."

His gaze flickered. Jayden raised his elbows to the arms of the chair, bringing his fingers to steeple at his lips. His torso barely moved.

She still had no idea what he was thinking, but she was pretty certain she had his attention now. Interesting.

"The team meets bimonthly, more if necessary," she continued, partially driven by her bad-girl self who liked that she had the hot parole officer's attention, but, professionally, she had to say exactly what she was saying.

"Everyone reports any suspicious activity they might have noticed, sharing any reports they might have received." She took a quick breath, adding, "A school counselor who noticed that a child was suddenly skittish or exhibiting sudden personality changes. A teacher who notices bruising, or unkempt circumstances. A counselor whose victim might lead professionals to believe that her abuser's anger is escalating. Or a doctor who reports signs of physical abuse noted on a patient. The police report all domestic violence calls they've gone on since the last meeting. We're all there on a volunteer basis and some team members come and go as, say, one physician takes over for another, and so forth.

Right now, other lawyers with information for the team report to me, but there are others who volunteer as team members from time to time, as well."

Dropping his hands, he adjusted his torso in the chair. Nodded. Met her gaze. And she, the professional, was glad he was there. She also wondered if he was uncomfortable in her hard-backed chair. Wondered if she could scare up an upholstered one. Officer Powell might be a risk-taker, the wrong kind of man for her, but he was exactly the kind of probation officer she needed. He wouldn't take any crap from Bill Heber. And he'd keep the man firmly under watch. No matter what it took.

"I'm guessing you know why I've asked to meet with you," she said and smiled.

He smiled back, looking at her as though they'd already sealed the deal.

"You need my help," he said, sounding confident. Assured. Not the least bit egotistical, though how he managed that, she didn't know. He had a lot to be proud of. He sounded…willing to help.

"Yes," she said, opening Bill Heber's file.

"You want me to join the High Risk team, and I have to tell you, I'm intrigued…"

"No!" She hadn't meant to blurt out the word. But there was no way she wanted to work with the man on a regular basis. "I'm sorry," she said, glancing at the file that would right her brain instantly. "I just need your help with a case."

She couldn't lose Suzie Heber. She just couldn't. And it was in his power to help her make certain that didn't happen.

* * *

He'd help her fly to the moon if she asked. Or do his damned best and die trying.

Okay, maybe nothing that drastic, but Jayden was ready to deliver whatever the sexy prosecutor needed. Domestic violence was an insidious disease that had to be wiped out.

"There are several different tools we use in assessing risk. One is something we call a 'risk indicator,' which is a list of nineteen conditions that could lead to a domestic violence death. If a suspect exhibits at least eight of these indicators, the team at least looks at the case. We then put it through a couple of other assessments," she noted. "Of those that come out with high scores, we form an individualized plan of action to keep the victim, or victims, safe. From frequent drive-bys, school monitoring and counseling, to removing them from sight and giving them alternative living situations if need be. Everyone in the victim's life who could play a part is put on alert, if necessary."

Made good sense. He liked it. A lot. Was seriously wondering if the team had room for a parole officer. If he had time to be of good use to them. Some of his offenders had the potential to turn violent, and most had families. If he reported concerns, perhaps he could help make a difference in a new way. Might help his personal résumé—the one only he was privy to—in the second chance department.

"I have someone I'd like to refer to the team as a potential assailant," he said, starting to sit forward until his ribs reminded him that he'd rather not. "A recent parolee," he continued, barely noting the stab of pain.

She looked surprised and…really interested.

"Tell me about him," she said, her eagerness to hear what he had to say openly evident.

"He was in for assault with a deadly weapon," he said, gaining momentum as pieces came together. This was how the world was supposed to work—bringing the right means together at the right time, to make things happen.

"Nearly killed some guy in a bar for saying something to his wife as he passed."

She frowned but said, "Go on."

Yeah, it wasn't a pretty tale. And unfortunately Jayden was struggling to see possibility of a better ending.

"He's been out a week and called last night to tell me that his young daughter is in the hospital and asking for him. Said his ex-wife, who'd divorced him while he was in prison, had called, asking if he could just stop by the hospital for a visit. They're up north, and conditions of his release prevent him from leaving Santa Raquel County."

Her frown deepened as she glanced at the file in front of her and then back at him. "Are you asking for a motion for temporary travel allowance?"

"No." He shook his head. "Not at all. I told him he couldn't go. And then I called his ex. She hasn't spoken to him since he was arrested. She'd already taken a restraining order out on him and had filed for divorce. And his daughter is fine. Hasn't been in the hospital since she was born. Apparently he beat up on his ex but left the girl alone."

Thank God for those huge favors that came along.

"You think he's going to go anyway."

"So does she. Said she was going in for another re-straining order."

"They aren't as effective in these cases as we'd like them to be."

"Which is why I called law enforcement in her area and alerted them to the possible danger to both her and her daughter, but I wasn't satisfied that it was enough. I'd rest a whole lot easier if she had an individualized plan…if people could be put into action to help her…"

Emma picked up a pen, pulled a pad toward her. "We don't have jurisdiction outside Santa Raquel, but I can make some calls, see if they have a team in her area, and if nothing else, get the local shelter involved, even if just by offering the ex-wife some counseling and being on alert. Since it's summer, there's no need to notify the school, but if she's in some kind of summer program or day care, and if there's security wherever the ex-wife works…the team's whole mission is prevention—trying to bridge the gap that only allows law enforcement and justice to step in after the fact. Hopefully we can help."

The woman was remarkable. Her job was to prose-cute crimes, not to tend to victims. And yet, she seemed to find a way to do both. And her work ethic…anyone who had anything to do with the prosecutor's office knew how many hours she put in. He sat there in awe, truly impressed. Even after he realized he was star-ing at her.

"What?"

"You…this isn't even your first area of responsibility and you're like… I'm impressed, that's all."

She shrugged—and he was kind of thinking he saw a bit of red on her cheeks, too. "I had a case that lead me to the team," she said. "And now I'm committed to them. In cities where teams have been implemented, there've been marked decreases in DV deaths. Marked. In one city, at least, they've been completely eradicated since the team was formed."

The passion that poured out of her as she spoke was unmistakable. And lead him to wonder if she was personally involved with someone who'd suffered abuse. He almost asked.

"I need her name," she said. "And the name of your parolee."

Right. Back on track.

He gave the names of Luke and his wife, and their addresses, too, after bringing them up on his phone.

"I'll make some calls as soon as we're done here."

"You said you had a case to discuss with me," he said, remembering. "And then I lay one on you. I'm sorry."

"I'm not. At all. But yes, I do have something that involves another one of your parolees. One of our doctors reported on a patient of his yesterday morning. He said that though she denied having been abused—said she fell off a ladder in a bathtub where she'd been doing some painting—her injuries weren't at all consistent with a fall. Of any kind," she elaborated. "He said there was obvious blunt force trauma, most likely from a male fist, on several parts of her body. When he asked her if someone had hurt her, she was obviously nervous and just kept shaking her head."

Jayden's gut sank. He'd done things he'd never get done paying for; had a death on his conscience that sat with him every minute of every day and would go with him when he died. But he'd never understood physically abusing a woman. Not any woman, in any capacity, for any reason. That's where he drew his line with his parolees, too. If they slid a bit when they first got out, maybe had a drink, or missed a day of work, he'd help them out if he could, but if they ever, ever hurt someone else…he'd get a judge out of bed if he had to, to get the abuser back behind bars immediately.

"A counselor from the local women's shelter, The Lemonade Stand, has since spoken with her, and while Sara is convinced that the woman has been abused, the victim is refusing at this point to admit as much."

"Are there children involved?" He was running a mental check of his client list.

"Not now, no."

Not now. An older guy, then? Out of the thirty men on his roster, that left about half. He was about to ask who they were talking about, so he could offer immediate solutions, when she spoke again.

"Here's the thing. I prosecuted the guy four years ago. His wife was a little over three months pregnant and he beat her so badly she lost the child and nearly died herself."

He lost any appetite he might have had. And wondered why he didn't know about this type of offender on his roster.

"And he's already out?"

"I lost the case because I went after him for murder, thinking I'd get him away from her permanently, not just five or ten years. That turned out to be an overreach."

Now he was frowning. "You said he was one of mine."

"He went away on another charge the next year."

Were they talking about the same guy he'd just told

her about? The thought occurred and was quickly replaced. She'd have said something...

"Santa Raquel police have been alerted. They'll be driving by the house more frequently, keeping a watch on the neighborhood... But without her help, there's not a lot we can do. Yet. And that's where you come in."

He held her gaze with the strength of his intent. "Whatever you need. Who are we talking about?"

"We can't arrest the guy. She won't admit she's been hit, let alone file for a restraining order, so the only other legal avenue we have for keeping a watch on the guy at this point is you. We need you on him like glue."

"Fine. Of course." He'd camp out in the guy's bedroom if that's what it took. "Who is it?" He'd go over—wherever his file told him the guy was supposed to be—immediately. Rearrange the rest of his day if he had to.

Good thing about his job was that his visits were supposed to be surprise sometimes. Or anytime.

She pushed the file toward him. "Bill Heber."

No.

Jayden didn't reach for the file. Didn't need to see what was there. He'd been working with the man for three months, so much so that Bill had become someone he really knew. Someone he cared about.

The man had been in prison for breaking and entering when all he'd been after were his own things from his former home.

Bill had admitted it had been stupid to go to his ex's home when she wasn't there. He'd truly thought that it was best for both of them if he just cleared out his stuff without them having to see each other.

He'd paid dearly for that choice. Had lost a career as

the owner of his own auto repair shop. Had lost almost three years of his life. Was forever a felon.

And doing everything by the book. Everything. All Bill Heber wanted was a life back.

Jayden knew that feeling. And knew that Bill Heber was working as hard as Jayden did to live a life worthy of society. To be given a chance.

To not be judged by his worst mistake. Or to be defined by it. Just three months postprison, working as a grunt in someone else's shop, the last thing the man needed was to be accused of something he hadn't done.

And Jayden was certain Bill hadn't hurt his ex. The man told him about the past case before Jayden even had a chance to ask him about it—though it hadn't sounded at all as the prosecutor had just told it, so much so that he hadn't recognized Bill as the offender she'd been referring to. And all that aside, Bill adored Suzie. Had a picture of her next to the bed in his small apartment. Carried one in his wallet. Not in any hope of ever getting her back. But as a reminder of the man he'd been. One Suzie had fallen in love with and married.

Bill's end goal was to be a man that Suzie could someday forgive. Not for breaking into her home, but for the things he'd done that had led to their divorce in the first place. His jealousy and possessiveness. His inability to believe that a woman as young as beautiful as her would love a crusty guy fourteen years older than she was. The way he'd checked up on her. Hadn't trusted her. The things he'd accused her of. He'd told Jayden about all of them over the past three months.

Even the death of his child. He'd caused it, but not by beating up his wife. Bill told Jayden that Suzie had lost the baby because Bill's constant doubts—even wondering if he was the father of her child—had stressed her to the point of not being able to eat or sleep and she'd miscarried.

And not once, no matter how many surprise visits he'd made, or what time of day or night he'd called, Bill had always been exactly where he was supposed to have been. And he'd been sober, too. Every single time. The man had passed every pee test. Was at work every day when he was supposed to be, and volunteered for all overtime.

In ten years of working with ex-cons, Jayden had never felt as strongly that one of his clients was innocent of reoffending.

Problem was, there was always a chance that he was wrong. Lord knew, he made mistakes.

But his job became clear to him as he sat in the prosecutor's office, looked her in the eye and promised her he'd protect Suzie from her ex-husband.

He'd keep an eye on Bill, all right. He'd catalog every move the man made, if that's what it took to prove to law enforcement, to judges, and to one far too alluring prosecutor, that Bill Heber was not a wife beater. And if he was wrong about Bill, he'd find that out before the man had a chance to hurt anyone again.

In the meantime he'd pray for all he was worth that whoever was hurting that woman was caught and dealt with.

Chapter 3

Most days Emma was confident. Sure of herself and of her place in the world. Felt good about her personal contribution to the universe. She really believed she knew herself, had a handle on her faults, was accountable to her mistakes, and understood her limitations. She paid attention. She owned her shortcomings.

She'd been through counseling after her last disastrous relationship. And again, when, six months before, her biological clock had been ticking double time, and she had to face the fact that while she didn't want to marry the type of man she fell for—didn't want a relationship with that type of man—she did most desperately want a family. She hadn't doubted herself at all as she'd gone through the testing process to have herself inseminated with anonymous donor sperm, chosen from a catalog at the clinic.

But as she sat in the fertility clinic office an hour after her meeting with Jayden Powell on Wednesday morning, she was quaking. Inside and out.

She could have taken a home pregnancy test. Her insemination doctor had given her time tables and suggestions for doing so. She just wasn't ready to bring the whole concept home yet.

Her friends thought she should get a cat. If they only knew…

Marta, her law school study partner and more of a soul friend than the others, would get it. Lori and Stef, she wasn't sure, which was part of the reason she hadn't yet told them what she was doing. They'd worry about her juggling a career that took as much emotional energy as hers did—one that tended to harden a person due to the dregs of society that she dealt with more often than not—with being a single mother.

Especially Stef, the oldest of the four of them. A grandmother who'd opened a small family law firm and dealt with broken families all day every day. Stef would probably think she was being selfish.

Was she?

Maybe the procedure hadn't been successful. Dr. Mobin had explained that it often took more than the one try.

She'd been devastated by the way her marriage had ended. Had taken years to get over the damage it had done. Whatever of it she'd ever get over, that was. Her ability to trust would never be what it was.

And she'd been equally destroyed, in a completely different way, by her only other live-in relationship. She'd hurt a dear, sweet man by her inability to fall completely in love with him. Or to feel any passion for him at all, really.

Drake, the duplicitous risk-taker she'd married in law school, had turned her into a wild woman. And John, one of the few men she'd really trusted, hadn't ignited a single spark. Ms. Shadow Side lived on the wrong track, forcing Emma to shut that train down. Permanently. But she still wanted to be a mother—longed to be a part of a family of her own—and this was the best way for her to do that.

"Ms. Martin?" the dark-haired receptionist called from the door.

She jumped up while her stomach did flip-flops. A baby in there? Upset that she'd moved so quickly?

Oh, God. What if she *wasn't* pregnant?

Her mom and dad, who lived near her younger sister in Florida, already had a slew of grandkids. Their grandbaby expectations where she was concerned weren't high. And Anna, her sister, would definitely prefer that Emma not procreate. She'd always been jealous of Emma, though loving, too. She'd made it no secret to Emma that while their parents were hugely proud of Emma professionally, she liked getting all the grandkid attention.

Emma stepped on the scale. She weighed in one pound heavier! Because she was pregnant! Was she really ready to be a single mom? To have her life change so drastically.

And forever?

Did you want to consider a future with no family of your own? No! came the immediate mental response. She'd always pictured herself as a mother someday. Raising a child. Giving all of the unconditional love that waited down deep inside her. And the past year, she'd felt like every day she was getting older and her whole life was going to be empty if she didn't start the process. Career success wasn't enough anymore. If it ever had been. Wanting a family had always been there. She'd just always figured she'd figure it out in the future. That there was time. Until her birthday had come around again and she'd started to panic.

Taking a seat on the chair in the examining room—she was only there for consultation that morning, for results of the blood test she'd submitted to the day before—she looked at the table, remembering how she'd felt during the insemination process.

How hopeful. And excited.

And how scared she'd been that night, home alone. Lying in bed in the dark, knowing that it was too late to change her mind.

When she realized her thoughts were going in circles that only made her dizzy, she tried to focus on work. On the fact that Jayden Powell had agreed to keep a tight watch on Bill Heber. He'd never said whether or not he'd suspected Bill capable of hurting Suzie again, but he'd shown no surprise when she'd told him what she knew. She was looking forward to a relatively quick arrest, as the probation officer found his client breaking the terms of his probation. Not that Bill seeing his ex-wife was one of those terms. Suzie wasn't getting a restraining order—or even admitting that Bill was hitting her again.

And Emma knew why. The woman didn't trust the system to protect her. Because the system had screwed up on her—*Emma* had screwed up—and Bill had walked free the last time.

Suzie hadn't trusted them enough to let them know if Bill had threatened her again. Hurt her again. The High Risk team hadn't been fully formed back then. Who knew what hell Bill had put her through before he'd been arrested on a completely different, but probably related charge?

He'd broken into Suzie's home. She hadn't known it was him and had called the police. Their investigation had pointed straight to Bill and this time there had been an eye witness...

The door opened. Heart pounding, Emma met the compassionate gaze of the woman standing there, trying to read her results written in those eyes.

Was she pregnant?

Here she was, contemplating her own motherhood, all while thinking about a woman who'd lost a baby to her husband's cruelty. How could she consider bringing a child into such a world as hers?

And yet...how could she not? There was so much good love in the world—who better than someone like Emma to create some more of it?

The doctor was washing her hands.

Did Emma already have family forming?

Was she irrevocably changed? And alone with the responsibility?

"So?" she asked when the doctor didn't immediately announce the news.

"Let me look," she said and walked to the computer screen attached to a rotating arm from the ceiling and started typing.

Oh. My. God. More waiting. Would they haul her to the emergency room if she passed out in the doctor's office? She couldn't afford to miss her afternoon appointments.

Click. Click. Click. She got that the lovely woman standing there in the white coat had to type passwords. That her information was protected. But come on…

Was she?

Was she!

"The test is negative…"

She wasn't.

That was good, right? A relief. No more middle-of-the-night panic attacks about having a child alone. She was glad, really. Had probably been acting prematurely.

So why were there tears pouring down her face?

Emma had herself firmly in hand by the time she walked into the Santa Raquel probation office just before closing that afternoon. She'd put her own personal wants back into the secret place inside her, and was just focused on getting help for Suzie, who had lost her chance to have a family.

Jayden Powell had asked to see her case files pertaining to Bill Heber, as well as the jury poll after she'd lost the case. While she dreaded reliving that horrible time, she would do whatever it took to keep Suzie safe from the fiend Emma'd failed to put away.

Jayden was the way, and the more he knew about Heber, the better able he'd be to recognize tells: those little things a person did that gave them away. Like a gambler who always chewed his lower lip if he had a good hand.

His door was closed. She could hear voices coming from inside, figured his last appointment of the day— one he'd told her about—was running over. With her folders clutched to her chest with both arms, she leaned back against the wall. The hall was sterile. Deserted. Most doors closed with lights out. She'd known that would be the case, too.

What she hadn't known when she'd agreed to the nearly dinnertime appointment in a day that had been fully booked for both of them, was that she'd be attending the meeting not pregnant.

Sadness engulfed her again, as it had been doing in large waves on and off since she'd seen Dr. Mobin. The second the doctor had said the word "negative," her heart had grieved.

The door opened and an older woman in a long, colorful skirt, loose, light green flowing top, and flip-flops came out and moved quickly toward the exit. If she saw Emma, she didn't acknowledge doing so. When Emma glanced back at the doorway, Jayden was standing there. Watching her.

"You ready?" he asked, giving her a smile that was probably professional and warmed her sad heart anyway.

Nodding, she pushed away from the wall and followed him into his office, discarding the absurd thought that she should have gone home and changed at some point she didn't have in her very busy day. The colorful skirt that had just left had been...nice. Nicer than the black pants and white-and-black jacket he'd already seen her in that day.

"She's one of your offenders?" she asked, following him into the small, unadorned room with its two metal desks, each fronted by two plastic chairs. File cabinets lined the walls.

"She is," he said.

He was still in the jeans and shirt he'd had on earlier in the day, too, she noted as he took a seat in the chair with arms and rolling casters behind one of the desks. If she hadn't seen him brace himself slightly on the chair arms as he'd taken his seat, she'd never have known he'd been shot the day before.

"She looks about seventy."

"She's that, too."

"What was she in for?"

"She was caught with stolen property. I don't believe that she took it, but she chose to spend three years in prison rather than tell us who really took the stuff. She's been out a month and having a hard time staying put."

It wouldn't be so bad sticking around if I had Jayden looking after me on a regular basis. Hearing her wayward side in the background of her mind, Emma scooted to the edge of her seat and put the files on the edge of Jayden's desk.

"Were you able to connect with Bill Heber today?" she asked, all business now.

"I was. Goes with the territory of my job," he said with not quite a grin. "My people might not always like to see me coming, but they all want me to see or hear from them if and when I choose to do so."

Because evading their PO was usually grounds for more jail time. For some, that could mean ten years or more. She'd been responsible for sending more than a handful of offenders back to serve the remainder of their sentences for parole violations.

She didn't just want Heber back for the duration of his five years. She wanted him in the cage for the rest of his life.

"And?" she asked the man whose sexiness had no role to play in her current dilemma.

"He was at work, doing exactly what he should have been doing. I told him that I'd be making a random stop-by within the next three days," he continued.

"So he'll make sure he's where he's supposed to be until you do so," she concluded, liking his work style almost as much as Ms. Shadow liked the rest of him.

His shrug was a half nod. Lifting his ankle across his knee, he leaned on the right arm of his chair, looking more like an athlete than an officer of the law—if you ignored the weapon hooked to the belt at his hip. He'd been mostly clean shaved that morning, but had a definite growth of dark stubble now. Together with that weapon, it made him look dangerous.

A dangerous athlete.

"You can't take anything for granted in this business," he said. "I'll be checking up on him without him knowing it, you can rest assured of that."

Thank God. A bit of the tension that she'd been carrying all day started to slowly seep out of her.

"So, what have you got there to show me?" he said next, dropping his foot to the floor as he sat up to the desk and reached for her files. "Let's start first with what the jury thought of him."

Even that she applauded. Knowing how Heber appeared to others, in conjunction with the assessments Jayden already would have done on his client, could help him predict what the man might do next. Or not do.

What did Bill Heber show the world—knowingly or not? Where was he convincing? And not so much?

It was the same type of work she did when trying a

case. How did you expose the perpetrator side of a man who'd probably done some good, too?

Pulling the jury poll from the file, she handed it to him. Waited while he read. Knowing every word by heart. Feeling the knives in her gut all over again.

When Jayden looked back at her, she was surprised to see no change in his expression. No loss of respect. Or sympathy, either.

"Based on testimony, if you'd gone for the abuse charges, you'd probably have won."

Yep. She nodded.

"Why didn't you?"

No one had actually asked the question before. They'd probably thought it. Or answered it for themselves because the answer was obvious.

"He killed his unborn child. He'd have killed her if she hadn't managed to land enough of a heel to his balls to be able to get away. He needs to be behind bars until he's old and feeble."

Jayden's look was pointed. Assessing. Was he judging her?

And then he nodded.

Approval?

Why should it matter?

"Did you interview Suzie Heber?"

"Of course. Multiple times."

"Did her testimony ever waver?"

"No." Not when it came to the beating she'd taken at her husband's hands. Not the tiniest little bit. It happened. There was evidence to prove so. Just not enough to prove that he'd actually killed the baby. The defense had contended that Suzie would have miscarried anyway: that the loss of the baby hadn't been due to blunt force trauma, but rather, Susie's lack of proper nutrition and rest.

That also came back to her husband. The woman had been terrified of the man since he'd first found out she was pregnant. He'd insisted that the baby hadn't been his. DNA of the aborted fetus had later proved that it was. And there'd been no indication to the jury that Bill Heber had ever intended to kill his wife, so the attempted murder charge had failed, too.

Suzie had never wavered on any of her testimony. The only unanswered question, and the only time Emma had had the least sense that the woman had been prevaricating, was when she'd asked if Bill had ever said who he thought the father of her baby could be.

He'd never said. Neither had she. But at one point Emma'd felt like there'd been something there. Something neither of them was telling her. She'd never been able to find anything to support that theory. And when the fetus's DNA had come back matching Bill's, she'd dropped the angle altogether.

"Was there ever evidence to show that she'd been cheating on him?"

Was the man a mind reader? Honing right in on what could have been the only weak point in her case.

"None." She told him. The defense had looked. Hard. Combing through phone records, asking everyone Suzie knew or worked with. The woman never went out of the house, other than to work, without her husband.

He nodded.

So did she. Relaxing as she sat there in the hunky PO's office.

They were on the same page. She could trust him to keep Bill away from Suzie until the police, who were working diligently, could find some evidence that he'd been near his wife recently—and had hurt her. There were impression marks from the first time. The doctor didn't have actual photos this time, but if an expert could take the descriptions in the doctor's report and somehow match them up...

She was going to get Bill Heber. Finally.

And Ms. Shadow Side? She was going to stay tucked away in her small dark corner. Bad boy on the premises or not, she'd hurt Emma for the last time. She would not get in the way of Emma having a baby, either.

Chapter 4

Thankful for the challenge of work, Jayden focused on the pages in front of him, the files Emma had brought with her. He'd given her valuable documentation on Bill Heber and while he read, so did she. They'd ordered dinner—made sense with the reading they both had to do. He wasn't turning over his files. Neither was she. They were just sharing their content.

He'd ordered his usual combination platter from the little family-owned Italian place around the corner from his office. She'd opted for the eggplant. They'd moved to the break room in the now completely deserted office suite and after a full day of work, he was feeling sore.

The files he was reading were probably adding to the tension in every muscle in his body. The light, flowery scent coming from his companion wasn't helping much, either.

While he appreciated women as much as the next guy—more than some of the next guys—he wasn't a man who walked around randy all the time. Most particularly when the woman he was with was pissing him off.

And after reading most of Prosecutor Martin's files on a man he was striving so hard to keep above water, Jayden was definitely pissed. It was people like her—people who were so certain they were right to the point of not looking at the other side of the story, people who judged a man because he'd made mistakes, without finding out which ones he had and hadn't made—that made life so difficult.

Everyone made mistakes, right? Not everyone was a criminal who deserved to be locked up forever.

Emma Martin's notes made Bill Heber, Jayden's most promising case, sound like a total threat to society. It wasn't right.

So, yeah, she was pissing him off.

So why in the hell, every time he looked up, did he feel jealous of the fork that kept crossing her lips and making contact with her tongue?

She caught him staring at them.

"You read these reports cold and it looks like we're talking about two different men, his word against the facts. Instead of taking accountability, he's reframing what happened," she said, acting as though she hadn't noticed his inappropriate gaze.

Thankful for the reprieve, Jayden pushed away his half empty plate, having lost much of his appetite.

He hadn't eaten much the night before, either. Bruised ribs were a bitch.

"I've got a way to go yet here, so give me a few more

minutes," he said, putting off further discussion until he had a chance to take in every fact to determine where he went from there.

The position he was in was as much of an inconvenience as his ribs. He needed the prosecutor to think he was on her side—which he was, completely, concerning Suzie Heber's safety—so that he could run interference between her and a man whose second chance lay in the balance. He needed to know if Emma Martin had gathered any new evidence, to know what she was thinking, so he could help his client. Keep an innocent man out of jail.

After three months of continuous contact with Heber, Jayden was as convinced as he was able to be that Bill loved his ex-wife and that he only wanted to do right by her and by society, too. He'd seen his faults and, while in jail, had put himself in counseling to learn to manage his jealousy-based emotions. He had real desire to live a life that contributed to society and to make up for the wrongs he'd done in his marriage and not to repeat them.

He kind of reminded Jayden of himself in that area: himself back when he'd realized he'd made a horrendous mistake, did something he couldn't take back, and became determined to spend the rest of his life taking accountability.

There were differences between them, to be sure. Jayden would never ever have knowingly hurt someone. Had never in his life even started to strike another person.

And there was another key difference, too. Bill Heber had gone to jail for something he shouldn't have gone to jail for. And Jayden hadn't gone for something he probably should have.

The law hadn't found him prosecutable, but he prosecuted himself every single day. And found himself guilty.

Yeah, he was in a pickle. He served at the interests of the public—to keep them safe from reoffenders. And yet, he was the best hope his clients had of living productive lives. He served them, too.

Bill Heber hadn't touched his wife since he'd gotten out of jail. Jayden wasn't certain the man had ever hurt his wife—despite what he was reading. There was no clear proof. And Bill's confessions to Jayden explained, just as astutely, the actions that had taken place in the past. Suzie Heber had fallen. Or, another theory: someone else had hurt her and she was covering for whoever that could be.

She'd blamed Bill. Bill didn't blame her for that. He'd been a jealous ass who'd made her life miserable.

But he swore he'd never physically hurt her.

Whatever had taken place in the past, Jayden didn't see how Bill could be guilty of the current abuse. Jayden was too on top of the guy, conducting surprise visits, phone calls, checking in at work, driving by his house, all of it. He was putting in extra time because he had a sense that this guy was doing what he said he was going to do and Jayden's job was to give him the best chance for success. Sometimes that meant having someone watching over you in case of low moments where you might get discouraged and slip, so Jayden was watching closely. And if Bill wasn't hurting Suzie, that meant someone else was. Someone that no one was looking for while they were only seeing Bill.

Emma Martin, based on her notes and reports, was only seeing Bill. "You did a thorough job," he told her, finishing with the last of the paperwork she'd given him. She seemed to have known how many times a week Bill changed his underwear. Or darn near close to it. Assigning motivation to every move he made.

Unfortunately, just because she assigned a motivator, didn't make that motivation true.

"You documented every single meal he had—"

"Only the meals he had when Suzie was outside the home. He ate out at least three times every day that she went to work, and that was with her making breakfast and dinner at home, which he also consumed. Every single meal was taken at fast-food restaurants within sight of her office complex. He was watching her..."

"He admits that he was insanely jealous. That doesn't make him a wife beater. To the contrary, he adored the woman and, while he had doubts about someone as young as beautiful as Suzie being satisfied with him, he also wanted to make certain that no one messed with her," he fired back.

"Did he tell you that he was abused as a kid? By a stepfather?"

"I read about it here," Jayden conceded. "And while I know, statistically, abusers have often first been victims, it's completely wrong to use someone's past abuse to try to prove he's an abuser."

"According to his mother, who refused to testify, Bill hadn't told her what was going on as a kid. He'd just said that he'd been playing football, which accounted for his bruises." She paused to take a breath before filling him in. "She didn't always see him right afterward, but it got to the point that she'd known he was hurting because every time he was physically hurt, he'd eat chocolate ice cream. She'd notice the container in the trash, or notice some missing from the freezer. Apparently he started getting into fights in his later teen years and her first sign of trouble was the chocolate ice cream containers... Says she can't stand to have the stuff in her house. He'd changed, though, when her husband died and left him the body shop. Said that there'd been no trouble since."

"There you go, then," Jayden asserted.

Emma frowned slightly before continuing. "Suzie told me that every time Bill hit her, he'd go out for a bit and always bring back back ice cream for her. A sundae. She can't stand the stuff because of it. When I checked, Bill's bank card reflected charges to an ice cream shop down the street from them that correlated with every single incident. He'd always place two orders. Two scoops of chocolate in a bowl, which he'd eat there, and then a hot fudge sundae to go. The owner remembered because it was so sad, seeing him sit there alone eating. She always wondered who the sundae was for."

Purely coincidental. A man's penchant for ice cream in no way convinced Jayden of anything. "Why didn't you bring this up at trial?" he asked.

"Because without his mother's testimony, I only had a man who brought his wife ice cream."

"Kind of hard to believe his mother would tell you all of this and then not testify," he noted.

"She didn't tell me. She told the investigator I sent to question her. And she, the investigator, just asked if Bill liked ice cream, as though making conversation. She was trying to lead the woman into giving up something that we could use. I'm sure his mother was merely explaining her son's behavior, not meaning to implicate him. She really wanted to believe that her son was a happy, good husband."

Jayden planned to ask Bill about his relationship with his mother. He wouldn't ask direct questions. He didn't want his client to know that the law was looking at him. Or why. Either could tip the fragile balance between staying straight or reoffending.

If a man thought there was no hope…that he'd always be judged on what had been…

"I'm not sure it was necessary to bring up his former relationships when there was no accusation of abuse there, only of jealousy," he told her. "But you make it sound like he's unstable when there was no indication of that."

Before meeting Suzie, Jayden knew Bill had been with a woman for five years, who'd then walked out on him. He'd had a few other relationships, all of which he'd ended with little or no explanation. And then he'd met Suzie. She was just twenty-four to his thirty-eight, and he'd apparently fallen deeply in love for the first time in his life.

"My job is to anticipate every question that might be in a juror's mind, and any defense that could be presented, and find answers to all of it."

"Answers that satisfy the jury, yes, but what about the truth?" If he'd been a little less irritable, he might have managed to keep the question to himself.

Her gaze narrowed as she leaned toward him, as though issuing a challenge that went beyond their current conversation. His body took up the challenge even as his mind prepared for a fight.

There was nothing overt. With Emma Martin there never was. Nothing he could hold up as evidence of the connection between them. How did you describe an intimate look in her eye? Or prove that it was there? Or take an account of heat emanating in the space between them?

"The only answers I seek are truthful ones," she told him quite succinctly. Enough so that had he been sitting on one of her juries, she'd have convinced him. "I have no desire to put away someone for a crime they didn't commit," she continued, a shadow coming over her face. "Taking away people's lives, even if they are guilty...it's not easy."

His hand fell to the table as he felt himself being converted. And fighting to maintain complete control of his own mind.

"I have Bill on an app through his phone that allows me to see where he is at all times," he told her, hoping he wasn't hurting his client by doing so. But getting her to see that Bill wasn't the man she was looking for was the only way Suzie was going to win.

And the way they'd all win.

"You don't trust him," she said.

"I give all of my clients the opportunity to be monitored so they have an alibi if they're wrongfully accused. They tend to get looked at first because they're ex-convicts. Bill chose to take me up on the invitation." He paused, distracted by her dark blue gaze, angry enough to want to issue a few strong words in her direction, yet wanting to know the taste of her lips at the same time.

Must be the gunshot getting to him. He'd fallen to the ground, didn't remember hitting his head, but if he'd been stunned, he wouldn't know, right? They hadn't checked him for blunt force trauma to the brain since he'd never lost consciousness and had no cause for, or sign or symptoms of, concussion.

And he was the only protection, the only potential champion, Bill Heber had.

"My point was," he explained, returning to the conversation, "that if I have suspected times, a window even, of when Suzie was hurt, I can see what area of town Bill was in at the time."

"Oh." She relaxed. Smiled. Not really at him, but it hit his gut anyway. "That would be great," she said. "Thank you."

He nodded. She thought the app was going to deliver Bill up to her. He hoped it would get her people out there looking for the right man. Before Suzie was hurt again.

"So… I'll get you a listing of potential abuse dates from Suzie's doctor and anything her counselor at The Lemonade Stand has, and then you'll let me know what the app shows ASAP?" she asked, stacking her files into a neat pile to take out with her.

"ASAP," Jayden said, collecting his own paperwork together.

"And in the meantime, now that I have Heber's address, I'll have someone check for any ice cream shops in the area, since he seemed to prefer them. But I'll have someone check any other establishments that serve ice cream, as well. It's a long shot, unless it turns up something."

Seriously?

The man had done nothing but get out of jail and work hard. He didn't deserve a witch hunt against him.

And…what if Emma Martin was right? What if Bill wasn't who Jayden thought he was?

"Why don't you let me do that?" Jayden said. If Bill

was in trouble, he wanted to know immediately. If that was the case, it was Jayden's job to get the man off the street.

Heber wasn't the first guy Jayden had believed. He wasn't even the fifth. And every single one of those who'd earned his faith were was still on the outside, living productive lives. He knew. He still kept watch.

He didn't stop looking out for his clients when they were off parole. With their permission, he kept in touch.

"I'll be in the area anyway, keeping a watch on him..." And by doing so he'd be keeping Bill off the investigative radar as much as he could. And then he was going to have to see what he could do to warn whichever detective was on the Suzie Heber case to look into whoever else in Suzie's life could be hurting her. Abusers were like bombs with faulty timers. You never knew what might set them off, or who they could strike. And if Emma was getting involved in Suzie's life, as a way of doing her own penance for what Emma saw as letting the woman down before...if she was going to push to the point of looking up any establishment that sold ice cream...without even considering that Bill wasn't the time bomb...who knew what else she'd delve into, who else she might make nervous? She could inadvertently trigger the real bomb while she or Suzie was in the vicinity of the explosion and get killed.

"That'd be great." She smiled at him again, distracting him from borrowing trouble.

Reminding himself that, ultimately, they wanted the same thing—Suzie Heber safe—he smiled back at her.

And then lost all track of time.

She stared at the man. No reason. No explanation. She just stared. When Emma realized what she was doing, she looked away immediately, her only consolation being that he'd been looking at her, too.

Which didn't make it okay.

Work was work. Her more impulsive side was another part of her life. The two didn't interconnect. That was an unwritten law inside her.

"So…" she finally said. "I wanted to let you know… the Lincoln situation is being handled." His parolee would most likely not be his parolee much longer. But Luke's wife was going to be safe. Emma was pretty confident about that.

"They had no High Risk team in the area, but Lila McDaniels Mantle, director of The Lemonade Stand, spoke with the director of the local woman's shelter, who contacted Luke's wife, Gina, immediately. They've moved Gina and her daughter into a secure residence, but are making it appear as though their home is still being lived in. When Luke shows up there, if he does, he'll be met by a policewoman who closely resembles Gina. Assuming he shows up in the next day or two."

"My gut tells me he will."

Emma hardly knew Jayden, but was aware of his impressive recidivism statistics—they were the lowest in the county—and couldn't help but admire his work ethic, since it mirrored hers.

"The shelter up north is interested in the High Risk team. I think they're going to try to start one of their own," she added for no particular reason other than she wanted to keep sitting there with him. She had no choice but to trust him to do his job where Bill was concerned. And had no justifiable reason not to do so.

"I'd seriously like to be more involved with this team," he told her, adjusting his back in the chair.

Slowly. Reminding her that he was nursing badly bruised ribs.

"You're welcome to join me at our next meeting," she told him. "It's next Tuesday, weekly instead of bi-weekly or monthly since we have an active case. I'm sure the Hebers will be the top priority, so it's fitting that you be there. You're our main source of containment at the moment."

What was she doing? Inviting him to participate in a group in which she was consistently active? Inviting him further into her life?

The reasoning was legitimate, she argued with herself.

"I'd like that."

He asked for the time and place. She gave it to him. And then they were looking at each other again. Until she stopped.

He'd only eaten half his dinner. She'd finished a bit more of hers. Starting to pack up the remainder, she thought about urging him to take them home, but figured they'd been sitting out too long to be good as left-overs.

And reminded herself that he didn't need her fawning over him. If he wanted his food, he'd grab it on the way out.

"You seeing anyone?"

She stared at him.

"Personally, I mean. Are you in a relationship?"

No. Ms. Shadow Side felt all warm and important inside her.

"Is that pertinent to our business here?" her prose-cutorial side asked, maintaining eye contact with him *again*, probably on behalf of her lesser self.

"It's pertinent to the fact that, unless I'm way off

my mark, we seem to have something kind of relevant in common."

The only thing they had in common was work. Personal relationships had nothing to do with work.

"What's that?" she asked anyway. Just to know what she was dealing with.

"An inability to stop looking at each other."

Emma wanted to stand and walk out. Her muscles felt like mush. Maybe that was why her lips opened to give him an unequivocal "no" message and then her mouth just hung open.

"I'm not currently seeing anyone." He dropped the information on her.

She nodded. "Good to know," she said. And suddenly energized, was able to stand. To gather her things. She was going to get out of there without making a fool of herself.

Or be in any danger of losing her good sense. Of making another bad choice over a bad-boy character who would only be trouble in her life. She knew the ropes. Had climbed them and had the burns to prove it. Had left burns, which stung even more.

Emma waited for him at the door, pretending not to notice the wince he made as he stood. It was only good manners to hold the door for him, and to do so as they exited the building, too.

Drawing the line at opening his car door, she split from him as soon as they were outside.

"You didn't answer my question," he called as she crossed the parking lot away from him.

"I know," she called back. Wanting to say more.

Before she gave in to the warmth pooling in places he had no business knowing about, she got into her car and locked the door.

Chapter 5

He'd made the offer. She'd declined. That should be the end of it. It would be, too, in terms of him ever again even hinting to Emma Martin that there could be something personal between him and her. A casual reference without pressure, when one had been mutually stared at, was fine.

Anything more than that and he crossed a line.

He could call her out for staring at him with that heat in her eyes.

Except that he'd kind of liked it.

And so it went with Jayden on Thursday morning. In the shower. Stepping out. He cringed as he dried off and contorted to get his shirt on without pulling on the muscles surrounding his ribs. He'd picked up the recommended wrap that would help reduce swelling and speed up healing but had declined the prescription pain meds. He'd been hurt a lot worse playing football in high school and still gone on the field.

There was no time for rest, either.

Leaving his shirt open, he put a slab of frozen packaged bacon on his chest while he made some toast and drank milk from the carton. The fewer dishes he had to do, the better. The fewer actions that required movement, the better. He'd woken himself up half a dozen times in the night, turning in his sleep. Or attempting to. Back to the recliner for him that night. He'd been dumb to insist on the bed the second evening out from having taken the hit.

He'd driven by Luke Lincoln's place on the way home the night before. The man had been there. He'd stopped earlier in the day, too, to make sure there was no gun on the premises; it would be his first stop this morning. Another gun check. Jayden wasn't just going to ask, he wanted to take a look around.

He'd be seeing Harold Wallace that morning, too. Wallace's son was going to be arraigned. And then, after a couple of workplace checks, it was on to Bill Heber. He was going it solo, partially because he didn't need backup, and partially because he didn't want anyone else to know he was checking into Heber. Not unless he found something that gave him cause to report anything.

If evidence that implicated Bill turned up, he would report it. But until then, he wanted nothing to hinder Bill's chances for successful reentry.

Luke, who'd done time for physical assault, among other things was at home. Wearing a bulletproof vest under the shirt tucked into his jeans, Jayden kept his expression serious and calm as he asked to enter.

Inside he was smiling; Luke was at home. The man

hadn't broken parole—at least not that he knew of. Success, even momentary, felt good.

"I need to come in," he told the twenty-two-year-old who'd opened the door dressed only in a pair of flannel pants. "Is anyone else home?" Luke was living with his younger sister and boyfriend, both of whom had passed the home inspection stage before Luke's release.

"No." Luke stood back, his expression grim as he let Jayden inside.

Having Leon or other backup with him would have been the safest choice for this call. And would put Luke immediately on the defensive, which would have blown any chance Jayden had for establishing even a small bit of rapport with his least-trusted client.

As far as he knew, Luke hadn't reoffended yet. And though he didn't feel as positive about the young man's potential for success as he had some others, he had to give Luke the chance to surprise him.

"I need to search the place," Jayden said as he walked into a living room that had definitely been lived in. Warrantless searches had been a part of Luke's parole stipulation, but if they hadn't been, he had reasonable cause, which, as a probation officer, was all he needed.

Dirty plates and glasses sat on the coffee table. Three of them. As though that small family had shared a meal sometime recently.

A blanket and pillow were on the couch, like someone had just taken a nap. Three remote controls lay on three different cushions. And there was an ashtray filled with cigarette butts.

"Have at it," Luke said, waving an arm toward the rest of the small house. Picking up a remote, he dropped down to the couch and flipped on the television.

Jayden knew Thursday was Luke's day off from the restaurant where he worked as a busboy. But he also knew Luke had to be at the convenience store where he stocked shelves later that afternoon.

The free morning had been partially what had brought Jayden straight to Luke even before Jayden's day had officially started. He'd more than half expected the man to track down his daughter.

Home searches were a fairly normal part of his job, and Jayden knew well what to look for. And where and how to look. Messy housekeepers often simplified the job. At the leg of the twin bed frame and mattress set up in the room designated as Luke's, he found a torn piece of cardboard: part of the top of a box of ammunition.

Finding the weapon and more bullets was fairly routine. Luke had them both stuffed inside the pillow, which was inside a pillowcase matching the one on the couch.

So much for building rapport with his offender. Who was now a *re*offender. Which put Jayden in a bit of a prickly situation. He was alone in the house with a man who could be considered dangerous—one of the few of his parolees that he'd struggled to believe in at all. He'd had to give Luke the chance the courts had granted him, but the man had never looked him in the eye. Not once. That didn't set well with Jayden.

Sore ribs were the least of his worries as he made a split-second decision. If he made a call, requesting backup, chances were he'd be overheard. Luke might run. Or attack.

Percentages said he'd run. Jayden might or might not catch him. And being a hunted man would make Luke more desperate to see his young daughter—since it could be the last time in a long time he'd have the right to do so.

Jayden could make the arrest on his own, and hope all went well.

Or he could pretend he hadn't found the gun, leave, keep a watch on the place, and call for backup. During which time Luke could arm himself with the gun hidden in the pillowcase. Or do something with it so Jayden couldn't find it again.

Texting Leon, he went to the living room to make the arrest.

With back-to-back hearings on two different cases in two different courtrooms, Emma spent Thursday morning fully engrossed in work. She was just getting back to her office, her feet hurting in the three-inch heels she'd put on that morning because they made her legs look sexy. She was cursing herself for letting her shadow side out long enough to influence her wardrobe choices that morning—knowing full well they'd been made with the thought in mind that she might run into Officer Powell.

The black slim-line short skirt and matching jacket was her power suit because of the red cami she wore with it. She'd left her hair curly and wild, rather than trying to tame it as she usually did.

And after a morning in the courtroom, she was disgusted with herself for her early-morning lapse. Her feet hurt.

"Hey, boss, this came your way this morning. I figured you'd want it first thing." Kenny punctuated the last two words with his typical head bob, as he came into her office with a file in hand.

"What is it?" she asked, taking and looking at the file. Kenny would give her a speedier and as equally accurate rundown as her cursory glance was going to do.

"That probation officer, Jayden Powell, requested that it come to you specifically," Kenny said. "One of his offenders, Luke Lincoln. You know him?"

"Yes!" She looked at the front page of the file.

"Jayden made the arrest?" She looked up at Kenny.

"Found a gun during a home visit this morning," Kenny said. "Powell's lucky he didn't get himself shot again. You'd think, after what happened Tuesday, he'd at least have had backup there."

You'd think. If you weren't Ms. Shadow who found the man's courage rather admirable.

"He was there alone?"

"That's what I hear. He had the guy down on the ground at gunpoint and then called for officer backup."

Wow. Emma was impressed. Thankful. And a bit wary, too. Powell didn't play by the safety book. Officers like that muddied waters, too. Powell finding that gun—it could come down to his word against the offender's. And Emma would be left to prove who was telling the truth.

She hoped to God Jayden had some definitive proof that he hadn't planted that gun just to keep the guy away from his daughter. She could hear the defense already.

And while she admired Powell's ability to get his job done, his dedication to keeping innocent people safe, she also had to wonder just how big a risk he'd be willing to take to do so.

Like planting a weapon?

Why, after having just been shot, had he gone to

the home of a serious offender alone? Unless he hadn't wanted anyone else to be privy to what he was doing. Hoping to cash in on the fact that a panel would believe him over a dangerous offender.

Part of her wanted her to call the man, to see what he had to say about this morning's visit and arrest. The untrustworthy part that was attracted to him.

Thanking Kenny, she dropped the open folder in front of her on her desk, turned on her computer and told her shadow side to shut the hell up.

Jayden went home for lunch. With the rib wrap and bulletproof vest he'd been wearing in July heat, he stank. He was stripping as he came in the door from the garage, stopped at the refrigerator, thinking about a beer from the six-pack on the bottom shelf—probably would have had one if he hadn't had a full afternoon of work facing him—and settled for a grape energy drink instead.

He'd put in a good morning. Hated to lose one of his own to reoffender status, but was glad that he'd stopped Luke from doing something much worse than possessing a gun. Luke would serve out his time in prison, with a bit more tacked on, he'd expect, once Emma got through with him, and maybe get himself straightened out. It happened sometimes, prison knocking some sense into a guy. Maybe he'd get some counseling. Or find religion.

Did Emma have the file yet? He'd give her until after his shower and then he'd call her. If she hadn't already called him.

She'd said she'd get him windows of time and dates for Suzie Heber's injuries, to check against Heber's file on Jayden's location app and also to use as he canvassed ice cream shops and establishments that sold ice cream in Heber's area to see if there were any Heber visits that coincided with Emma's dates. He'd been waiting all morning to hear from her.

She had other cases. A lot of them. So did he. So he showered. Fed the feral cat who hadn't been outside since consuming the fish in his tank. Ate a peanut butter sandwich and then rewrapped his ribs. They were a bit better, though perhaps a little challenged by the morning's events. He couldn't say for sure. At the time that he'd pulled his gun, aimed it at Luke and told him to lie facedown on the floor, he'd been so filled with adrenaline, he hadn't felt a thing.

The twinges had come later, when he'd stood over the man, called for backup and waited, poised to act at any minute movement from his soon-to-be ex-client. Other than breathing. Luke was allowed to breathe.

They'd twinged a bit during his meeting with Harold Wallace, too. Jayden wasn't pressing charges against the boy, but the state was. He was to be remanded to juvenile detention while awaiting trial. His father was an ex-con on parole—they weren't going to give the child to him.

But it was a first offense. The kid had been crying in court when he'd told the judge that he was only trying to protect his father on their property. Harold's eyes had been moist, too. Jayden promised his client that he'd write to the judge personally, suggesting that the boy's charges be lessened, and asking him to be placed with his father's girlfriend, who was the closest thing to family he had. The woman was clean, had never been a user herself, and had been on her job for ten years. The fact that Wallace lived with her didn't have to be a bad thing. Depending on how he spun it.

He'd told Wallace, if need be, he'd do whatever he could to take personal responsibility for the boy. But he wasn't sure how that would look. Still, he was determined to try. That boy needed serious counseling, and deserved a second chance. The kid could prove him wrong. Could come after him and finish the job he'd started at his dad's house. But it was a risk Jayden had to take. He had a good sense when it came to assessing people. And if not for second chances, he wouldn't be the man he was.

He'd be a deadbeat drunk without a college degree, still trying to find a good time. If he was alive at all.

Still shirtless, and feeling better standing, Jayden called Emma from the back patio of his walled-in yard. Only a mile from the beach, he saw no point in a swimming pool, but he kept the place nice. Grass mowed. Flowering bushes trimmed.

Nothing like the opulent home he'd grown up in south of LA. Or the home he'd one day inherit. But far more to his taste.

"Jayden Powell here," he said when she picked up.

"Your name came up on my phone," she replied.

He slipped a hand into the front pocket of his jeans. So she had him programmed, huh? He grinned.

And then stopped. He had all of his work associates in his Contacts, too. Meant nothing.

"I'm waiting for the dates and times Suzie might have suffered injuries." He turned his thoughts to his earlier offer. He'd invited a more personal relationship. She'd declined.

Not something he was used to, but he'd definitely survive.

"I was just getting ready to put in a second call to Sara," she said. "I've got what the doctor could give us. I wanted to get it all to you at once."

Made sense.

"I've been in court all morning."

He walked along the pavers he'd put in across the lawn that lead to his built-in barbecue patio. He'd been heading toward a chair at the table, but once there, opted to remain standing.

The distraction didn't work. He was still grinning from the realization that she hadn't been specifically ignoring him. She'd been in court.

"I requested you on a case," he told her. Maybe she hadn't been assigned to it. There was always that possibility, though it was just now occurring to him.

"I've already read the file. Need to talk to you about it, actually. Can you swing by my office sometime today?"

"I can talk now."

"I want the interview recorded."

"Right." He nodded. "For the record." Because she was that good. He'd known he'd made the right choice, turning Luke Lincoln over to her.

"For the record," she reiterated, but her tone had softened. Perceptibly. He imagined she had a look in her eye, the same look that had accompanied that tone in her voice the night before.

"What time works for you?" he asked, kind of hoping she'd rush him through in between other important things. Like court appearances.

"I'm done at four," she said. "Would that work for you?"

He could be free at four. And would force himself to be the height of professionalism when he showed up, too.

Chapter 6

Emma took Jayden Powell straight to the interview room after he checked his gun into a locker. She didn't look at him. So how did she still note that his jeans and button-down white shirt looked fresh. Not wrinkled from a day's work.

Ms. Shadow was that good. A brief glimpse with peripheral vision and that girl could fly to the moon and back.

Or send Emma to hell, was more like it.

She'd once had Emma on the back of a motorcycle, throwing reason, good sense, and her conscience to the wind, all because she'd had the hots for the guy who owned it.

The story of her life: what made her happiest also made her miserable. That was why she'd chosen only unselfish happiness by serving others, being a mother, but having no partner, doing work that energized her, captivated her and made society a better place to live.

"We're doing this alone?" he asked when she shut the door to the little room behind him.

"It'll be on tape." Emma nodded at the equipment on the table as they each took a seat, her on one side, him on the other. She'd already set up the Lincoln file, and typed on the keyboard to access it, naming the new document *"Jayden Powell Interview."*

She switched on the recorder so fast, her fingers fumbled and pushed the wrong button, closing the file, which she then had to reopen. Thankfully she was the only party in the room privy to what was on the laptop screen built into the tabletop.

As soon as the recorder was in play, she relaxed. No chance for anything but professional conversation now. Her shadow side could just go hide.

"Tell me what happened this morning, starting from when you pulled up to the residence where Luke Lincoln was staying."

She had a list of questions and made it through most of them in record time. Powell made a great witness, her shadow side was quick to point out, and this time Emma concurred with her lesser self. She was starting to feel better about her chances in court with his succinct, appropriate and immediate responses. Not only was he giving her facts she could corroborate, first off with his location app, which would validate timing, but the man also recorded every one of his visits.

He was that good.

And would make an excellent witness. She was picturing him dressed in a blue blazer over his jeans and white shirt, probably with a tie, his longish hair somewhat contained, sitting in the jury box, before she realized that Ms. Shadow was spending more time with her than in the box where she belonged.

Part of the problem was that she and her darker side were starting to agree on a thing or two where the probation officer was concerned, and that just was not acceptable. She'd decided a couple of years before, when she'd broken a wonderful man's heart, that her mental and emotional health, and the good of those with whom she might relate, depended on her keeping her lower tendencies in their place. She'd tried with all her might to fall in love with the good man with whom she'd been living, had even pretended to herself that she'd succeeded, but it hadn't happened. And he'd known it…

She was almost through her list of questions.

"Why did you go there alone?" she asked, although she believed now that he'd found the gun where he'd said he had.

"I do the job I do because I believe everyone is deserving of a second chance," he said, surprising her with the…personal tone…of his answer. He wasn't being any less professional, wasn't giving her looks or smiles—hadn't since he'd walked toward her in the lobby of her building when she'd gone out to meet him—but somehow she felt like he was sharing something real with her. Real to the man, not just the officer.

"Go on."

"If I didn't go alone, I'd be making Luke immediately defensive, without having a chance to talk to him, to convince him to stay put," he said. "During our first interview, he asked if I'd be the only one visiting him. He didn't want his sister upset with a bunch of different cops showing up at her house at any time of the day.

She'd said she was okay with it during our preplacement interview, but Luke said he felt bad enough, having to put his little sister out. Said, as her big brother, he should be protecting her, not humiliating her in front of her neighbors." He looked her in the eye. "At which time I told him that as long as he complied with my rules, I'd visit alone most often. I knew if I showed up today with Leon, or anyone else, I didn't have a chance of keeping him on the outside."

"You knew he was potentially dangerous and you just walked in there anyway."

"I was pretty sure he wasn't going to do anything stupid, like attack me."

She stared at him. He could have been hurt. And didn't seem to get that. For such a smart man, he'd made a very stupid choice.

At least in terms of his safety.

"And I was right," he added, having held her gaze for the past several seconds.

A hint of desire crept through her.

Emma looked away. They were doing it again. Saying things with their eyes that her mouth could never say. Or follow through on.

"Like you were right on Tuesday?" she challenged.

"I was right about my offender."

"So why are you so hell-bent on giving second chances that you're willing to risk your life to give them to virtual strangers?" Not a question on her list.

"It's my job."

She turned off the recording. Looked at him. "The job you do, as I understand it, is to oversee parolees to make certain they comply with the terms of their release in order to keep the public safe."

"Yes, that's what it used to be, and still is, of course, but today we're trained to help our clients, to support their efforts. We're counselors some days as much as we are enforcement officers."

"So you've had training in counseling?" She couldn't help the tone of disbelief.

"I have a duel degree in criminology and social work, with a master's in counseling. And I made it through the police academy, too."

He was drawing her in with his eyes again. And seeming to listen to things she wouldn't say. As if he were listening to Ms. Shadow.

Emma couldn't breathe for a second there, fearing that he knew about her deepest desires. And then realized that she was smarter than that.

"Forgive me for saying so, but you sound a bit overqualified." The words came out wrong. "Only in that you could have your own practice, or some high-level position within the police department. You know, counseling officers and—"

"I knew when I was still an undergraduate what I wanted to do," he told her. "My training is job specific, with the end in mind."

She'd been that sure of herself, too, getting a degree in psychology with the sole purpose of going on to law school and becoming a prosecutor. Because of an emotionally sensitive, and spoiled darling, younger sister, her childhood had been emotionally turbulent. Anna was a drama queen who'd controlled them all with her moods and her needs. Her little sister loved fiercely and was a horrible enemy, too. She could cut a person to the quick without even seeming to notice. Her parents had certainly never seemed to see the undisciplined monster they'd created by never telling her no. Or teaching her that she couldn't have everything she wanted. Emma's friends had gradually stopped wanting to hang out at her house because her little sister always had to be included. Anna would want things her way and then throw a tantrum, even at thirteen, if she didn't get what she wanted. The time she'd called Emma's best friend an ugly bitch was a standout.

Emma, the practical, reliable older sister, had been the one responsible for keeping her sibling in check at school, too. When Anna got in trouble, her parents held Emma accountable. Why hadn't she stepped in? She knew how sensitive Anna was...

Like she'd had any control at all over her sister's choices or actions.

Emma had longed for a life that she could control. That would be driven by written rules, things she could count on. Black and white. And so she'd become a prosecutor.

Maybe it hadn't turned out exactly as she'd planned, but she loved what she did. Believed she was making a positive difference in the world. And...

Was ready to take the next step in her life: becoming a mother. Having a child in her life who she could love as much as she'd loved Anna—one she could raise to be aware of others and who'd learn to love in return.

Jayden was still watching her. Assessing her?

Seeing...what?

And what did it matter what he saw? She was the one in control here. Conducting an interview—even if she was no longer recording it. Everything she gained was for her to pull on in court if she needed it.

"Why is it so important to you to spend your life giving second chances?"

"Because I'm living mine."

He fidgeted in the chair and she wasn't all that sure it was rib discomfort that was bothering him. He'd looked up at the grate at the top of the wall that let in daylight.

She couldn't take her eyes off him. The man had layers. A lot of them. She wanted to unpeel them all.

And not for the case.

Which meant that she couldn't.

Whatever he'd done…clearly it hadn't been prosecutable. Not on a felony level. He wouldn't have his job if it had been. And therefore, it was none of her business—her shadow side be damned.

Jayden didn't talk about his past. It had happened. He couldn't change it. Whatever condemnation he deserved, he gave himself. Every single waking minute of every single day.

And whatever commiseration or understanding his telling might possibly elicit, he didn't deserve it.

His friend, a guy who'd looked up to him, was dead, because of him. And part of Jayden had died, too. It was just that simple.

And that tragic.

Even more upsetting to him at the moment was how close he'd come to telling Emma Martin about it. He couldn't even comprehend the temptation to tell her.

"Did you ever hear from that counselor at The Lemonade Stand? About Suzie Heber?" He had to get things back on track. And get home. Crack one of those beers. Find a comfortable position in his chair and maybe get some sleep.

"Yes." Emma pulled a sheet from beneath the yellow legal pad in front of her. "Here are approximate time frames Bill is suspected of having been in the area. This is based on when Suzie said she fell, but also on other things she said. Times she was upset, or just not herself. A day she didn't make it into work, but said she wasn't sick. As well as doctor reports. She's been to the ER twice in the past three months and also to see her regular physician and her chiropractor."

"All of this has happened in the last three months," he noted, looking at the information she'd printed out for him. He just couldn't believe Bill was responsible. And yet…clearly someone was hurting Suzie and it made sense that Bill would be a suspect. The incidents had started after his parolee's release…

"She claims that all of the ailments stem from a fall that has created issues that have caused other falls. She hurt her foot and says she stumbles a lot, but all medical reports say the same thing—the injuries aren't ones you'd sustain on your own. They're blunt force caused mainly by human hands and, on occasion, a fist."

"Is there evidence of a foot injury?" he asked, feeling the tension grow within him as he listened. It sounded as though things were escalating, and if Suzie was being hurt, as apparently all medical personal reported, they had to get the guy before he killed her.

"Yes, a cracked bone that is healing incorrectly. It appears, from bruising, that someone grabbed it and deliberately twisted it."

"That broke it?"

"No, that was after the initial injury."

Good God. Just to be sure, he pulled out his phone.

Checked his app. Bill was at work. Right where he belonged. Half an hour south of Santa Raquel.

But that didn't mean Suzie was safe.

"I'm assuming they're doing something for her foot now? So that if it was causing her to fall, that won't keep happening?"

"Yes. Eventually she'll probably need surgery, but they have her in a boot."

He glanced down at her list. "I'll check all of this tonight against the app. And head to Heber's neighborhood in the morning to check out ice cream vendors."

She nodded. Smiled. He didn't smile back.

"You want to go get some dinner?"

Her question knocked him out of line. She'd very clearly blown off his advance the night before. And he...

Had work to do.

Jayden looked at her, knowing he had a beer waiting in his refrigerator.

"Are you seeing anyone?" He repeated the question she'd ignored the night before, expecting her to back away again.

"No."

"Then yes, I'd like to get some dinner."

He was no fool. Or...maybe he was.

Chapter 7

They drove separately—her call—and she was going to ask for separate checks, too. All the way to the restaurant—a pub she'd suggested close to the new hospital, not some romantic place on or by the beach—she reprimanded herself for having made the invitation.

Unless...

The idea hit her as she pulled into the parking lot. She wasn't planning to live her entire life without sex. Without men. She just wasn't going to have a committed relationship. Once the baby came, she'd have to reconsider the casual sex idea. But for now...

Could it be that she could let her dark side out to play for a bit without anyone getting hurt? Could she have fun with the risk-taker in her path, without undue consequences?

Lori, one of her three study partners from law school,

had done it. And swore by it. Sex was healthy, she said. She was right, of course, but it was more than just a physical activity.

The point was to take control of your life, not to let urges and temptations take control of you. She was already in the process of starting the next phase of her life. All those years, growing up with Anna, she'd told herself that "when she had a child of her own…"

She would not let herself be controlled by urges, by drama inducing emotions…

Hot shards of desire shot through her anyway, her entire system on high alert, flooding her with adrenaline. Could she do this?

Was it possible to allow all parts of herself to live and breathe a little bit?

Parking, she got out of her car and, satchel over her shoulder, met up with Jayden at the door of the restaurant. She looked at him, her nerve endings sizzling with awareness.

He requested a table for two, sounding so…professional, she was embarrassed as hell by her earlier thoughts. Just because she had the hots for the guy didn't mean he'd want to have meaningless sex with her.

How could she even have thought that?

Been about to do that?

How had Ms. Shadow fully escaped without Emma knowing? She could generally shut her down.

Life wasn't going to be good if she couldn't trust herself to remain in control.

Longing for the single glass of wine she allowed herself when she was driving—most particularly after coming off weeks of no alcohol while she waited for the insemination results—Emma chose iced tea. Jayden did, too.

They decided to share a veggie appetizer while waiting for their dinner to arrive; that made split checks awkward and she told herself that if he grabbed up the check, she'd just pay him her half when the bill came.

At a high-top table, they'd sat perpendicular to each other. When her knee bumped his, the wave of heat jolted inside her again.

What was it about this man?

"Why did you need a second chance?" What about him was she reacting to so strongly? She couldn't control what she didn't know. She justified asking while Ms. Shadow popped up eagerly to listen.

"Why aren't you seeing anybody?" he shot back quickly.

"How long has it been since you've been in a relationship?" she countered.

"You want to have sex?"

Her entire body burned. Head to toe, bone to skin. She was the first to look away. "You said you have that location app on your phone?"

"I figure the clients who allow me to track them, when they aren't required to do so, are asking for my help. I keep a pretty close watch."

He was looking her in the eye again. Not flirting. Not coming on at all. She turned on anyway. His open intelligence, the way he made her feel like she was the only person in the world when he talked to her...

She was lonely. That had to be it. She'd been battling it for months. Needed the family she was in the process of starting.

"Then maybe we should look at it. Did you bring in

the list of dates I gave you?" Had she seen him carry in a file? "Forget that, sorry. I have them here, in my email…" She grabbed her phone out of the satchel she'd hung on the back of her chair. There were files in there, too, just not Bill Heber's. She hadn't planned to work on the Heber case tonight.

With a hand on top of hers, he stopped her. "Would it be all right with you if we don't work through dinner? I've promised to go check the Heber dates tonight, and I will. I'd just like to eat my food without a rock in my gut."

"Oh. Yeah. Sure!" She put her phone away. Folded her hands in her lap while she tried to erase the memory of the warmth of his touch. Like some silly teenager who was discovering her sexuality for the first time. Not sure what to do with it.

The man was gorgeous. A temptation. She wasn't a schoolgirl. She was a mature adult; a woman who knew the ropes, and then some. A woman who knew that no matter how great he seemed on the surface, there'd be a shadow side to him, too.

Everyone had them. She wasn't the only one.

She was a woman planning to be a mother.

And he was a man on his second chance. Meaning that he'd blown his first one and had learned from it?

Did that blown chance have anything to do with why he was single? Had he been married, too? Maybe been unfaithful? Was that why someone as tempting as him was alone and a workaholic?

"Have you ever been married?" she asked, testing her theory. Needing answers.

"No. Have you?"

She should have seen that coming. "Yes."

His brows rose.

She'd surprised him. It felt good—surprising him.

"You don't have to look so shocked that a guy would actually want to marry me!"

"It's not that. It's just…you're like… I thought we were two of a kind. You know, married to our work, so to speak…"

So he'd felt it, too, then, like she'd first thought? This whatever-it-was that was drawing them together? A sense of sameness between them?

"I am. Now." She felt compelled to give him that.

He nodded. Sipped from his iced tea. Toyed with the straw wrapper. "So…how long were you married?"

"Two years."

"Recently?"

"No. I married him fresh out of law school. He was in my graduating class."

"What happened?"

She shrugged. Not that she wanted Jayden to find her irresistible—even if her darker side was pushing for it—but Emma didn't relish him knowing that she didn't have what it took to keep her man, either.

Of course she knew that Drake's issues weren't about her. That she could have been a porn star or a centerfold and he'd still have strayed. Knowing didn't seem to take the sting away.

"Work get in the way?" he asked when she didn't find any words that satisfied her.

She finally just put it out there. "Other women did."

Drake had been a Harley-riding wild man, the one in their class who bucked the laws and found a way to argue himself out of every single predicament he got into. He'd been the star of their moot court team. Ms.

Shadow had adored him. With all of her big, open, emotional heart.

"He was unfaithful to you?" His voice rose an octave.

She'd surprised him again. It was nice.

"Multiple times." He was so big on second chances, she wouldn't want him to think her a woman who couldn't give them.

Or hadn't given them. She wouldn't be doing that again, giving a man a chance to be unfaithful to her. She had to be in a committed relationship for that to happen.

"Wow. I'm sorry. I just…" He shook his head. "The man must have been blind."

"I don't think it was his eyes he was using," she said, wanting the subject to change.

"Is he still practicing law?"

"I have no idea. I assume so. Last I heard, he'd moved to Las Vegas."

"Was he your first love?"

What was this? Twenty questions about her? She was about to not answer. And then saw that warm, caring look in his eyes again.

No wonder he had such great results with his offenders, having the best success rate of any of Santa Raquel County's probation officers. As a counselor, the man seemed to have what it took to get others to open up.

"No, he was not," she told him, figuring, since she wasn't entering into a relationship, there was no harm in spilling her beans. They wouldn't come back up on her. "That was Keith Scott." And her worst mistake ever. The high school quarterback—a guy who had it all and knew it, who thought he was above the law. She'd been an idiot, drawn to his assurance that he could do whatever he wanted and all would be well. She'd done what he wanted, and all hadn't been well at all.

She'd been out of control. Had caused her parents so much stress, sneaking out to be with Keith. Lying to them. And then…when she'd needed Keith the most—when her entire being had been grappling with loss, he'd stopped answering her calls and had gone off to college.

Her parents had tried to warn her. To tell her that he wasn't a good guy. She'd thought she'd known better.

"Was Keith before or after Drake?"

Jayden's words brought her back to the present. The tender smile on his face…she wanted to touch her lips to his. To lose herself in the promise she read there.

He was a risk-taker. A charmer. And successful, too. That was all part of the excitement. Emma recognized the signs of her alter ego's takeover.

And knew that if her shadow side didn't disappear, she might just ruin Emma's life for good this time…

"Keith was before Drake," Emma said, munching on the celery stick that had just been delivered, as though she didn't have a care in the world.

Or care any more about the previous relationships in her life.

"Have you dated anyone?" He listened as Emma told him about the last serious relationship she'd been in. The guy had been faithful, kind, smart and funny. Everything she'd always wanted. And she just hadn't been in love with him.

"I broke his heart," she said, her attempt at a smile failing as her eyes teared up. "I hate that about me. That I did that. I tried so hard to love him…"

"I'm guessing that you did him a favor, letting him go," he said.

"Because he was too good for me?" she asked with a chuckle.

That hadn't been what he'd meant at all, but at least she was smiling again.

"Because it freed him up to find the person who was meant to love him," he said.

Her smile faded as she looked at him. People moved around them. Other diners talked, laughed. Waiters and waitresses took orders, delivered food and drinks. A bus person cleaned the table just beyond them. Jayden was aware, and yet couldn't really hear them. The silent communion between him and Emma held him captivated.

"You really think there's one person out there for everyone?" She broke the silence between them.

"I think that if there *is* someone out there, being caught in the wrong relationship would be horrible. Criminal, even. Lord knows, there's enough challenge finding happiness in this world without being trapped outside of the love you feel."

"Have you ever hurt a woman?"

"Probably. But not that I'm aware of."

"You never broke a girl's heart?"

He'd once slept with a sorority girl who'd made her way around the frat house, something he wasn't proud of, but he didn't think she'd been hurt. To the contrary, she'd invited the attention, but he thought what they'd all done with her had been wrong. They'd used her, not respected her as a woman with feelings of her own. No one had hurt her. She'd come on to them, one at a time. But no one had bothered to ask her what she'd really wanted. Why she was doing what she was doing. Maybe she'd just wanted fun, and that was great. He wished he knew, and wondered for a second what had ever happened to her.

"I don't think I broke any hearts, no. I was too busy having a good time to slow down and commit to a relationship."

Until he'd been too busy finding a way to live with himself to be able to commit to a relationship.

"You've never had a serious, committed relationship?" she probed.

"Nope."

"How old are you?"

"Thirty-one. How about you?" he returned.

"Thirty-two."

They munched veggies. His mind filled up with questions he didn't ask. He didn't want to have to answer any more questions. They were getting dangerously close to things he didn't want to talk about.

"You ever see yourself getting married? Having kids?" she asked.

"Nope."

"Seriously."

If that disappointed her, and he assumed it did, best to just get it right out there. "Seriously," he repeated.

"You have it bad growing up?"

"No. To the contrary, I had a great childhood." Loving parents. More money than he'd ever known. Opportunity. Fun. "I have casual relationships, just no desire for commitment or to have kids."

Not quite the truth, but true, just the same. Part of him had the desire. Deep down. He'd always thought he'd be like his folks, fall in love for life, raise a family. Maybe a bit different, too, in that he'd wanted more than the one child they'd opted for. Maybe if he'd had siblings, hadn't had all of his parents' attention focused so completely on him, he wouldn't have been so full of himself...

"Why not?" she queried.

He could see her curiosity was killing her. Wanted it to be more than that. Wanted her to want to know about him.

So maybe he should just tell her. The bigger he made it, the more it would bother her. The more she'd care about finding out.

"Because I don't intend to have what I robbed from someone else. My sense of fair play won't allow it."

Chapter 8

The choice to remain alone was unequivocal. So yeah, Jayden lived and breathed when Emory didn't, but he was using his breath to give to others, not to better his own life. He lived to serve others, not to serve his own happiness.

"What did you rob from someone else?"

Their dinner had arrived: a barbecue chicken ranch salad for her, whiskey chicken breast with a baked potato and broccoli for him.

"The chance to be happy," he said, taking his time cutting his food.

He waited for more questions. Would figure out how to answer them, how much to tell Emma, as they came. And reminded himself why he didn't engage in casual relationships a lot, either. People wanted to know who they were involved with.

Should know.

And he should know better. Why was he there, eating with her? Why had he opened the door to begin with?

Why was she such an enigma? She was just another coworker, not a big mystery to him.

"You said you go for casual relationships, though."

"Occasionally." He was a healthy man, whether he deserved to be or not.

"Is that what this is?" she asked as she stabbed another bite.

"That would be up to both of us, wouldn't it?" he asked. The chicken wasn't bad. And when he loaded up the potato, it was pretty good, too.

"We're both married to our work," she pointed out.

"True," he agreed, trying to focus on being busy with his. They'd come together that afternoon for work.

"We know the score." She punctuated the sentence with stabs of her fork in midair. "Which means no one will get hurt."

He had a mouthful and so he nodded.

"So, what do you say?" Her gaze seemed to grab his.

"What do you say?" He was playing with her now and enjoying himself more than he probably should.

But she seemed to need his attention as much as he wanted hers. He wasn't going to snub her. It wasn't his way.

And when it ended, he'd feel a pang. That would be worse than the guilt he felt at getting what he wanted.

"I'd say that by being who we are, and being here, we've both already said yes."

She'd swallowed the food in her mouth, was watching him. He leaned over and kissed her. Right there in the restaurant. His ribs be damned.

Lips only. And only for a second.
But the deal was sealed.

Emma wanted to think that she wouldn't have slept with Jayden that night even if she'd had the chance. She wanted to think that, no matter what they ultimately did with each other, she'd at least have had the where-withal, the good sense, to see him a few more times before falling into bed with him. But she never got the chance to find out.

As it was, he'd gotten a call toward the end of dinner—a parolee of his had failed to come home from work and his wife was worried. After throwing money down on the table to pay for both of their dinners, he'd left his food unfinished and hightailed it out of there. She'd understood completely. Would have told him to hurry, if she'd been given the chance. And still felt... let down...as she sat there alone.

More relieved than disappointed, she told herself, she took the time to finish her dinner and then, pocketing his cash, put the meal on her credit card. She'd asked him to dinner. She'd pay. And hand his cash back to him at the next opportune moment.

Maybe they could have a casual fling. She knew she'd have one or two along the way. Was okay with that. Single parents weren't all sexless. She'd just have to be circumspect.

And she had to make certain that any sex she had didn't interfere with her family life, didn't involve her child's life at all or affect her work. And she was fairly confident that as long as neither she nor Jayden had any expectations of one another, any fling between them would not affect the jobs they were doing together.

On her way home from dinner, she called Sara Havens Edwin at The Lemonade Stand, to check on Suzie Heber. The woman was supposed to be attending daily counseling sessions but hadn't shown Thursday afternoon. Sara told her that Chantel Harris Fairbanks, a detective on the High Risk team, had already done a wellness check and that Suzie was at home. She'd been alone and said she was fine. Emma did a drive-by, just in case. Like she'd know what to look for. Mostly just because she felt compelled to be close enough to the woman to somehow be able to save her life.

She was taking this one personally. She knew she was. To the point that for a minute or two after turning off Suzie's street, she actually thought she was being followed. A truck of some kind had made a couple of the same turns she'd made.

And then it hadn't. You'd think she was her little sister with the drama she was concocting.

At home. Emma wished she could call Suzie herself. To question her. She'd been able to get through to Suzie four years before, when most people had failed, but didn't know that the woman would trust her again. Suspected Suzie wouldn't and didn't blame her, since Bill Heber had gone to jail for another unrelated incident, instead of for the murder of their child.

Hoping that Jayden would call yet that night with Bill Heber's location statistics, she set to work on the Luke Lincoln case. The man's arraignment was the next day and Emma had to make certain that he went straight back to prison for parole violation. Any other charges she might file, like illegal possession of a weapon, could come in the next few days.

By ten o'clock, there'd still been no call from Jayden.

Her sister had called from Florida, worried that their father might be having heart problems, talking about the pressure it put on her, to carry the burden of their parents aging all alone. She called her mother, immediately, to find that her father had had heartburn after a Mexican dinner two nights before and was as healthy as could be.

She took a shower, standing there until the water ran cold, and then, in a short robe and bare feet, headed out to the small walled-in pool in her backyard. Not to swim. She just liked sitting out there at night, with the pool lights on, listening to the quiet. Her home was in a gated community. She felt safe. And yet...yearned for air.

She'd had a message from her doctor that afternoon, wanting to know if she was ready to schedule another insemination. She was physically ready. But hadn't called back.

Probably a good thing, since she'd practically made an agreement to have sex with a hot probation officer. Her life plans, her baby plans, weren't changing at all. But it might be best to get her little "thing" with Jayden out of her system before having a baby planted inside her.

She didn't want to wait long, though. She was already thirty-two. And it might take a year for her to get pregnant.

Yes, it was all very practical, she thought as she sipped from the half glass of wine she'd poured on her way outside.

Sure, she was curious about the circumstances that had led Jayden Powell to believe that he'd stolen his happiness from another, but she didn't need the details. The man was owning whatever mistakes he'd made. That was all she needed to know. It wasn't like they were entering a relationship. There'd be respect, tenderness, absolutely, but they weren't about warm fuzzies.

Leaving her wineglass next to her phone on the table between two loungers, she crossed the cool decking to retrieve the pool cleaner and skimmed the top of the water. There wasn't much to collect. A small bug or two, a wayward leaf from a bougainvillea plant close by. The pool's automatic vacuum system took care of much of the cleaning.

She liked to skim, though. Spent a lot of hours at the pool in the dark, slowly clearing the top of the water while she worked through prosecutorial strategies in her mind.

Maybe she should go see her parents. A two-day dose of her sister would be enough to take away any immediate loneliness she might be feeling. Loneliness that could make her more susceptible to Jayden Powell. And in the meantime, spending time with her folks, assuring herself they were as healthy as Mom had assured her they were, and seeing her nieces, too, would fill up her emotional well. Children had always done that for her, even Anna, before she'd been spoiled to the point of rottenness. Yeah, a dose of those two sweet girls would ease a bit of the sting of waiting for her own baby.

She'd check flights. As soon as she had a break in her caseload that would let her get away. And after she'd been successfully inseminated. It would be good, to tell them, in person, that she was pregnant.

Yeah, it was a plan. A good plan.

The pool was clean, and the probation officer still had not called.

In fact, he didn't call until just before midnight. She'd given up and gone to bed, had been lying there playing a puzzle game on her phone, hoping to relax enough to fall asleep, when the thing rang.

Just before she'd reached the top of a mountain, too. She'd been about to win a big prize—in the form of extra game tools—and there was Jayden's name, interrupting her moment.

"Hello?" she answered, wishing her increased heart rate was due to not being able to claim her rewards but knowing it was not.

"Is this too late? You said you worked late every night, and since we seem to have similar work habits, I thought you'd be waiting to hear what I found on the app."

"I was waiting, yes, and I was still up." Sitting up in bed. With only a short, spaghetti-strap nightshirt on. Without panties. Her secret. A concession to Ms. Shadow, who'd announced several years before that she preferred to sleep in the nude. Emma insisted on a nightshirt. The lack of panties was a compromise.

"I'm just on my way home now, calling to let you know that while I'll get to it when I get home, I'll call you in the morning. It's been a long night."

"Is everything okay or should I be expecting another case file on my desk in the morning?" She was half teasing. Obviously he wasn't going to send every one of his cases her way.

"He didn't break parole, he broke his leg, among other things," Jayden said, sounding tired.

She figured it might be nice for him to have someone waiting up for him at home with a cold beer, or a glass of wine, and a few minutes to sit with him before he tended to more work. Someone who'd understand that, though it was late, he still had work to do. Someone who'd support him in that endeavor.

Not her. At all. Just someone. He was a nice guy.

"He was in a car accident on the way to work," Jayden was saying while she reeled her mind back into appropriate spaces. "He took a shortcut on a country road that cuts through some groves, was thrown from the car and then hobbled and dragged himself, thinking he was heading back to the road, but ended up being farther into the groves."

"Oh my God. That's horrible." She was there in her mind. Lying in pain with no way to call for help. "Is he going to be all right?"

"Yeah. I waited with his wife until he was out of surgery and the doctor came out to talk to her. They expect a full recovery."

"And was there alcohol in his system?" She knew Jayden would have waited to hear about the toxicology report.

"Nope. The report was clean." He sounded pleased, as he would be.

She was pleased, too, to know that they were on the same wavelength. "How did they find him?" she asked.

"He'd agreed to be on my location app, so we found his car almost right away. His phone was in the car, in a holder, with the GPS still on. It took us a while to find him in the dark, in what was really more woods than anything."

He'd had one hell of a long day. "You need to get some rest," she told him. "Bill Heber's information can wait until morning. It's not like we're going to be able to do anything with it until then. And you can see that he's where he should be, right?"

"I check every hour."

"Except when you're asleep, I hope."

"I've got an alarm set up to let me know if there's movement outside of a perimeter. It tells me anytime he travels enough miles in any direction to get within five miles of Suzie's home."

Emma'd known she could rely on him. She'd just had no idea quite how good he was.

The thought made her squirm a little bit in her bed as her shadow side suddenly tried to engage a takeover—imagining his enriched performance in much more personal endeavors.

"I'll get to it yet tonight," he said. "I have a full day tomorrow. So I should get off of here."

For a split second she thought about telling him she thought she'd been followed on the way back from Suzie's that night, but didn't want to lose his respect by making issues where there were none. The truck had disappeared from behind her long before she'd made it home. And she'd had no legitimate business driving by the woman's house in any case.

"Right. Okay. Thanks for calling…"

"I've been thinking about you on and off all night," he suddenly admitted.

That wasn't good. She was smiling anyway. Because she'd been thinking of him, too.

"I've been thinking about what we talked about at dinner," he continued, sounding hesitant, and her spirits dropped several notches.

She pulled her nightshirt, which was already covering her crotch, down even farther, yanking her bed-sheet up to her neck.

"Thinking what?" she asked. There weren't going to be any complications, either way.

"That even though we're not starting anything, relationship-wise, my goal is to make you feel good. If ever there's a time when that stops, *this* stops."

Heart pounding, grinning, her body on fire, Emma sat there for a second, having a hard time believing she'd actually met someone so much like her. Even stranger was that she'd known him peripherally for a while and hadn't known this about him.

"That works both ways," she said. "If I'm not making you feel good, it stops."

"Agreed."

"Okay, good."

So when were they going to do it? Part of her was dying to know. Pushing her to ask him to stop by right then.

But Emma knew better. She told him good-night. Hung up. And left the rest just hanging there.

Anticipation, the buildup to release, the tease, would make it all that much better when it finally happened.

And it was going to happen.

Finally, something she and Ms. Shadow could agree upon.

Chapter 9

Crap. Just not good.

Out of the four time frames Emma had given him, Bill Heber had been in Santa Raquel for two of them. Not at his wife's home. But close.

Jayden's faith in Heber had been rocked a little, but he still had the sense that Bill wasn't lying to him. He'd sworn he hadn't been to Suzie's house, and he hadn't been.

But Jayden had some questions to ask the man. Unfortunately, one in the morning wasn't an appropriate time for him to call a parolee unless he wanted to alert the guy to possible serious ramifications for perceived actions.

He wasn't ready to alert Bill yet. He wanted this done, and Suzie's abuser found, before Bill caught wind of the fact that his wife had been hurt.

And before he knew he was a suspect again.

Both facts could seriously jeopardize Bill's chances for successful reintegration into being a contributing member of society.

He couldn't call in the middle of the night, but he had to get the man on the phone before he had to turn over his findings to Emma. Had to be able to give her logical reasons, with alibis for Bill's whereabouts on both occasions in question.

That was why he was up at six Friday morning, showered and, forgoing the rib wrap, dressed and out the door by seven. That, and because he'd been lying in the bed thinking about sex with Emma Martin, which wasn't a great sign. Wanting it, even doing it, was passably acceptable. Mooning over it made it more than it could be.

Bill was already expecting an in-person visit sometime, so his showing up wouldn't send up any alarms at all, where a phone call asking questions might.

Bill was due at work at eight in the little town just north of Santa Raquel where he was currently renting a trailer from a friend until he found a little place to buy. He still had money, savings that had been his part of the divorce settlement, but while it was enough for a down payment, it wasn't enough to support him.

Unlike some of Jayden's parolees, Bill had friends who were upstanding members of society, respectable family men. Friends from high school. Clients who'd always come to his shop for any of their car repair needs. People who trusted him.

Right now, what Jayden cared most about was making sure that Bill continued to trust him. He figured if he showed up right before Bill had to leave, he could ask a few questions, as he always did on visits, and let the other guy get on his way. Show Bill that it was just a cursory stop-by, because he was required to make them, not because he believed Bill might act out.

Then he'd check for any ice cream shops, or shops that served ice cream, in the area. He'd already done a search for shops near the areas Bill had been during the two visits that had him near Suzie during critical times, and come up with two. He'd be on both of those later that morning.

In jeans and a T-shirt, Bill was just locking up the door of the trailer when Jayden pulled up. Jayden's car wasn't fancy. A dark blue sedan, four-door, relatively new. But nothing like the sports cars Jayden had driven as a young adult. He still owned one, garaged at his parents' house down south, but he only kept it because his father, who'd purchased it for him, had begged him not to sell it.

He met Bill at the door of Bill's truck—an older red pickup that he'd paid cash for upon his release. Bill had sold the newer pickup he'd owned before his incarceration rather than pay to have it stored and have to make truck payments while in jail. The man was responsible.

Accountable.

"Hey, Officer," Bill greeted him, holding out his hand for a shake.

Jayden noted the strength of Bill's grasp, tight enough to show familiarity, comfort, affection, confidence, but not so tight that it gave hints of aggression, power, control.

"How's it going?" Jayden asked, squinting against the rising sun. It was piercing in spite of the sunglasses he wore.

"Good." Bill shrugged. "Can't complain."

He could. Living in a trailer instead of the three-bedroom home he'd once owned. But he didn't.

"Doing a quick check, like we talked about," Jayden said, keeping to the point, like it was all just red tape. "Give me some alibies about a few random places on the location app and we're good to go."

"Let me have 'em," Bill said. He stood with a hand on his door handle, a hand at his side, looking at Jayden straight-on.

He named a location not far from Bill's home.

"A taxidermy place," Bill said immediately. "I caught a twenty-five-incher six weeks ago and had it mounted. I can show you the fish and the paid receipts."

"When you get a chance—" Jayden nodded "—just email a copy."

"I'd do it now, 'cept I'm not going to be late to work. You'll have 'em tonight."

Jayden then named one of the Santa Raquel addresses.

"A park I used to go to with Suzie. We carved our names in a tree there, a long time ago. I was having a rough night, thought about drinking, and went to take a look at the tree instead. To remind myself why I'm where I'm at and how much I know I ain't never goin' back. I bought a hot dog from a vendor there. And took a picture of the tree on my phone."

He pulled out his phone as he was speaking, and showed it to Jayden, who noted the time stamp. And then Bill scrolled farther. "Here's the fish, too," he said.

"Wow, that's a nice one!" Jayden asked what kind of bait he'd used and what time of day it had been.

And then he asked about an address closer to LA.

"An autobody shop," Bill said. "I was there on official business, picking up some parts for work. I'll take a picture of my time card when I get to the shop and send it to you."

It wasn't necessary, but Jayden didn't say so. He wanted Bill to be accountable. To be able to feel accountable.

He gave one more non-alarming address and then the other Santa Raquel one.

"You know I haven't been to Suzie's house," Bill said, giving him a more pointed look.

"I do. But you were arrested for breaking and entering in Santa Raquel. You aren't currently living there. I have to check…"

Bill nodded. Frowned. "I was looking at a place," he said. "It's for sale. It's right off the freeway, needs some work, but I can afford it."

Bill was thinking about moving back to town. Where Suzie lived.

"I passed on it because I figured it was too soon," Bill explained. "When Suzie and I can talk, and I can make sure she's okay with me moving back to my hometown, then I'll buy."

As one of the conditions of his release, Bill wasn't allowed to contact his ex-wife, since he'd broken into her home. But he was allowed to speak with her if she contacted him.

"Has she called you?" Jayden asked. And knew he'd gone too far when Bill took a deep breath.

"You're checking my phone records, right?" Bill asked.

"Yes."

"Then you know she hasn't called. You also know I haven't called her."

He did.

He nodded. "I'm here to help, Bill. I know you can do this. I also know there will be tough times. I hope you'll call me, anytime of the day or night, if you get to a point where doing so is the only thing that would stop you from doing something you don't want to do."

"I'd dump myself at the bottom of the ocean before I hurt that woman," his parolee said. "But yeah, I got your number on my speed dial."

Bill showed Jayden his phone.

He nodded. "Then we're all good, man. I'll be checking by again within the next few days. You're at the three-month mark and I've found that to be critical timing. I like to keep a tighter watch between three and six months, if that's okay with you."

"Like you did for the first two weeks," Bill said, climbing into his truck. "I hope someday when I see your ugly mug it'll be over a beer at a pool table somewhere." He pulled his door closed behind him.

Jayden didn't get a chance to tell the older man that he'd like that. A beer and a game of pool sounded good. *Too* good. Reminding him of days gone, college nights that he and his frat brothers would drink and shoot pool until the sun came up, and then drink some more…

It was one of those days when Emma felt like no matter what she did, it wasn't enough. She'd been disappointed from the get-go when she'd missed a call from Jayden. She'd been in court when he'd left a message, telling her that not only had he been over Bill's locations, but that also he'd talked to the man himself.

He'd told her that Bill had not been within two miles of Suzie's home since he'd been out of jail and that he had alibis for every single location Jayden had questioned him about. Bill would be sending receipts as proof and Jayden would forward them to her if she had to see them.

Of course she didn't need to see them. She didn't need to do his job with him. She wasn't that much of a control freak. Jayden hadn't said if any of the times Bill had been in Santa Raquel coincided with times she'd given him, but assumed not, since he wasn't sending up red flags. And she appreciated his diligence in following up.

Because if any of those occurrences had been during critical times, Bill could easily have left his phone someplace, gone to Suzie's, and gone back to get his phone. Maybe that type of thinking was paranoid, but in her line of work, she had to be that way.

She spent her days unraveling all of the ways people managed to do evil things to each other, or to innocent victims. There were no lengths, apparently, that some wouldn't go to…

So yeah, maybe she was a bit hardened by it all. And a bit paranoid? She'd been certain, when she'd first turned into the parking garage at work, that she'd seen in her rearview mirror the same truck from the night before come from around a corner and pass by. The stress of Bill on the loose, of Suzie not being in protective custody, was getting to her.

Maybe she needed to be a bit more like Jayden, looking for the good in people instead of always assuming the worst.

Maybe that's why he'd come into her life right then,

while she was taking steps to bring a baby into her world. To remind her to see the good.

No way a child should grow up seeing only the bad. Expecting the bad.

Like she did.

And what more perfect way to make certain that she didn't make anything more of the fling with Jayden than to take steps to conceive a child on her own? She was remaining practical. Not even thinking about changing her life goals for him—or including him in them. If she got to the point of telling him her plans, and it scared him off, all the better.

Staring at her computer screen shortly after leaving her message for Jayden, she sat completely still. Shocked where her thoughts had led her.

She *did* expect the worst. Not just from the defendants she tried, but from everyone.

When had she become so hardened, bordering on bitter when it came to humanity?

She used to have so much fun. Used to love meeting new people because of the new experiences they'd bring to her life.

Certainly all the stuff with Drake had soured her. How could it not? But she'd thought, when she'd tried her second live-in relationship, that she'd gotten beyond that.

Wow.

Not the kind of home she wanted to provide for her baby.

So she had some thinking to do. Some self-watching. From that moment on she'd be more aware, make conscious attempts to find good in every situation.

Her resolve lasted through lunch. And two cases in

court. She prided herself on how well she was doing as she came from a successful plea agreement, applauding the defendant for taking accountability for her actions and wanting to make amends.

And then she went to Luke Lincoln's arraignment. She'd expected the proceeding to merely be a formality. She'd gone armed with her recorded copy of Jayden's testimony, which she'd also printed to give to the judge. The arraignment was for the gun violation charge for which he'd been arrested. The defendant was to be held without bail, while awaiting his hearing before the parole board. They would likely send him back to prison to serve out the remainder of his original sentence. She could have handled the case during her first year of law school. It was that clear-cut.

Except that not only did Luke Lincoln have an attorney, he had an überaggressive one—one who sought to convince the judge that Luke had been unaware of the gun at the residence. The home didn't belong to him. He was only staying there until he found a place he could afford, as had been approved by the system prior to his release.

Not only was the gun not his, he hadn't known it was there, or he'd have called Officer Powell immediately and made arrangements to be somewhere else. His attorney was asking, on Luke's behalf, that the charges be dropped and that Luke be released, at least until the parole board hearing.

Emma objected, of course, vehemently. And asked the court to listen to Officer Powell's interview with her.

When the defense had no objection, the judge allowed her to play the recording. Watching the judge's face, Emma relaxed again, confident that, in spite of the little glitch she hadn't anticipated, the hearing would end with the expected result.

It didn't. At all.

In spite of the risk Jayden had taken, the good work he'd done.

And therein ended Emma's temporary ability to find the good in every situation.

Jayden was at home, typing up reports from his visits that day, when his cell rang with a call from Emma.

He picked up, ready for her. She'd had her hearing with Luke. Though the results were a no-brainer, he'd expected her to call, just to confirm. And had steaks thawing in the kitchen for the invitation he planned to issue.

Maybe they'd finally sleep together that night. If they gave his ribs another night or two to heal, that was fine. If not, he'd be just as "feeling good," as she'd ever need him to be.

"The judge dismissed the charges."

In his recliner, with his laptop across his thighs and a grape energy drink on the table beside him, Jayden wasn't sure what she was talking about.

"Come again?"

"Luke Lincoln. The judge dismissed the charges. Obviously, you haven't had a call yet. He's still in jail on the parole violation and chances are he'll be back on your list soon."

Slamming down the footrest, he dropped his laptop on the seat and stood. He'd changed into sweats and a T-shirt when he got home—only until he knew for sure she'd be joining him for dinner—and paced barefoot to the kitchen.

"What the hell! What happened?"

"He's got some high-dollar attorney who pulled out every obscure case on the books to substantiate his claim that since Luke neither owned nor was aware of the weapon on the premises, all charges against him should be dropped."

"What the hell!" He was repeating himself. He had no other words. He didn't blame her, at all, but…what the hell!

"I found the gun in his room, stuffed in his pillow-case. I took pictures before I left the scene. They're time stamped."

"I know. The arresting officers took pictures, too. But Luke claims that he doesn't sleep in the bed. That he sleeps on the couch. He says the room is too small, reminds him of his cell. And that the bed is too big. He's more comfortable on the couch."

"It's still his room. His pillow. The damned pillow-cases even matched—the one on the couch and the one on the bed."

"So you saw the one on the couch?"

"Yeah."

"And the blanket?"

"Yeah, there was a blanket wadded up on the couch. Looked like he'd been taking a nap shortly before or when I got there…" He stopped. His words. And his tracks. Damn. He'd forgotten to tell Emma about the pillow and blanket on the couch—and had thus tainted her case.

Chapter 10

"I didn't tell you about the pillow and blanket on the couch." Jayden resumed pacing, silently cursing himself. "I didn't find them relevant."

"No one else did, either, except his attorney. She claims that Luke only uses that room to keep his clothes. He's never slept in that bed or touched that pillow. There were no fingerprints on the gun, or on the pillowcase, other than yours…"

"I did not plant that gun there."

"No one's claiming you did. They weren't going to take a defense that would put the burden of proof on them. Or put your word against theirs. They say the gun belongs to Luke's sister's boyfriend, according to the story they're all sticking to. He wanted it in the house for protection from Luke. Just in case."

"That's bull. I talked to him during the prerelease

home inspection interview. He keeps his gun in his vehicle, which he keeps locked at all times, and said he'd park on the street until Luke found a place of his own. And it's a Beretta. I found a Glock 9."

"The Glock was unregistered, and the story is the boyfriend bought it off the street when he knew Luke was coming to stay with his sister. For her to use if she needed it."

"So the sister knew it was in the pillow."

"That's the story. And that, because Luke had no knowledge it was there, he can't be held accountable to it. I had a chance to question both the sister and her boyfriend and their stories seemed too practiced to me, but the judge bought them. Luke's out. At least until the parole board has a hearing."

That Jayden would attend. If they still moved forward on it. The judge had thrown out the gun violation charges. There would still be a parole hearing. Luke had still been on premises with a gun. But with the court's ruling, there was little likelihood that the board would revoke parole. Feeling like he'd let Emma down didn't set well with him, but what bothered him a whole lot more was Luke's wife and daughter being in danger again.

The same instinct that told him Bill Heber was not hurting his wife was yelling loud and clear that Luke would do that to his family, the first chance he got.

"The preliminary is Monday," he told her.

"I've already called up north, letting them know that he might be back out. His wife and daughter will be at the shelter until after the preliminary hearing on Monday anyway."

"And after that?"

She sighed. He felt it clear to his bones. Somedays were harder than others to find the energy to keep fighting the fight.

More so for Emma than for him, he imagined. Every probation officer he knew was on the same side. But for Emma…she fought her own peers every single time she stepped into court.

"Did you know the attorney?" he asked.

"No. She was someone from LA."

"I wasn't aware Luke had the money to hire an attorney from anywhere…"

"Apparently she knows his sister. Took the case on, gratis."

"You think they're all three lying to her, too?"

"I wouldn't put it past them. The sister was a particularly good witness."

A schoolteacher with impeccable credit and a no-nonsense attitude, she'd impressed Jayden, too, during the preliminary home visit, which was why he'd allowed Luke to live with her. But if she'd lie for him…kind of a wrench in the gut.

"You still at the office?" he asked.

"Yeah."

"You want to come by for dinner? I laid out steaks and am pretty decent at the grill."

"Only if I can bring the wine."

He hadn't had wine…ever. Unless he had to. Back when he'd been a drinking man, he'd regarded wine as being for weaklings. Beer, he'd taken down in gallons. Whiskey. Tequila. Vodka. Rum. He could take them all, in straight shots, one after another.

Made no sense to him that he hadn't become an alcoholic, developed some kind of addiction to the stuff.

When he thought about how much he could consume, how hard he'd partied…

"You can bring whatever you want," he told her. He had his six-pack.

Or maybe he'd sip on a little wine. If it would make her feel good.

Emma wasn't going to get to know him much better. She couldn't. If she did, she'd start to care, to take on his concerns and go into problem-solving mode. It was her way. She knew it.

No, they were going to be colleagues who respected each other, and who were going to deal with the lust that had sprung up between them.

Tingling with anticipation, Emma took a good six or seven minutes just trying to choose the wine. Did he like red or white? She wasn't a big drinker, usually just chose a semidry white wine because it was mostly unassuming.

But tonight…she wanted something bold. Daring. Maybe a little dangerous.

She'd had a really bad afternoon at work and wanted to forget it for a few minutes. To put it out of her mind. Just long enough to regroup and go back to believing she made a difference.

The only way she knew how to get that necessary step away was to let her darker side out. On a leash, of course, but to let her run ahead a couple of steps, to lead her down the block.

As long as she chose the block, they'd be fine.

"'Aphrodite's Touch,'" Jayden read, taking the bottle she handed him at his front door. His house was smallish, in a nice neighborhood, non-gated, but well land-scaped. Clean. Fairly close to the beach.

"It's from our local winery, run by Tanner Malone," she explained, though she didn't say it was described in the Malone winery catalog as a step out for a woman needing more than a good dinner. "He grows a variety of the Aphrodite grape," she continued, fighting self-consciousness. Where was Ms. Shadow when she needed her?

She'd paid for the damned wine and then gone into hiding. What the hell?

"Aphrodite, the goddess of sex, love and beauty." Jayden's voice was laced with…something that made her tingle. And yeah, leave it to him to know about Greek mythology.

"I like Malone Wines." She tried to play it all off with nonchalance.

"This is one of your favorites, then?" He'd carried it into the kitchen. Already had a corkscrew in the top—with two wineglasses on the counter behind him.

"I've…um…actually never had it." She couldn't lie to him. Her shadow side might have been able to, but Emma would have stopped her. "I usually just drink his Riesling, when I drink wine at all."

"You prefer something harder?" he asked, a tiny grin on his lips as he poured.

"Nope. Just wine." So now he knew. She was a light-weight when it came to alcohol. If he didn't like it… if he was a heavy drinker…didn't really matter. They weren't starting anything that was meant to last.

Turning to her, he handed her a glass. Held his up to hers, looking fresh and way too hot in his jeans and button-down shirt—with at least three buttons undone.

Gaze fixed on his chest hair, suddenly nervous, she willed Ms. Shadow to get her ass up out of wherever she went when she was banned, and held her glass while he clinked his against it.

"To what's to come," he said.

She'd have felt better with a simple "Cheers," but took a sip. Saw the steaks prepared and waiting to go out to the grill. Wanted to see his backyard and so she walked over and looked, feeling…drained from her long day. So…yesterday in her light brown skirt that hugged her thighs nicely but was way more businesslike than sexual. The off-white silk blouse and brown pumps she wore with it—ditto.

She'd dressed for court, not seduction. And now that she thought about it, wasn't even positive what underwear she'd put on that morning. Could she hope it had been anything with lace?

"You want to come out and sit with me while I grill?" he asked. It was July, but Santa Raquel didn't generally swelter. They were a seaside town with enough breeze to keep things moderately comfortable.

Feeling like she'd been given a huge reprieve, Emma followed him outside, finding his cute ass about as nice as anything she'd seen that day.

Jayden figured, about a second after Emma had handed him the wine she'd brought, that he wouldn't be getting any that night. Sex, that was.

And quickly rephrased the thought in his mind. He wouldn't be giving any. The gorgeous blonde, with her curly hair, looked tired, about as ready to fly as an ant.

"You had a rough one," he said as pulled out a seat for her at the pagoda table on his way to the grill.

"When you get your thrills from work, days like today really suck."

He might have thought she was leading him to more…thrills…personal ones, but the way she sat there, staring out, sipping her wine, surveying his yard, not meeting his gaze, told him differently.

"Luke's getting to you."

"And Bill Heber," she said. "I couldn't get the man the last time, couldn't protect Suzie, and it looks like he's going to do it to me again."

"Unless he didn't do it." It bothered him that she didn't seem to give that option any consideration. For Bill's sake, of course, but more for Suzie's at this point. If they didn't find the abuser, she was likely going to be hurt again.

"He did it." She met his gaze then. "I know he did it. I just have to outsmart him. And believe me, I will." She sipped.

He admired her bravado. The attitude it took to fight the kinds of fights she fought every single day.

Any chink at all could lose her this case. And police officers relied on their prosecutors. It was a heavy burden she bore.

"You aren't drinking your wine." She was looking at him now. "You don't like it? I'm sorry, I should have asked what you preferred…"

He took a sip of wine. Found it…not bad. Not bad at all.

"I'm more of a beer man," he told her. "But this is good."

"It's not going to hurt my feelings if you drink a beer."

He shrugged.

"Seriously," she said. And then, "Or are you out? I can go get some…"

Her desire to please was genuine and he realized how much he really just liked the woman. "I've got a six-pack in the fridge," he told her. "I'm happy with this."

He was just plain happier having her around.

Sitting in Jayden's smallish, but nicely manicured backyard, Emma finally started to relax. The wine tasted good. The steaks cooking on the grill smelled good. And the man...

Every part of her approved of him.

Her ringing phone interrupted a feeling of content-ment she hadn't experienced in a while. It was Luke Lincoln's arresting officer.

She listened, nodded, and hung up, noticing that Jayden had also taken a call.

"Luke?" she asked as he also disconnected.

"Son of a bitch."

"You have to go?"

There'd been a miscommunication between court deputies and, instead of being taken to the holding cell to wait for a ride back to jail that afternoon, Luke had been released.

"No. Not yet, anyway. Officers have been sent to get him. Technically he hasn't broken the law by leaving. He was told he could go. Might even think, with the win in court today, that he really is free."

Technically. "I have to call up north again." She was thinking aloud. "I know his wife and daughter are safe, but I need to let them know..."

"I was told someone from the department already made that call."

The relief she felt, knowing that she didn't have to put her work hat back on right then, was a bit startling.

Emma was always ready to work. Was energized when she was needed.

Had to be the wine.

It most certainly could not be the man.

Refusing to be an animal that jumped the bones of his dinner companion without foreplay, finesse or tenderness, Jayden forced his libido to calm down and tried to focus on the food they were sharing. He liked to eat. He just didn't bother to put forth the effort to eat well. Mostly he settled for canned stuff. Frozen stuff. Fast-food stuff.

When he saw his parents—at least once a month to keep them happy—he ate all weekend.

Emma had done his steak proud, though. She'd scraped right down to the bone with her knife. And devoured the baked potato and salad, too. He liked that she wasn't so conscious of calories that she couldn't eat a good meal.

And wondered where she put it all. She wasn't skinny, but there was nothing extra on her, either.

He'd noticed. Again and again.

She'd finished her glass of wine. He hadn't, but he'd enjoyed what he'd had. When he offered to pour her more, she'd declined, reminded him she was driving.

A sign that she wasn't planning to stick around awhile.

And yet she didn't get right up and leave, either.

They cleared the dishes and when he offered her an iced tea, she accepted. And followed him out as he closed the grill, sitting back down as though she was in no hurry to leave.

He was in no hurry to have her gone.

And was growing more and more increasingly bothered by her determination to see Bill Heber back in jail. They'd been talking about work on and off all evening. In between general discussions about their work lives.

Seriously, what else did either of them have to talk about? They were workaholics.

And not falling in love.

"What is it about this Heber case that has you so bothered?" he asked when she brought them back to the fact that he'd found no substantial evidence against Bill Heber that morning. He hadn't yet mentioned that he'd found an ice cream shop not far from Bill's house and that Bill had been there enough to be known to the owners.

He was keeping the information to himself at the moment for a very good reason. Bill's visits didn't coincide with the times Emma had given him. The man just liked his chocolate ice cream.

And Jayden had to figure out how to help Emma see that.

"I'm bothered by all my cases that feel like failures. In this instance, I've got a chance to make it right. I'm not going to blow it."

"Is this the first case you've had that gave you the ability to right a wrong? Surely you've had someone reoffend and gotten another go at him or her." She'd been at the job for eight years. Some failures happened.

"Of course I have, and no this isn't the first time I've faced this situation."

"So why is this one so bothersome to you?" The woman was clearly deflated, as though she'd hung everything on his location app nailing Heber. That was understandable. But he was far more bothered by the

Luke Lincoln issue. Emma was bothered, too, clearly, but not as much as she was by Heber.

"They're all bothersome to me."

"Forgive me for overstepping…" She'd stayed, which invited the conversation as far as he was concerned. Plus, he just plain wanted to know. "But it seems… almost…personal."

"Like you feel Bill's right to have a second chance, you mean? That's personal."

Her jab hit its mark. "Probably."

She held his gaze. "It's the baby," she finally said. "He killed his baby, while it was still in its mother's womb. That's heinous."

"You were not able to prove that at trial."

"Suzie told me it was him. She just got scared and wouldn't testify because she didn't want to be pulverized by the defense attorney."

"Bill told me that she miscarried because of ill health. She wasn't eating or sleeping. Was a nervous wreck."

"Yeah, because he was beating her."

"He claims he was insanely jealous of her," Jayden said, hoping he could bring some good to both of their days by putting this one to rest. "He was scaring her, making her life miserable. He was guilty but he wasn't hitting her."

He looked Emma right in the eye. Willed her to see the truth.

"That's not what the facts say."

Suzie's testimony. That she wouldn't give in court. The medical record stated that blunt force trauma had contributed to the miscarriage, but if Suzie had been healthy to begin with, the baby might have survived.

The doctor's opinion was that the trauma was likely the result of another human being.

Likely. Not proved.

Like Suzie's current injuries.

They could tell from bruise marks, indentations, directionality of blows, that Suzie's current injuries were human inflicted. There'd been no such clear marks four years before—and he'd proved Bill hadn't been around Suzie and able to hurt her since his release.

"Bill takes full accountability for the miscarriage, for causing Suzie so much anxiety that she'd lost their baby. His remorse is real. Palpable. This is not an aggressive man," he told her. "He wants only to do what he can to make her life easier, and if that means staying away from her, that's what he'll do. His location app proves it. He's working his ass off, taking way more hours than he needs to, so that he can send money to her."

"He's required to pay alimony."

"He's doing it because he wants to. Because he needs to." And as soon as Bill made more of it, he'd send more to Suzie.

Jayden didn't like the hesitancy in her gaze as she looked at him, like she was doubting *him*. Not Bill. "Are you telling me that you aren't going to keep him on your radar? You've decided he's not a danger?"

"Absolutely not." He wasn't just saying that to get back in her good graces. He wouldn't do such a thing, just in theory, and certainly not to Emma. "I'm fully aware that I'm human and could be wrong. I've been wrong. I just want to make sure that, in case we're wrong, someone is still looking for another abuser."

"Chantel is all over it. If there's something else out there, she'll find it."

So...why wasn't she relaxing a bit? Luke's ex-wife and daughter were in more immediate danger, in Jayden's opinion, and yet Emma trusted the system to take care of them.

Maybe because they were currently in a secure shelter.

The answer was valid. He acknowledged that as it came to him. He just didn't think that's all there was to it.

As a probation officer, he'd gone as far as he could go.

As her possible future lover, he'd already gone farther than he should.

Jayden had no acceptable reason for pursuing the conversation. But he felt compelled to anyway.

"Suzie Heber...it's personal, somehow, isn't it?"

Chapter 11

Emma had no idea why she was still sitting there. As hot as he was, as much as she was turned on by him… she just wasn't feeling the sex this night.

She was too sick inside to feel wanton. And Jayden was part of the cause. She knew he'd done his job well. That he'd risked his life to get Luke in custody. She couldn't say that she'd have thought to report evidence of someone napping on the couch in relation to an illegal gun possession. But there it was…

Luke was loose. She'd somehow lost control of something she'd thought a sure win. Not somehow. She knew how. Jayden hadn't given her the full information and Luke's judge had found his sister credible.

There was still the parole hearing. At least a preliminary to determine if Luke was going to have his parole revoked for being in the home with a gun.

"I take it, since you aren't answering my question, that I'm right. The Suzie Heber thing is personal…"

He'd admitted to her that giving Bill a second chance was personal to him. That second chances were personal. He'd given her as much knowledge as he'd thought she needed.

If she was going to do that job, partnering with him as she'd chosen to do, she had to acknowledge her own weakness, didn't she?

She stared at him, seeing the counselor more than the officer. Maybe because he wasn't wearing his gun.

Maybe her shadow side was choosing this most inopportune moment to surface. Maybe she didn't need to tell him any more about herself.

She sipped her tea. What would it hurt?

"I got pregnant my senior year in high school." The words flew out while she was still debating whether or not her desire to tell him something that no one in her professional life knew of was valid, or the result of her shadow side rearing her head.

His head tilted to the side a little, his gaze a new kind of warm as he looked at her. But he didn't push. Or probe.

"The father…he didn't seem all that fazed by it. Said I could do what I wanted with the pregnancy. That things would work out either way. He also didn't offer any real support. But he didn't dump me. My parents were devastated, of course. And me…my whole world changed…every breath I took felt different. My future looked different. And yet… I wanted that baby. Hard to believe you could love something that you wouldn't even know was there if not for a test you'd taken…"

Here was the time when she shut up. Walked away.

She couldn't even look away.

"Did your parents pressure you to abort? You can't blame yourself if you did as they asked…"

She almost went with that story. It fit closely enough for her current purposes in telling him anything at all. Though, what exactly that purpose was, she wasn't altogether sure.

"They talked over all of the options with me and then asked me what I thought I should do." She remembered, smiling a little through the profound sadness. She'd thought she was over the critical intensity of that feeling. Hadn't experienced it quite this badly in years.

Ms. Shadow and her drama.

"I wanted to keep the baby," she said, looking Jayden straight in the eye. She was doing this—telling him—and she was going to do it right. "I'd created a life, and it wasn't about me anymore. It was about that baby."

Until the night…

"How did they react to that?" His words came softly into the soft light of the moon as he reached up and turned off the light in his pagoda. She hadn't even noticed darkness had fallen.

"They were worried, of course, but also excited about the baby coming. At least, my mom was. She was making plans, volunteering that she'd babysit so that I could still go to college, that she'd turn the spare room in our home into a nursery, but wanting me to make all of the decorative choices because it was my baby…"

Tears pushed up from inside her, far more dangerously close than they ever got these days. Her mom had been so great. And Emma had taken it all for granted. A kid who'd been so hooked to the wild man who'd impregnated her that when he'd begged her to get on the back of his motorcycle and ride the drag race with him, she'd hopped on.

"A group of guys had been racing bikes for about six months. Spectators would all chip in money. Each time there was some new challenge that they'd get right before the race began. That night the requirement was to have three people on your bike. And the prize money was a thousand dollars. The baby counted as his third person…"

Jayden's brow furrowed, but otherwise his expression didn't change.

Finding her throat inordinately dry, Emma took a gulp of tea.

"The stretch of road was fairly simple and everyone knew Keith was the best biker around. He'd never had a wreck…"

But he had that night. He'd slid out at the turn, had to lay down his bike…

"I was thrown from the bike," she said, swallowing. Taking another sip from her glass.

Whatever the hell was happening, she was in way over her head.

"You lost the baby," Jayden said when she was pretty sure she'd finished talking about it.

She nodded. And now he knew. She'd basically killed her own child. Not really. Not in any legal or maybe even moral sense. But under her own accountability test…

There was no way she could fail to save Suzie a second time.

"I've prosecuted and lost a couple of other cases involving fetal deaths," she said, finding half a brain somewhere in the midst of the emotion and waywardness attacking her. "One a domestic violence case. The other a landlord who refused to fix faulty wiring and a fire broke out. The mother suffered severe enough smoke inhalation that she lost her baby."

As difficult as the conversation was, it wasn't overpowering her now. She was back in her element. In control. Jayden was a good listener.

"My point here is that I know Suzie Heber told the complete truth four years before. I know what her husband does to her. I know this based on the evidence before me, the interviews Suzie gave, the compelling reports that were offered live in court. Not based on what I might want to believe. And this time? Yeah, maybe I feel some personal emotion to it all, but I'm out to see justice served for Suzie. For the baby she lost through no choice of her own. Not for myself."

Emma had no doubts. No wavering. Nothing but a sense that she was doing what she had to do. What was right to do. No matter what Jayden thought.

Jayden leaned in then and kissed her. Probably the absolute wrong thing to do. He did it anyway. Just leaned over, ignoring the slight twinge in his side, and planted his lips squarely on hers. She'd bared her soul to him, and he'd just needed to connect with her in a tender, personal moment. A sign of caring. Of support. Not of desire.

It was possible he'd have straightened right afterward. Apologized. But when her lips moved against his, opening slightly, he pressed harder, opening his mouth to taste her more completely. To let his tongue talk to hers and come to an agreement the two of them couldn't seem to reach any other way.

Their jobs took everything. And somedays, it raised emotions that needed an outlet. Something that would dispel built-up tension when winning the case wasn't an immediate option.

Without breaking from the kiss, he put his hands at her waist, and stood, helping her up with him. She took a step, he leaned, and their bodies came together, moving side to side, just enough to create friction where he was hurting most. Reaching a hand down, Emma cupped him there. He swelled even more, eager to do what they must to deactivate the attraction that would inevitably detonate at some point and kept distracting them from what mattered most to both of them.

The job.

He was ready to lay her down on the lounger not two feet away. To push her skirt up her hips, get her panties out of the way and come.

Condom. The thought floated in and out. *Wallet.*

She was rubbing slowly, methodically, on his fly, her tongue kissing him with more fire than he'd ever felt from a woman. Her nipples were rock-hard. He could feel them against his chest. Arms around her, he pulled her closer, meaning that they touched with more pressure, not more completely. The only way to be more complete was to get unnecessary clothing out of the way and be inside her.

Moving against her hand, Jayden had to remind himself to slow down. No matter how urgent the business matter at hand, she deserved a man who respected her womanhood, not an animal about to devour her.

"You want to move this inside?" he asked, thinking that the bed would be more comfortable to her. And his wallet...was it in his back pocket?

"Something wrong with that lounger?" She moaned against his lips, sending more shuddering need through him.

"Hell no," he muttered back. Having sex outside... hell yeah.

She was reaching for his fly. He went for her breasts. Cupping them simultaneously, no padding there, moving his palms against the tips while she worked the button on his jeans. The closure gave and the relief of pressure was both a blessing and a curse. He slid his hands inside her blouse, liking the thin silk separating his skin from hers. So thin, he slipped beneath it easily and then around to undo the clasp. Almost as easily as she yanked down his zipper.

He sprang free. He had to have her. The pain was almost excruciating.

Her breasts were partially bared now, the nipples exposed to the warm night air. Had he undone those buttons? Hoped to God he hadn't ripped them.

Pushing her backward, holding her tight as he guided them toward the lounger, Jayden sank his tongue deeply into her mouth, mimicking other things he'd like to do with it. Thinking about them. And still somehow managing to get her on her back without falling on top of her.

Or dropping her.

He dropped his jeans instead, stepped out of one leg, and then, with a knee between hers, he lowered himself down, sliding her skirt up as he went. The material was tight, as though teasing him, and he pushed harder, exposing silk-laced cotton underwear.

The thin silk he'd been expecting would have seduced him. This...this conservative piece of fabric, that screamed "good girl" to him enticed him on a whole new level. He had to stop a second, hold on to his release with every ounce of willpower so that he could give her the pleasure he'd promised this coupling would be for her.

"I need to get a condom," he said, shocked at the tension in his voice. Like he was being strangled.

"I've got one." She pulled it from the waistband of her skirt. A little pocket there? Or had she been wearing it there, between her waistband and that delectable skin all night?

If he'd known, he'd have been hard all through dinner.

He almost exploded when she ripped the packet open with her teeth, and yanked at her panties as she sheathed him with her delicate hand. It should have been awkward. His big body on that lounger for one, but she moved in tandem with him, doing her jobs while he did his, rubbing her crotch against his hand as he bared her to the openness of his backyard.

He entered her effortlessly. Gloriously. As smooth and tight and right as it had ever been. Expecting it to be quick. Hard. Instead he slowed as he moved. Looking at her. Finding her staring right at him. Into him.

And he didn't want it to end. Didn't want to finish. Stilling himself inside her, he kissed her. Softly. Mating their tongues in a quiet conversation that was no less passionate. He touched her breasts, exploring their fullness in a hello that would stay with him. While she held him.

When his lips left hers, she was watching him. Smiling at him.

He smiled back and started to move. Slowly. Drawing out the seconds into minutes until they both moved, coming together so hard he could hear the touch of their bodies.

Her gaze narrowed and her breathing changed. She was close. They were both so close. And…

As soon as she started to pulse around him, he let go. And kept letting go. So much, it was almost embarrassing.

What an experience.

The most incredible sex ever.

He wanted to tell her how special she was. How glad that she'd come into his life. To ask her to spend the night.

Their agreement didn't leave room for those kinds of words. They weren't in love. Or starting a relationship.

Scooting to his side on the lounger, he helped her turn to hers, spooning her just while they caught their breath.

Holding on.

Chapter 12

She almost fell asleep. Catching herself just as she was dozing off, with her naked butt nestling against Jayden on his backyard lounger, Emma told herself to get her ass in gear. Her darker side suggested that she just go ahead and doze. See where the night would lead them. Maybe wait to see if there'd be more sex.

Or an invitation to spend the night sleeping in the man's arms.

She listened for a second. Until she started imagining how that might feel, snuggled up in Jayden Powell's embrace between the sheets. Then she sat up.

"I have to go," she said right out loud. She'd tried for her court voice. Managed a weak rendition.

Still, it worked. Jayden was off the lounger, handing over her panties by the time she was on her feet, smoothing her skirt back down her thighs. Stuffing the underwear in the satchel she'd left by the table, she was embarrassed as hell to realize she still had her pumps on. And her blouse was missing a button.

Without another word, she grabbed her keys out of her satchel, flung the bag over her shoulder and walked to the door that would lead through his house to the front door and her car just beyond.

"Thanks for dinner," she called over her shoulder, briefly aware that he'd followed her, and let herself out.

"Thanks for dinner?" During the entire three miles from his neighborhood to hers, through the gate into her community and then to her house, she stumbled around that last line. Replaying it, out loud, in all kinds of ways.

Not a single version sounded anything but inane.

Thanks for dinner. They'd had mind-blowing sex and that's what she came up with? *Thanks for dinner.*

What could he be thinking? That she had sex as nonchalantly as some people ate dinner? You could eat with those you cared about, or just as easily do it alone? Or with strangers? That you were satiated and went home?

That she'd just experienced a life-changing event and was scared out of her wits?

No. Not that. He couldn't think that. It just wasn't true. Was it?

She pulled into her garage, pushed the remote on her visor to close the door behind her and got out of the car.

In any event, it didn't matter what he thought. They weren't starting anything.

No, they were finishing off whatever waywardness was between them in a practical and emotionally healthy manner—

Ms. Shadow's *hogwash* was cut off midstream as she came through the garage door into the kitchen and saw something written on the sliding-glass door leading to her pool. In her private, walled-in backyard. With a locked-gate access in a gated community.

Leave it alone.

The words were roughly scrawled on the glass, as though written by someone who'd just learned to write. Or written backward. They were uneven. Big. Red. Legible.

Retreating immediately to her car, she locked herself in and, willing her garage door to open quickly as she started her vehicle, dialed 9-1-1.

Jayden was in bed, watching TV since he wasn't going to kid himself into thinking he was going to close his eyes and go to sleep—rather, he'd be closing his eyes and getting hard as he relived the after dinner feast he'd enjoyed—when his phone rang.

Emma.

"Hey!" He grabbed his phone up immediately, sliding the answer button across the screen with his thumb with the phone already on its way to his ear. "I'm glad you called."

She wanted to talk as badly as he did, he assumed. Was unsatisfied with the way things stood between them. Deeply so.

"I need you to check Bill Heber's location from tonight." Her terse words didn't fit into the postsex daze.

Sitting up, he muted the TV, some documentary about the way cheese was made, and flipped on the lamp on his nightstand.

"Come again…"

"The locations app, I need you to check it, please." She was sounding professional…but…familiar, too…

like she had the right to call him at ten at night to ask a favor.

He yanked on a pair of basketball shorts to cover his nudity, stumbling a bit as he tried to step into them while holding them with one hand.

"What's going on?" he asked, half hopping toward the bedroom door on his way to his office. He could check the app on his phone, but didn't want to take it away from his ear. To stop talking to her.

"Someone was at my house tonight. They wrote 'Leave it alone' on my sliding-glass door in red."

"When tonight?" She'd only been gone a little over an hour.

Holding the phone with his shoulder, he quickly backtracked to the chair by his bed, grabbed the jeans that were always laid out in case of emergency, pulled them up and reached for the shirt.

"While I was at your house."

A dozen questions sprang immediately to mind. "Are you there now?" he asked, his unbuttoned shirt hanging on his shoulders as he grabbed his wallet, keys and gun, and slid into the shoes at the bottom of his bed.

"No. I'm at the police station, making a report. They're there now, checking things out."

"I'm on my way down," he told her, disconnecting before she could even attempt to tell him his presence wasn't necessary.

Only to himself did he admit that, for once, his needing to be "there" didn't have a whole lot to do with the case.

He checked his app and Bill's whereabouts that evening, while waiting at a red light. Tossing his phone on the passenger seat next to him as the light turned green, and picking it up again at the next red light.

Bill's phone had been in the same place all evening. His home. Right where he was supposed to be. He'd driven there from work, right at the time that fit the schedule that Jayden had for him. The man was free to come and go, of course, without reporting to his parole officer, but Jayden knew about any scheduled events like church or meetings, just because Bill had chosen to report them to him. And Bill knew that if he went anywhere without the phone app he'd agreed to carry, all bets were off as far as Jayden was concerned.

On his way into the station, he called Bill, just to make certain his phone was on. And with him. He asked Bill how he was doing and heard how the man had been watching a baseball game and his team had won. He chatted about a couple of game-winning plays. Things he and Jayden talked about pretty regularly as they both followed the same team.

The receptionist at the front desk of the Santa Raquel police station was expecting him and directed him to a small private meeting room just feet away from Chantel's desk. The detective, a transplant from Las Sendas, just north of San Diego—via upstate New York—had worked with Jayden a time or two. And anyone who took her slender, blond frame to mean the woman lacked the strength of a larger officer, or who attempted to test that theory, would find himself hurting. How badly depended on how pissed she was.

That night she was pissed.

"Do you know where your offender, Bill Heber, was tonight?" she greeted him, standing from one of the four chairs at the wooden table—the only furniture in the room. Emma was all business, sitting next to where Chantel had been, leaving him one of the two chairs across from them. She looked expectant, waiting for him to hand over his client.

"I do," he said, his gaze traveling over Emma quickly, but thoroughly, assuring himself she was okay without alerting anyone to the fact that he knew her intimately.

That she'd left his house dressed in the exact same clothes, but without her panties on, a little over an hour before.

He was sure she'd put them back on. And by the look on her face, she'd put their time on his lounger completely out of her immediate consciousness, as well.

"He was at home all night. Just as he should have been."

"At home." Chantel's tone was skeptical. As if he'd said the man was on the moon rather than somewhere normal—like the place he lived.

"Yes."

"And someone can verify that?"

"He lives alone, but yes, I'm certain I can get neighbors to verify that he was there. His phone moved from work to home at exactly the time it should have, and never left."

"I'm sorry, Jay, but you and I both know that that means nothing. He could have left the phone at home," Chantel returned.

"He never knows when I'm going to call. He knows if I do and he doesn't pick up, he could be heading back to jail."

"How often do you call him in the evening?"

"Once or twice a week." He made a point of checking in randomly, unpredictably, for his clients' own protection.

Jayden glanced at Emma. Her lips were white, her eyes wide and slightly shocked-looking. Like she couldn't believe any of this was happening.

She'd been threatened.

He wanted one minute alone with whoever had done it.

"Bill watched the game tonight." He named the team and the time. "He gave me a blow-by-blow of the game, not just highlights that were on the news." He knew because he'd watched the highlights since he'd missed the game itself.

He'd been too busy having sex with Emma to even remember the game had been on.

"Whoever did this… We have a prosecutor in danger, and we can't play around here," he said, checking himself when he'd been about to make it a lot more personal. "I suggest you look at her other cases," he continued. "Luke Lincoln comes immediately to mind. He's also one of my clients. He refused the app, but we all know he's out tonight…"

Pulling out his phone, silently castigating himself for not thinking straight enough soon enough, he dialed Lincoln, the offender no one had been able to reach on the phone since his arrest.

Luke didn't answer. No surprise there. Officers hadn't found him yet, and they'd been searching since dinnertime. At his sister's house. His job. Talking to people in the area. Law enforcement in Northern California had been notified, as well.

"I'll put out an APB," Chantel said, leaving the room as she pulled out her phone. Leaving Jayden alone with Emma.

Her hair was mussed—from his lounger, he knew—but with the wild, curly look she normally wore, and with the fact that it was getting closer to midnight, a bit of disarray would look more ordinary than not.

"You okay?" he asked, trying not to make it personal but failing as her gaze met his.

She nodded. "You think it's Luke?"

"Makes sense, doesn't it?"

"I don't know." She wrapped her arms around her middle. "He won in court today. What's there for me to 'leave alone'?"

"His parole hearing. He's warning you not to show up at that hearing." The facts were completely obvious to Jayden.

"I have nothing to do with that. I'm not the prosecutor on that case."

"No, but you know as well as I do that the parole board will welcome any input you have to give them."

She nodded but didn't look convinced. "It makes more sense that it was Bill. You questioned him today. Maybe he figured out that he's being looked at."

"Unless he knows that Suzie's been hurt again, I highly doubt that he'd jump to that conclusion. I check up on him regularly."

"Asking him to verify things you found on the location app?"

"Not always," he told her. "But sometimes. I hardly think that would have him jumping to conclusions…"

"Why else would you be asking him about times he was in Santa Raquel?" Sitting forward, her arms on the table, Emma faced him. "He knows I know he got away with murder. And that I'm going to do everything I can to be sure he pays for that."

There was no reaching her on this one. She was so damned convinced.

That meant that for all three of them—her, Bill and himself—Jayden had to stay on top of every aspect of the case, everything she was pursuing where Bill was concerned, to prevent a grave injustice.

Chapter 13

The last thing Emma needed was to be all alone in a quiet little room with Jayden Powell. A detective's office that was usually buzzing with energy, activity and noise when Emma visited was mostly dark and quiet on the other side of the glass from where they sat.

It was all too intimate. And emotional. Way too tempting to a shadow side that refused to go away. Her lesser self was pushing her way up and out with such force, Emma was having a hard time controlling her.

"How long were you home before you noticed?" Jayden's soft voice, that look in his eye, made her forget, for just a second, that she was completely creeped out.

"Less than a minute," she told him. "I saw it as soon as I walked in the door." From his house. Where they'd had wild and intense sex. *No.* She shook her head. "He was in my backyard," she said, needing him to understand just how dangerous his offender really was. She loved that he gave his guys the benefit of the doubt. Many deserved it.

But some just did not.

"He got in through the community gate, which he could have done by waiting close by and following someone else in. Our gate takes a moment to close because it's so big and heavy, and there's time for a second vehicle to slide through..."

"There should be surveillance, then, if that's the case."

"Chantel has already put in a request for a warrant to view the tape. Hopefully they'll have it yet tonight." And then he'd see that Bill Heber was a serious threat.

"It's possible that whoever was there climbed a wall to get in."

"Officers are checking the perimeter of the community," she said, feeling creeped out about the whole thing. All the manpower on her behalf...it was more attention than she wanted.

And yet...she didn't want to just go home and pretend it hadn't happened, either.

"A prosecutor being threatened...that's a big deal for all of us. For so many reasons. It puts our judicial system at risk."

"I know. And the fact that he climbed my wall—it's six feet of brick—or made it over my back gate, which is also six feet..."

"I'm assuming someone checked to see that the lock on the gate hadn't been tampered with?" he asked.

"It hadn't been. I wish it had. Then they'd know where to brush for prints. As it is, they're brushing randomly, hoping to get something..."

Jayden's hair was askew, like he'd been in bed when she'd called him. She was only now noticing. That told her just how out of sorts she really was. The shirt and jeans? Those she recognized. Figured if she got close enough, she might smell herself on them.

Could Chantel?

Oh, God, if anyone knew what they'd done, she'd...

"I thought I was being followed a couple of times this week." She blurted the words to distract herself from thoughts of needing to be safely back in his arms.

She could take care of herself.

"I told Chantel about it."

And she hadn't told him. Either time. Because it hadn't seemed professionally necessary for him to know since she'd been certain she'd been overreacting. And personally...well they weren't...personal. They were just...having sex.

You wouldn't know that by the way he spent the next several minutes grilling her. And then checking Bill Heber's phone app to verify that both times she'd thought she'd been followed, the man had been no-where near Santa Raquel. And then passed another long minute as he attempted to call her out for not tell-ing him about it.

"There was nothing to tell," she said, her tone firm-ing enough that he backed off.

Sat back. Studied her.

And made her want to crawl back into his arms again.

"I had a great time earlier tonight." Did his voice really just drip sex? Or was she losing all control? And was he reading her mind, too?

"I did, too." She couldn't sit there and lie to him.

But added, "It was just like we said it would be...just physical."

The way he was studying her made her uncomfortable. She shifted in her chair, pulled her skirt down underneath her thighs. Worried about the missing top button on her blouse. Nothing but the edge of her bra showed. A lot of women displayed more than that.

She wasn't a lot of women.

And her breasts tingled. Her nipples hardened. Remembering.

"My physique wants to know if you'd be interested in a repeat performance sometime."

"Of course." The words slipped out. Inside, Emma slapped her darker side down. But it was too late. Jayden was already smiling. Not a big smile. Not sitting there in what was really an interrogation room. But a smile that reached her baser instincts with a thunk. "If...you know, the whole idea was to rid ourselves of the magnetism. Even in relationships that fades with familiarity."

"Right."

He nodded. Didn't look challenging at all. Good.

They'd get rid of their desires and be done.

Chantel wanted to send Emma home under police protection—just until Luke Lincoln was found. She understood the concern, she'd said. Shared it. But added that in her neighborhood cars weren't allowed to park on the street. Of course, they could get permission from the homeowners' association, due to the circumstances, but she was loath to draw undue attention to herself. In small communities like hers, word spread. It was bad enough that they'd note the police car out front. Still, she could play it off as minor vandalism. She hadn't been robbed. There was no reason for anyone else in her community to be afraid. And she liked her current anonymity.

Those who knew of her at all, knew her simply as a lawyer who worked all the time, was quiet, lived alone. She explained herself to him and Chantel quite clearly.

Jayden could hear a hint of fear in her voice, though.

There were other options. Cars in her driveway, for one. Surely her neighbors wouldn't find it completely a shock for her to an overnight guest.

"I just…there is so much real crime out there," she said. "I don't want to waste personnel watching my house while I sleep."

He got that. The attention wouldn't feel right to him, either.

"I'll just stay in a hotel. At least for tonight."

"Luke's my responsibility." Jayden spoke up for the first time since Chantel had come back into the little room to let them know that the warrant to pick Luke up had been sent to departments all over the state, but no one knew where he was. His sister said she hadn't seen him since he'd left court earlier that day. He hadn't been due to work, because of the court hearing. And, so far, no one up north had seen him, either. "I can follow you home. Sleep on your couch."

Or in her bed. Whichever she preferred.

He half expected her to stick with her hotel plan. Didn't like the idea that he really didn't know what to expect with her. Usually, when he slept with a woman, there was at least a modicum of expectation…

"The city would most definitely put you up in a hotel," Chantel said when Emma didn't immediately respond.

"If I go to a hotel, I'll foot the bill," Emma said, standing.

Jayden stood, too. "I'll pay for it. As I said, Luke's my responsibility."

Seriously? It was past midnight and they were going to stand there and squabble about a hundred bucks?

"No." Emma put her satchel on her shoulder. "I'll just go home. And you can sleep on my couch, if you must," she said, glancing at Jayden and then back at Chantel. "I'd have to go back to the house anyway to get my things. Someone would have to go with me. And I'd rather sleep in my own bed. If whoever did this is watching the house—and somehow I feel certain that Bill is—then he'll know he won if I'm not there. And he'll know he's going to lose if he makes a move while Jayden is."

Just when he'd been relaxing into the idea that Emma wanted him in her home as badly as he wanted to be there, she came up with a perfectly valid, completely professional justification for his presence that had absolutely nothing to do with him personally.

"Just for tonight, then." Chantel nodded. "Because it's so late. We'll reassess in the morning. See if Luke's been picked up by then. If not, we can figure out whether or not we should move you out."

Emma nodded. Thanked the detective. And walked out the door.

Presumably expecting Jayden to follow her.

Emma had a few rough minutes that night. Pulling into her driveway was one of them. The police still at the scene told her they had checked her house, both inside and out, with no sign of anything other than the writing on her back door. Her desert rock landscaping prevented even so much as a footprint. They took some pictures, would analyze everything, but they had very little to go on. The perp had probably been wearing gloves, so what fingerprints they'd managed to collect—nowhere near the writing on the glass—would probably belong to Emma.

At least they'd cleaned the words away. A courtesy to her, she was sure. Because of who she was.

Jayden, who'd come in right behind her, having asked her to wait for him before entering the house, confirmed her thoughts. That whoever had been to her house investigating had been nice enough to wipe away the evidence.

He'd insisted on looking around one more time, too. It was his first time in her home. She kind of wanted to walk through it with him, but didn't. His being there was business. Not personal.

Still, she thought about each room as she heard him move to and from them. Wondered what he thought of the little trunk filled with flowers and antique perfume bottles in her bathroom. Or if he noticed that she hadn't dusted in over a week.

She held her breath while he checked out her room—the floral quilt ensemble on her bed, with all the matching throw pillows and wall art, made the room her happy place. She loved every single thing about that room. The way the sun came in. The view of the ocean in the far distance if you stood just right and knew what you were looking for. The plush carpet.

Definitely not a guy place.

She allowed the distraction of Jayden in her home, to keep her from the darker thoughts threatening…what if whoever had left that warning had actually come inside her home? What if he came back?

By the time Jayden had come to join her in the living room, she already had a sheet on the couch, a blanket and the bed pillows from the spare room. She'd thought about suggesting he just stay in the extra bedroom, but he'd better serve his purpose for being there by staying close to the entrances of the home.

He hadn't balked. Had wished her good-night. And she'd gone to bed.

Ms. Shadow had whined a bit. And in the middle of the night, when she'd sat straight up in bed from a sound sleep, she'd thought about going out to Jayden, maybe asking him to join her, but then she'd heard the flush of the toilet in the hall bathroom and knew why she'd woken in the first place.

It had taken a while for her to get back to sleep. Her fault, not his. Or rather, Ms. Shadow's. But, all in all, they made it through what could have been a hugely awkward situation with little discomfort. He'd gotten up before her, all of his bedding folded on the couch when she came out—dressed in shorts and a T-shirt because she had company—to make her coffee. She'd offered him a cup. He'd said he had to get home to shower and get to work and was out the door before she'd even put her pod of dark roast in the brewer. He was working on Saturday. That didn't surprise her.

It was what she planned to do, too. Just as soon as she'd inhaled her first cup of coffee. And cleaned her back window again. Hell, she'd clean all of her windows, just in case the creep had touched any of them.

By her second cup of coffee, she was feeling better. She was showered, dressed in a casual, tie-dyed summer dress and on her third cup of coffee, in her home office, when she heard from Chantel again. And then hung up and called Jayden.

"Luke's been picked up. And he has an alibi," she said the moment Jayden answered. He'd be hearing officially, she was sure, within minutes. Chantel had just called her immediately. "After he left court," she continued, "he went to spend the night at his mother's. She and his sister don't get along, apparently, and she sided with him, in that the sister shouldn't have taken him in if she was going to feel the need to put him at risk by having a gun. The mother verified all of that. They apparently were both confused to see police at their door, thinking he'd been released because he'd had the charges dropped."

"It wouldn't be the first time a mother lied for her son," Jayden noted.

"A neighbor saw Luke leave there this morning." She needed him to be on Bill. To not let up. Not for her sake. For Suzie's. "The police caught up with him when he went into work. He said he was going to try to get moved to his mother's house. Said that he didn't want to go back to his sister's since 'she'd done him wrong that way.'" She quoted Chantel's rendition of Luke's own words. "That's when they told him his release had been a mistake."

"A more accurate account might be that his sister refused to have him back after he made her lie for him in court. And that the gun is his," Jayden said. "I'm on my way to speak with her now. The preliminary parole revocation hearing has not been canceled. The board will hear from me and witnesses, and determine if they think Luke violated the conditions of his parole. It's set for Monday."

Emma hoped justice would be done. Trusted that it would be. It appeared that Luke had an alibi for that night. That he wasn't her stalker.

But that could be a lie, too.

Turning to her own case, she said, "The surveillance tape showed no instances of a car entering my community on the back of another last night. However, there was one walk-in. Looked to be male, six feet, two hundred pounds. Blue long-sleeved shirt. Jeans. Dark baseball cap with no logo visible. The image was blurry and the guy's head was turned away from the camera."

"As though he knew where the camera was," Jayden observed.

"Bill Heber once lived in a gated community. He fits the description."

"So do hundreds of other men, Emma, but I'll stop by to see him this afternoon. And see if anyone in his neighborhood noticed his truck gone." He didn't sound happy about the task.

"Thank you," she said, understanding that Jayden didn't want to crush Bill's chances of making it on the outside by doubting him. Hounding him. But the man wasn't going to stay clean, no matter what Jayden did. The only question was whether or not Suzie would make it until they had enough evidence to convict Bill this time.

"The message was written in red lipstick. The lab is testing further to see if they can determine a particular kind or brand," she told him. "Chantel said she'd send officers to canvass the local drugstores within a few miles of Heber's place to see if someone matching his description bought any lipstick recently, but I suggested that you might want to do it yourself," she offered the concession she'd sought for him.

"I do want to. Thank you."

He was on the wrong side of this one, but he was there for the right reasons. She'd help where she could. Just not when it came to putting Suzie at further risk.

"What about your other cases?" he asked when she'd thought them done with business and had been wondering what he was doing with his Saturday night. "Is anyone looking into the possibility that whoever left that message on your door was someone else? Neither Luke nor Bill Heber?"

"Chantel picked up my case files this morning and already has people checking through them. Really, at this point, it kind of seems like overkill to me. All the man-hours being spent on this. It was a note on the door. No one got hurt."

"Not yet."

Now he was scaring her.

With reason, she knew. She just didn't want to confront the degree of danger. It wasn't just a note. Behaviorists would find the red lipstick significant. The fact that it was her back door, not her front, factored into the severity factor, too. And her home, not her office. Or in the mail. The perpetrator was letting her know he could get to her if and when he wanted to do so.

She'd faced some really heinous people in the courtroom over the years. Put a lot of them away. Some cases she'd lost. And some of the offenders were out now. It was a downside to her job…the fear part. She couldn't let it get the best of her.

"I owe you a dinner," her darker side blurted.

Emma should call Sara at The Lemonade Stand to see if she'd talked to Suzie. Or Chantel. Emma wanted to talk to Suzie herself. Maybe she'd missed something the last time she'd been up against Bill. She'd underestimated him.

Jayden hadn't replied to Ms. Shadow's dinner comment. Emma noticed, even though she was trying her best to stay focused on work: the one thing she did that contributed to society. Both sides of her agreed on that one.

"My bourbon pork is decent," she said, admitting to herself that she wasn't looking forward to the evening there alone. Had the man been at her back door the night before because he'd known she was gone? Was he watching her? Still?

Or had she just been lucky she hadn't been home?

Of course, that all led to, what if he came back?

This person must be a proficient criminal. He'd left very little real evidence. Nothing easily traceable. Most men with an ax to grind against her, most likely had acquired that ax by being one of her defendants. Bill Heber had been slick enough four years before to get away with murder. And he could have learned a thing or two in prison, too.

"Do you want to come over for dinner tonight?" She finally just put it out there.

"I was wondering if you were going to ask." There was a hint of...pleasure in his voice. He'd been messing with her with that silence.

He'd gotten her to declare herself.

Points to him.

"I'm wondering if you're ever going to answer."

"That depends."

"On what?"

"On whether or not your invitation is professional or personal?"

"The threat is still out there." She couldn't believe she'd actually said that. That she was using a serious situation in such a way. "You don't want to keep me safe tonight?"

"I'll keep you safe. If it's professional, I'll be over after dinner."

He'd put it all right back on her.

So…fine. She wasn't one to back down from a challenge. "My dinner invitation stands."

"Under my specifications?"

"Yes."

"What time should I be there?"

Chapter 14

Jayden picked up a bottle of the same wine Emma had brought to his house the night before. There was still half a bottle at his house, but bringing that would be tacky.

He almost grabbed his six-pack, too. Then didn't.

Freshly showered and in blue shorts and a white polo shirt, with a pair of tennis shoes, he showed up at her door exactly on time. Six o'clock, just like she'd said.

Figured them for a nice dinner and bed by a little after seven. He wanted to take things nice and slow. Maybe snack in between sex sessions. She had a pool, he'd noticed the night before, and he had some ideas there, too. One thing he'd discovered about Emma Martin last night was that she'd walk on the wild side with him.

At least a little bit.

The thought had tantalized him on and off all day. At the most inappropriate times. It hadn't interfered with his work, though. If that happened, this was done.

When he first walked into her home, he was certain something was wrong. She'd pulled open the door but left it hanging there, telling him to come on in, and all he saw was her back.

The place was darker than his own. Far darker than it had been when he'd left that morning. Every curtain and blind in the place was drawn.

He had kind of an emotional reaction to that. Moved past it.

She was at the stove, stirring something in one pan while another large skillet held about twelve slices of tenderloin. Had she invited others over?

He'd only brought one bottle of wine.

And conversation for an intimate twosome.

"That smells good," he told her, refraining from a kiss on the back of her neck, but just barely. Her hair looked like she'd tried to contain it with a band, but a lot had sprung free. Her tight skirt was short, black, made out what looked like T-shirt material.

He reached out and touched her backside because… he just did.

She continued to cook. Her arms, slender and busy, lifted out over the pans in front of her. Pressing himself against her, he slid his hands around the white cotton hugging her torso to cup her breasts.

Her spoon slipped, but she recovered. Stirred.

"This has to reduce to half a cup in eleven minutes," she said. Her nipples hardened beneath his fingers.

"How long has it been?" he asked, watching her cook

from over her shoulder as he continued to gently tease her body.

"About nine."

He had two minutes to play.

"The pork is four minutes on each side. We're into two on the second side."

Timed perfectly. He wasn't surprised.

"It smells wonderful." His nose was just above the mass of blond curls.

"Yes. Well, if you want to eat food, you better back away. Another second or two of that and the pork can burn."

He was glad to hear it.

But went to find a corkscrew and tend to the wine.

She'd set the small table in her kitchen. It was just an eat-in alcove, and the table—a high-top—only sat four. But the walls were decorated with French cooking art and the alcove was cozy. This wasn't dining room entertainment. They weren't an item.

"I figured us for the table I saw this morning out by the pool," he told her, bringing their glasses of wine to the table. She'd said she was fine, but the drapes were all drawn and…if she was scared, they should talk about it.

"Since this is personal and we're not starting something, I'll just tell you that I had an incident last night and would prefer to stay indoors." She put the plate of pork in the middle of the brown wood high-top. Added a gravy boat of sauce. Pulled some little red potatoes and fresh green beans out of the oven.

"Let's toast," he said, holding up his glass before either of them sat. And when she lifted her glass to his, added, "To being friends with benefits."

She hesitated, studying him, and then clicked.

He sat.

"I'm fine," she said before he had a chance to figure out how to bring up the vandalism that had her hiding out behind closed blinds. "I just… Until…well… I felt like a sitting duck, being in here knowing someone could see in."

"I'm glad to hear it," he told her. "You're taking the threat seriously."

"It's my first," she told him as if that was some big secret or something to be ashamed of. "Others in the office have had them, but always sent to the office. And, like, in the eight years I've been there, there've only been three."

"Did they find out who sent them?"

"Nope. And nothing ever happened to the address-ees, either."

The threat against her had come to her home. "Is there anyone in your personal life—anyone who might think you could expose something?"

She'd said her ex-husband had been a high-powered attorney, not always working with the most law-abiding clients.

"What personal life?" she smirked. And then, "Seri-ously, I work all the time. I haven't dated in over a year. This person just told me to 'leave it alone.' That's not like someone who's mad at me personally. Or jealous or anything. It's someone who wants me to quit work-ing on something I'm working on. It has to be. Work is all I do. Chantel is going through my current cases…"

He agreed with her.

"I'm sure it's Bill."

He'd visited with Bill that afternoon. And with a couple of his neighbors. "He was home all night. I've got a witness who saw him through his living room window, watching the game."

"What time?"

"Around nine."

"I was almost home by then."

"I've verified that his truck was in his driveway at six. And again between seven thirty and eight."

"The security camera showed Bill walking in the gate behind a car at just after seven. And even if he was home, he could have paid someone in the neighborhood, or elsewhere, to do it for him."

She had an argument for everything—because, in her job, she'd seen just about everything.

He didn't want to spend the evening arguing.

Emma didn't really want to talk about this case any further. Or any of them. She wanted to forget, for a few minutes at least, that someone was going to be pissed when she didn't "leave it alone." Whatever that meant.

And that whoever it was was fairly certain she'd know who he was. The only defendant she knew who'd ever given her cause to fear for her life was Bill Heber. The way he'd looked at her in the courtroom…there was no way she'd imagined the anger simmering beneath his surface. The only thing standing between him and his wife had been Emma and he wasn't going to have that.

In the end, he'd been right. She hadn't been able to stand between him and Suzie.

There was a new end in sight now. And she wasn't backing down.

"Did you have a chance to check any of the drugstores for lipstick purchases?" she asked because they had to talk and she didn't dare venture into conversation that would make her like Jayden Powell any more than she already did.

She wasn't going to satisfy her curiosity where his life was concerned. Only his body.

Take it or leave it. That last was for her shadow side. The demon side that had been tempting her to throw all her lessons to the wind and hook up with the parole officer. If he'd have her.

One of her safety nets was that he didn't want a relationship any more than she did. Even if she lost her mind and begged, he'd say no…right?

"Two of the three places that sell lipstick within the vicinity of Bill's phone app activity have already been crossed off," he said. "The third said that the clerk who'd been on all week would be in on Monday. I'll check back then. And no, no one recognized him, or remembered any man buying lipstick."

He could have picked it up at the big-box store at the edge of town, she thought to herself.

"What's that?" Jayden was looking at the calendar on the side of her refrigerator. She never sat in that seat. Never noticed the calendar in view from there.

"A calendar."

"It's got X's on most of the days. You counting down for something?"

So, this was embarrassing.

"It's my cycle. So I'll know when I'm ovulating." Just one of those personal things that had nothing to do with him.

His face lost all expression. It was like he was there with her and then he wasn't.

"You're trying to have a baby?" She was pretty sure a guy couldn't look more horrified.

"No!" Standing, she carried her plate to the sink. Poured a tad bit more wine. "Well...yes, but not right now," she corrected herself, rinsing her plate and then moving back to get his. "I'm not using you for your sperm, if that's what you're afraid of. As a matter of fact, I'm making certain that we aren't...satisfying this thing between us...when I'm ovulating."

He stood, too, helping to clear the rest of the table. "Glad to have that cleared up."

With the water running, she stopped to stare at him. "You actually think I'd do that?" What did it matter what he thought? They weren't going to be together.

"I don't. But it's a bit of a shock to be having sex with a woman who announces that she's tracking when she ovulates."

He was looking more like himself. Topped off his glass of wine, though he'd only taken a few sips of what he'd had to begin with. He really should have brought some beer.

Or she should have picked up some. She'd seen the six-pack in his refrigerator the night before. She knew what he liked.

"It's all part of my life plan," she said. "I know I'm never going to marry again. Or be in a long-term committed relationship. I'm not looking for a man to father a child. But I want a family. I've had a child growing inside me. I've never gotten over losing it. That alone tells me how badly I need to be a parent. I've already got an anonymous donor picked out."

"You need to be a parent."

Leaning against the cupboard, he watched while she finished rinsing the sink, wiping down the faucet. "Don't you?" she asked. "Someday?"

"Absolutely not."

"You sound pretty sure about that."

"I've never been more sure about anything in my life."

Okay then, that was clear.

"I've been seeing a fertility specialist," she told him, taking her wine into the living room. Heading back to bed didn't seem like such a fine idea at the moment. It wasn't even dark outside. Maybe a movie would be good. Something a bit raunchy. "My first attempt to conceive was this past month. That's what the calendar was for. I was inseminated a little over two weeks ago and found out on Wednesday that the attempt was unsuccessful." And if the news scared him off, so be it. They weren't starting a relationship. They were having sex. And it was going to end sometime.

He sat on the couch, so close their thighs were touching.

"I'm sorry." His gaze was warm again. Sincere.

"For what?"

"I'm sorry you had bad news. And sorry that I over-reacted like a first-rate jackass."

She thought for a second. Nodded. "I'd say, given the circumstances, some bit of unease was natural."

Mostly what she thought was that the man got more incredible every time she was with him. He'd apologized. Acknowledged that he'd been a bit harsh there for a second. No one was perfect, but when you were with someone who was willing to take honest looks, to admit to mistakes...

Keith had never done that. Drake, either. Never. Ever. Both of them. Like it was in the wild man's genes to believe they were invincible. Never wrong.

Like Jayden believed himself about Bill Heber.

Still, he'd admitted he could be wrong. He'd see reason about Bill, too, once they had enough proof. And in the meantime, he was keeping close tabs on the guy so she knew Suzie would be safe.

"So why such a strong reaction?" she asked him.

"You know the reason. I'm on my second chance. What's left of my life is about serving others. About making them feel good. Not about me."

"So…you don't think you could be a great dad someday? Not now. Now with me. But someday? You're loyal. Hardworking. You give people the benefit of the doubt. And believe in forgiveness…some child could benefit from that."

He took another sip of wine. Not looking at her anymore.

"I'm not going to have what I took from someone else." He'd said something similar the other day. When they'd agreed to have a fling. Rather than a relationship.

"You took someone's ability to be a father?"

"Not directly, but yes."

"How?"

"You're breaking the rules now."

She supposed she was. "I told you about my past."

"I'm sorry, Emma. I'm not going to tell you about mine. Take it or leave it." His head turned sideways, their shoulders and thighs touching. He gave her such a serious look, she had to take a moment to absorb it.

Whatever had happened to him went deep. Too deep.

"Okay," she said, still holding his gaze, as serious as he was.

"You sure?"

"Yeah. I am."

Chapter 15

They had sex again and again that whole night. Jayden couldn't get enough of her, in enough ways. He thought about the pool, but didn't want to take her out to real-life memories that would intrude on them.

Her room was like some kind of womanly garden, a hive where desire swarmed thick as honey. It wrapped around them, creating some kind of masterpiece. Not a relationship. Or a future.

Or a child. He had no doubts about that.

But it was something that would always exist. Even if only just in that one memory.

They worked hard at it. Sweating, panting. At one point there were tears in her eyes. She'd been on top of him, had just had an orgasm, and as she'd looked down at him, he'd seen the moisture. She made a joke then.

Moved around on his body, distracting the hell out of him, and the moment was gone.

The next morning, though, it was as if the night had never been. Things were strictly professional again. The fact that she was so close to having a child made it a little easier for him to find his necessary distance. He'd been more than a little surprised to hear that.

"People remember what they see," Emma told him as she brought him coffee in bed. It was Sunday; he didn't have to rush off. Apparently she had things to do. She didn't join him under the covers, but rather, in shorts and a T-shirt, curled up in the armchair in the corner of the room. "They don't remember what they don't see."

"Okay."

"Bill's truck," she said, barreling right on ahead, as though they were sitting in either of their offices, a desk separating them rather than a few feet of bedroom carpet. "Someone saw it at six. Someone else around eight. No one saw it between those two times."

"No one saw him leave."

"But they didn't see him there, either."

Right. Grabbing his phone, Jayden checked his location app. Called up Bill's profile. It said he was at work.

At eight on a Sunday morning? Was it possible Bill was planting his phone on purpose? Outmaneuvering him? *Manipulating* him?

Excusing himself, saying he had to make a call, he pulled on his shorts and went outside, dialing Bill as he went. If the man was in Santa Raquel... If he—

"Bill Heber," the parolee answered on the second ring. As always. "And yeah, I'm working on Sunday morning," he said. He would have seen Jayden's number come up.

"The shop's closed."

"Johnson asked if I minded coming in. We got jobs piling up and he knows I don't have anything better to do. Besides, I'd rather be earning money than sitting in front of the television set."

"Okay, good." He'd overreacted. Was letting Emma get to him. Maybe in more ways than one. Pushing away a brief flash of the night he'd just spent—the physical and emotional power he'd allowed the woman to have over him—he focused on his client. "Everything going okay?"

"Since we spoke yesterday, you mean?"

"Yep."

"I'm a getting a bit nervous, actually," Bill said. "You being in touch so much. Like you think I might be up to something."

"Are you?"

"What do you think?" Bill replied.

"It doesn't matter what I think. Are you?"

"No." Then, "Of course not." Another pause and then Bill said, "I thought you were different."

"How so?"

"I thought you were giving me a straight shot. I trusted you with…like a weakling or something, telling you all that stuff about me. My regrets. You didn't believe a word of it, did you? To you I'm just an ex-con who can't help himself from screwing up again."

"That's not true." He *was* different. "Believe it or not, I'm protecting you, Bill." Jayden knew when the words came out of his mouth that he'd said too much.

"So they're looking at me? Someone thinks I already did something? Something's happened to Suzie, then? Is that what you're telling me?"

Jayden could almost feel the man's tension ratchet up along with the change in voice tone.

Damn. He was off his game. Too filled with sex. With Emma.

He'd said he wouldn't allow it to affect his work. He'd meant what he'd said. To Bill and to himself.

"Suzie's fine. At home and planning to go to work tomorrow, as far I know," he said. "Don't go getting all half-cocked on me and try to see her. I swear to you, she's fine."

At the moment. Because she was under police watch.

"Then why all the attention?"

"I just know I've been alerted to check in with you. And the more I do so, the more proof I have that you're innocent of anything that could come up in the future. You can trust me, man."

Unless the man reoffended. Then Jayden would be his worst enemy.

"I swear to God, I have not raised a hand to Suzie— or anyone—since my release. Nor am I going to do so."

Since his release. Bill had said many times that he hadn't ever hurt Suzie, and never would. It was the first time there'd been a disclaimer with the statement. Could be that Bill was specifying because they were discussing a current situation. But what if Emma was right? What if Bill *had* hit Suzie in the past? Did that change the now?

Having a second chance meant you'd blown your first one. What was past was past and you were starting over. Right? Getting it better the second time around. Had Bill lied to him about what he'd done the first time?

"Did you ever hit her in the past?"

"Not like that bitch prosecutor said." Bill's disregard

for Emma came out loud and clear, but that was nothing new to Jayden. Not from Bill or other offenders. Not many people were fond of those who put them away. To be rabidly accused, in front of a panel and courtroom of witnesses, in minute detail… Even if you were guilty, that was a tough gig.

And no matter how used he was to that kind of prosecutor battering conversation, it rankled more than a little to hear it directed at Emma. And made him a bit less fond of Bill Heber.

"But you did hit her?"

"I might have raised a hand to her a time or two. But I swear, Jayden, a slap, that's all it was. When I was sure she was lying to me about seeing another guy. I know it was wrong, unforgivable. But it was nothing like that Martin woman accused me of. Nothing. I die every day thinking about that baby we lost, all because of me. Because of my insane jealousy making her so stressed she couldn't eat. Couldn't sleep…"

The pain in Bill's words resonated with Jayden. After all the years he'd been doing the job, he'd learned to detect true remorse. Had always been pretty decent at reading people, even back when he'd been mostly about himself. Back then it had been a way to make sure his own world moved smoothly.

"Just stay away from her, okay?" he said now. "And if you hit a rough patch, call me. Or get to a group therapy session. Yeah?"

"Yeah."

"Talk soon," Jayden said, hoping to God Chantel and her people found the guy who was hurting Suzie Heber soon. Because he wasn't sure how much longer he was going to be able to keep Bill at bay. The man loved his wife. At some point he was going to give in to the need to protect her. It was an instinct, not a desire. Something that would push at him from the inside out and eventually win.

Just like Emma's belief that Bill was the culprit was pushing at him. Jayden had to find a way to do something about that.

Hanging up, he headed back inside.

Emma was in the kitchen, notes from Bill Heber's trial spread around her, when she heard Jayden come back inside. She had no idea who he'd been talking to. He'd been looking at his phone before he'd gone out; obviously had had a message that needed immediate attention.

She got it. He worked as much as she did. There was comfort in that.

She'd jumped into the shower, planning to head into the office for a few hours once Jayden left. Sometimes just being at her desk, especially when the office was quiet, settled everything inside her until she could find whatever puzzle piece she needed.

And she had a couple of court appearances in the morning. A manslaughter trial starting in a couple of weeks. There was always more to do than there was time to do it.

"I have to talk to Suzie Heber," she said when Jayden came into the kitchen fully dressed. She'd heard him go back to her room; figured he was probably getting ready to go. He emptied what was left of his coffee down the drain, rinsed the cup and put it in the dishwasher.

Not a single one of the men she'd been with in her life had done that. Not even her father. Drake wouldn't even have carried it into the kitchen, let alone put it in the sink.

"What's up?" he asked, stopping halfway between the sink and her spot at the table, car keys in hand.

"I keep feeling like there's something I missed before. Something that will tie then to now, to prove that Bill is back to his old behavior. That he's a diabolically dangerous man. I've been over and over the interviews, the testimonies, the reports, and I couldn't find anything significant. And maybe that's because, until this week, it was so insignificant I just let it go."

"What was so insignificant?"

He came closer, his gaze focused, and she had to pause a second while a wave of emotion passed through her.

It was nice, working with him. Someone as dedicated as she was. Who understood the dedication. The drive.

"I noticed earlier this week… Suzie answered every question I asked, in multiple interviews, when Bill was on trial with me. Every one of them. Except one. When she found out she was pregnant, she'd thought Bill would be thrilled. He'd wanted them to have a child together, said it would cement them together forever. Instead, when she told him, he flew off in a rage. Said the child couldn't be his. That she'd been unfaithful to him," she reported.

"He told me he struggled with jealousy from the moment he fell in love with her," Jayden shot back immediately. "He just couldn't believe that someone as young and beautiful as she was would really love him, an old fart. His words, not mine. He said the jealousy would make him almost insane at times, in his thoughts. And that he'd accused her of awful things. He also said that he'd take off, go for a drive, or just go mow the lawn, settle down, and come to his senses, and he'd apologize. That things would be good for a while, until the doubts started to eat at him again. He said that's what hurt Suzie. His doubts. That she never knew when he'd get jealous again, and was always watching every move she made so that she didn't risk feeding his doubts."

"Yeah, she told me that, too," Emma confirmed. "She was talking about having to watch every move she made, being afraid to answer the phone when he was around in case it was a telemarketer and he would think she and the marketer were lying to him and insist that it was a lover who'd called, not knowing Bill was going to be home."

Was he finally beginning to see Bill more clearly? The thought was a relief, and scared her, too. It made Bill as her perp that much more real. The man was unstable. Violent.

"So what question didn't Suzie answer?"

"I asked her who Bill thought the father of her baby was. I've been all over my notes, even listened to the tapes over the past couple of days, and nothing. She never said."

"It's my understanding that he worried about anyone and everyone, at one point or another," Jayden said. "She probably didn't know the answer."

Probably. Maybe. But unanswered questions made her uncomfortable. "It didn't matter to the trial," she said aloud. "Once we got the DNA results saying Bill was the father, I didn't need a name to go with the imaginary lover he'd concocted."

"What does it matter now?"

"It probably doesn't. I just don't like unanswered

questions," she said. She wasn't sure Sara was working that day. And didn't want to bother Chantel. But as soon as she could, she'd ask The Lemonade Stand counselor if she could try to arrange an interview with Suzie Heber.

And prayed the woman would agree to speak with her again.

Chapter 16

Other than preparing for Luke's parole hearing and monitoring the location app, Jayden took Sunday off. He was on call, of course—that was a given with him—but he didn't make visits or calls. Didn't even sit at his desk and do paperwork. He went to the beach, to surf for a couple of hours. To get some distance between him and Emma—to find perspective. And when the waves didn't take away his constant need to fight thinking about her, he headed down to have dinner with his folks.

They were as welcoming as always, clearly delighted to see him, doted on him like he was still a high school kid living at home, and asked very few questions.

"There's something different about you," his mother, Sheila, said as they sat at a restaurant on a pier out over the ocean. One of his father's favorite spots. Jayden

Sr., who went by Jay, never changed much. He had his ideas about how life went and didn't sway from them.

Take the steak he was eating. Always filet. Always with a bit of pink. And absolutely no steak sauce. His baked potato had both, butter and sour cream. Same ranch dressing on his salad—it never wavered. And he didn't touch the bread. There was something solid, reassuring in the sameness.

And it drove Jayden nuts. When he'd lived at home he'd felt…claustrophobic with the sameness. Figured maybe that was what had pushed him to take such risks all the time. Trying new things. Like he had to prove to himself that there was more to life than just…solid. And the same.

"Nothing different," he told his mother now. "I'm exactly the same as I was three weeks ago." He'd been home for two days that time. "Working the same job. Even have mostly the same clients."

"I'm thinking about retiring." His father's words interrupted his foray into a past that had often included him going off in his head, reliving some caper or another, during family dinner—just to survive the blahness. "Any chance you're ready to come home and take over my business?"

"Zero," he said lightly. They'd had the talk, seriously, when he'd graduated from college. His father knew he was going to spend his life doing what he was doing. And he knew why.

"Besides, you're only fifty-three, you'd grow old and die if you retired."

"That's what I told him," Sheila said, smiling at the man like they were still just high school sweethearts.

There'd been a time when he'd wanted that—to be

so in love, and so loved, that it would last a lifetime. If things were different, he'd still want that. But things weren't different and there were some things he couldn't change, no matter what he'd give to be able to do so. Some things money couldn't fix, the weight on his conscience being one of them.

"The world's changing," Jay said. "Not just with technology, but overall. More and more businesses have to get in the political arena to survive. Hell, you have an employee who misspeaks on his or her own time and you could end up in national news."

"And you'd love the free publicity," Jayden said, popping a bite of crab leg into his mouth.

"Maybe. Just saying…if you were ready…"

"I'm not." He continued to chew. Thinking of Bill Heber. In a way the guy reminded him of his dad— other than the jealousy issues and a brush with the law. Bill was a bit younger, but not much. He'd owned his own company, too, before his life had come crashing down around him. Both of them were in the automotive industry, though not at all on the same scale. Bill's had been a one-up mechanic shop and Jay's was a multi-million-dollar extrusion company that manufactured car parts for several of the major automakers.

"So…" His mother pushed away the big bowl that had held her chicken and Baja ranch salad. "You seeing anyone?" She always asked.

"No." The answer was always the same. They always moved on. He'd never told his parents about any women he'd slept with. And he wasn't about to start now, let alone with Emma.

"You're thirty-one, Jayden."

What was this? He looked at her. Sucked out another bite of crab. "I'm aware of that," he said, wiping his mouth with his napkin. She meant the world to him.

"What about grandchildren?" The question was softly spoken. Almost hesitant.

"Sheila." His father's voice, one word, in a tone they all knew. Not disrespectful. Not threatening. But one meant to get attention.

"I know," she said, pursing her lips as she shook her head.

Now he was confused. Glancing from one to the other, he asked, "What?"

"Nothing." They answered in unison.

He put down his crab fork and the leg he was holding. "Tell me what's going on."

Jay shook his head, but Sheila looked at him. "We're worried about you."

"Sheila." Jay's tone wasn't quite as commanding, but the message was the same. Accompanied by a bit of acceptance, as well.

"We want grandchildren," she added. "But we know that if we mention this to you, you'll just shut us out, so we don't," she concluded.

Jayden's first instinct was to get up and leave the table, leave them sitting there. The fact that he felt that way bothered him. He wasn't a high school kid anymore. And wasn't going to run from things.

The idea that his parents thought they had to treat him like his mother's fine china…

"You know I don't intend to have a family," he told them quietly. "And you know why."

They nodded, both meeting his gaze openly.

"So, I don't get it." He frowned. "Why would you think that's going to change?"

"You're maturing, son," Sheila said. She'd always been the one to have the emotional talks with him. His father had been the enforcer. "People change as they mature. Perspectives change."

"This isn't a perspective," he told her, completely confident in what he was saying. "This is a life choice. One I'm not going to change."

"Okay." She looked to Jay, who put his hand over hers.

"You're too much like me," was all Jay said. He wasn't like his father at all, but he let that go. Or at least, wasn't willing to accept that he had to be like him.

"And there's no reason to worry about me, either." Picking up his utensil, he went back to work on dinner. "If you must know, I spent the weekend enjoying myself, not working."

He had to give them that much. They were his parents, and he loved them.

Everything clicked for Emma on Sunday. Case files, prep for the morning, motions written and ready to file, grocery shopping down, bathrooms cleaned, and an email to Sara, asking her to call at her earliest convenience. She did, that same day. She wasn't at work, but she was checking email. And said that she'd try to set up a meeting with Suzie within the next couple of days—preferably at the Stand.

Emma made a big bowl of pasta salad for dinner, with enough to take in for lunch a couple of times during the week. And she thought about Jayden.

It was good that he'd left as soon as they'd gotten up. That she hadn't heard from him all day. They were doing it right. Sticking to their plan. It was working.

Remarkably, fantastically, well. All parts of her agreed on that one. For the first time in the couple of years that she and her dark side had been so critically at odds, Emma couldn't distinguish between herself and Ms. Shadow. She felt oddly…at peace. Buoyant, even.

Her life's map was on course. To the point that she'd openly spoken about the actions she was taking to start her own family. She'd told Jayden, knowing that it would put distance between them. That meant she could look forward to Jayden's return that night guilt-free. Even more so when he didn't call to suggest they dine together again. That would be too much like them becoming an item.

She'd expected to hear from him by seven that night, though. Hoped so, anyway. Not if he had an issue at hand. Of course not then. His work came first. She'd just had a thought or two about some fun they could have, things she'd like to try. Things she'd never even thought of before that day.

When Chantel called at seven forty-five, Emma's heart jumped. It was close to dark and she was nervous about being alone. Not afraid, exactly, but uncomfortable. She could leave. But had already made the decision that she wasn't going to let the creep push her out of her own home. She really just wished Jayden would get back. He knew the threat to her was still valid.

He was practically the one who'd made her aware of how very real the threat was. Wanting her to take it seriously.

"Just calling to let you know that I've got a couple of people stationed outside your home." Chantel's words didn't make sense at first. Emma glanced out the window. Saw no one. "The car in the driveway next door.

Your neighbor is out of town and gave us permission to park in the driveway. One or the other of the officers will check your perimeter at least once an hour."

"I don't understand." Had something happened to Jayden? "I..."

"The chief says a threat to a prosecutor, most particularly one with the personal and emotional issues you handle, is not to be ignored. We aren't taking any chances. Until we find out who did this, or have reason to believe you are no longer in danger, you'll have protection."

"But Jayden..."

"He called to say that he wouldn't be able to make it there tonight."

"Okay, well, thank you." Emma wasn't ready to hang up, though she didn't really know why.

Chantel gave her the names of the officers, as well as their cell numbers in case Emma needed them during the night.

Then Emma was alone with shades drawn and no plans for the rest of the evening.

All alone.

Jayden wasn't coming. He hadn't called and he wasn't coming.

Good. Right. They were keeping things impersonal and professional.

Exactly as they both wanted.

The only reason Jayden stopped by Emma's office after the preliminary parole hearing on Monday was for business purposes. There'd been no guarantee she'd even be there.

At her desk, in a blue skirt and jacket that hugged her

beautifully, aptly outlining all of the curves he knew firsthand, she looked totally engrossed by whatever was on the computer screen in front of her.

"Jayden!" She jumped when he knocked on her open door.

"You busy?"

"No!" She sort of smiled. Then said, "Well…yes, I am. But come in. What's up?"

Kind of seemed like his unexpected presence had given her a bit of the jitters. He liked that. Made suffering through them a little easier if you didn't suffer alone.

She watched him as he entered, took a seat in the sole chair in front of her desk. Had it only been five days since he'd first sat there? In more pain than he'd have liked to admit. At least the ribs were healing. The discomfort was hardly noticeable. Might be a little discoloration left, but that was fading fast.

She was staring at him. He stared back.

"You look nice." She said the words, then looked away, back at her computer. Clicked a couple of times and then folded her hands together on the top of her desk.

Feeling a bit manly about the fact that his court clothes—dress pants, shirt, and tie—hadn't gone unnoticed, he quickly sobered.

"I just came from Luke's hearing," he told her. "They didn't let him go. They've got thirty-some days to schedule a final hearing and then write their report, and he'll have to remain in custody at least that long. That should mean that his wife and daughter are safe to go home. Since you made the call for me on their behalf… I thought it prudent for me to let you know."

What a bunch of bull. He wanted to see her, he could admit that to himself.

But with his mother's talk about children and maturity and perspective ringing in his ears, along with Emma's ongoing fertilization process, he wasn't as comfortable around her.

He liked her as much, though, which was fine as long as it was only sexual. And she wasn't...

"When's your next doctor's appointment?" He'd wanted to know. Hadn't been sure he should ask. And yet he had. Her welfare mattered to him.

She frowned. "Excuse me?"

"For the insemination. I just think we should be done with doing what we're doing before you get..." He threw his hand in the air in lieu of actually saying the word "pregnant."

With a glance at her open door, she frowned again. "I'm not going back until we're done," she said softly, glancing toward the hallway again.

There was no one out there. Everyone was either in court or gone for the day, or wherever they went when they weren't at their desks. He'd noticed as he'd walked by, thinking that Emma's office would be empty, too.

"Give me credit for having some sense," she said. "I'm not going to...do things with you...if a baby is growing inside me."

"Pregnant women do have sex, you know." Why in the hell had he said that?

"Presumably with the father of their child, and even if not, I've never been one to do things just because someone else does."

Now that didn't surprise him. He liked it when she didn't surprise him.

"You get a chance to get out to that drugstore today?" she asked.

It took him a second to realize she was talking about the Heber case and red lipstick.

"Yes. The clerk wasn't there. She called in, apparently has a sick child. I asked if they'd mind showing me their surveillance tape, but they said not without a warrant. I've got someone working on that now."

Her nod seemed approving. He approved of it.

Wanted to ask her to dinner.

Or to just push some things aside and have sex right there on her desk.

He stood instead. "I have to get home and feed my cat." Headed for the door.

"You have a cat?"

"Kind of."

"Was it there when I was?" she asked.

"Yeah. It hasn't left in weeks."

"I didn't see it."

"It doesn't come out much when other people are around. Or when I'm there alone, either." He assumed the thing made itself at home when he was gone, though. There was cat hair everywhere.

"What's its name?"

Her round of questioning seemed to hold doubt. As though she thought he was making up an excuse to get out of there, which he was. He'd fed the cat that morning. He had to go because he wanted so much to stay. Emma Martin was becoming a threat to promises he'd made to himself, promises that could not be broken.

"I have no idea."

"You have a cat, but it doesn't have a name?"

"Well, it might have one, I just don't know. I'm guessing not, though."

"Is it male or female?" She sure was making a lot out of very little.

"Not sure of that, either," he admitted.

"Where'd you get it?"

"I didn't get it. It got me. Came walking in the door one night when I got home. No collar. I assumed it's feral."

"And you let it stay?" she asked.

"It's easier than trying to get it to leave. Damn thing scratches like hell if I try to pick it up."

"Seriously."

"Seriously."

Emma nodded. Was smiling. "Do you have a litter box?"

"You smell cat crap when you were in my house?" He sounded concerned.

"No."

Right. He had a litter box. He wasn't a complete moron.

"I had cats growing up," she said. "I loved them. My friends were just trying to talk me into getting another one."

"What friends?" She'd never mentioned hanging out with people outside of work. He didn't. Other than his parents. He had a lot of people he knew. Some guys he'd go have wings with, some he'd even die for. But he didn't hang out. Or follow sports. Not anymore. He worked. And did what he could to help others. He didn't deserve any more than that. Couldn't live with himself if he allowed any more than that.

The fact that she had friends made them even more different than he thought they were.

"My law school study group. We've stayed in touch. We get together once a month for dinner."

"And they want you to get a cat?"

"They don't know about the whole baby thing," she told him. "I figured I'd wait until the procedure is successful before I tell them."

Yeah. Good call. He'd probably do the same. If he had a group of friends he got together with once a month.

Or was ever planning to have a family.

"You mind if I stop by? To see the cat?" she asked.

His mood escalated a bit. A lot. Who knew the beast that had invaded his home and eaten his fish would serve a good purpose? "Suit yourself," he told her.

"Tonight? Around seven?"

He could tell her to come earlier. To have dinner with him. He didn't.

They were business and sex. Not companions.

Chapter 17

They were going to have to set a date. An end date to their fling. After Jayden left, Emma couldn't concentrate. All she could think about was seeing this cat. And him.

The oh-so-sexy parole officer had a cat. Or rather, the cat had him. He was a surprisingly tender person, evidently, and a tender lover, too, in addition to being inventive enough to speak to all sides of her. The more layers of him she uncovered, the more she liked him.

So yes, setting an end date was in order. Maybe the following week. Another seven days or so ought to do it. The honeymoon sex phase would be through. If it weren't after office hours, she'd call the clinic and set up her next insemination appointment right then.

Giving up on work, she packed up for the day. She was ready for court in the morning. And ready for trial the week after. The other fourteen cases needing imminent attention would wait another day.

She had to get this desire out of her system. Out of her life. She was trying to take care of the elephant in the room, but the more she tried, the bigger it seemingly got.

Stopping at a drive-through gourmet salad place, something new in Santa Raquel, she ordered avocado and tuna tapas and drove to the beach. She parked so she could see the waves coming into shore, opened her windows and sat there and ate. Every bite was delicious. Sensual. Taking her closer to the time she'd be at Jayden's house. She'd ordered tea with her salad. Thought about another bottle of wine, but decided that pouring it down the sink, as they'd done with a good part of the other two bottles, was a waste of money.

If he had any beer left, and they wanted libation, she could just sip on some of that. Like he'd sipped on the wine she'd chosen.

Wine made her think of chocolate. And chocolate led to dessert. A dessert of Jayden's long, lean body. She knew it fairly well by now. And still found it a mystery. All of the things she'd like to do to give him pleasure. To take pleasure from him. He was such a good man, too. Dedicating his life to others, believing in them when no one else did. Taking in a stray cat...

No. Wait. Their time together...she couldn't let herself start to actually feel things for the man. Only for his body. She had to get back to their sexual relationship. To stick to their rules.

She tried. She really, really tried. His body definitely gave her much to think about. As did the various ways he looked at her. The way he talked to her without words.

A couple was walking at the edge of the tide, holding hands. The woman stopped to pick up something in the sand. The man looked at it, then at her. Kissed her.

Emma swallowed a lump in her throat. Yeah, that was lovely. But it wasn't for her. She went for wild men, not the guys who were sweet. The ones who were content to settle for monogamy and sameness...she broke their hearts.

Was bored by them. Couldn't make herself love them.

So raising a baby on her own, a family on her own, wouldn't be what she'd once hoped for, but life was what you made it and she could make it great.

Stuffing the rest of her dinner in the bag she'd pulled it from, she started her Lexus and left the parking lot. She'd had enough beach time. She had to go get her some body time.

Halfway home, her mind busy planning to change into something a bit sexier and less professional, she had a call from Sara. Suzie Heber was at the Stand, in a group session. She said she'd only talk to Emma if Emma came to the Stand while she was there.

Changing course immediately, she thought about Jayden sitting at home, expecting her to arrive soon. Thought about calling him. About hearing his voice. Wanting to see him. Maybe agreeing to stop by when she was through.

And waited until she pulled into the Stand to text him instead.

As a prosecutor who worked with the Stand's victims, and a member of the High Risk team, Emma had a pass to the private parking lot behind the Stand, as well as a key card that allowed her admittance to the grounds. She met Sara at the counselor's office. Suzie wasn't there yet. An evening volunteer counselor was in with the group and she'd bring Suzie to them when group was done, which should be within minutes.

"I didn't expect her to see me," she told Sara, a married mother of two. While Sara was three years older than Emma, Emma still felt…less than…as she sat there. Like Emma had accomplished so much less in life than she had. The other woman had it all: a full-time career and a home with two kids. The husband was a bonus.

But the kids… She looked at the pictures on Sara's desk. They were adorable. Heart-stopping cute. Happy.

She definitely had to call the clinic.

"She didn't seem to mind speaking with you at all," Sara was saying, focused on work. As Emma should be. "My bit of concern came from the fact that it was tonight or not at all."

"As though she's not coming back," Emma reiterated from their earlier phone call. "You think that's because she's really okay? Or because she's in denial?"

"I think it's because she's scared." The woman's blue eyes showed concern. As slender as Sara was, as feminine-looking with dark blond shoulder-length wavy hair and sensible clothes, she was also as strong as they came.

And as calming, somehow. Sitting on one end of the couch in Sara's office, leaving the other end for Suzie, Emma faced the counselor in her usual chair across from her.

"Her ex-husband's getting to her again."

"That's my assessment. And we're up against a bit of a wall here since she cooperated last time and lost."

Her fault. She knew what they were up against. She'd blown Suzie's trust. Not that Sara blamed her—as she'd made clear multiple times over the years.

"But she agreed to speak with me."

Sara nodded. "I was encouraged by that, as well."

"You have any pointers for me?" Emma was a prosecutor, not a counselor. Building back lost trust…she wasn't sure how to do it—and in only one meeting, with no preparation time.

"Just be yourself," Sara told her. "You've got this just by being who you are. Truth and honesty, in action as well as word, are your strongest tools—"

A knock on the door interrupted them, followed by the door opening and a woman unfamiliar to Emma peeking her head in just enough to announce Suzie and usher her inside. She came in, limping in her black boot, and shut the door behind her.

Auburn-haired, with a model-like frame, Suzie's shoulders were hunched, her face makeup-less as she took a seat on the vacant end of the couch. She'd been dressed as drably, with her hair pulled into a ponytail and no makeup every other time Emma had seen her. She'd gained a little weight, but not enough.

None of that shocked Emma. What got her was that when she opened her mouth to speak to Suzie, she choked up.

She was a professional. Not once, in all her years of lawyering, or even studying to be a lawyer, in all the heinous photos and videos she'd had to study, all the details she'd had to relive, had she ever shown undue emotion in front of a witness, victim or defendant. Her ability to compartmentalize was one of the talents that made her so good at what she did.

"I'm sorry," she said, apologizing for her shocking emotionalism. "I'm so, so sorry, Suzie. I let you down and now..."

The other woman glanced over, her head still slightly lowered. "I don't blame you, Ms. Martin. You tried your best. I knew he'd win, but it just felt so good, having someone on my side, I wanted to let you try..."

She'd known he'd win? That was the first Emma had ever heard that. And a horrifying thought occurred to her. Was it possible Suzie had known Emma wouldn't win because she hadn't told Emma the truth?

Emma had never even considered that possibility. Not after seeing the doctor reports, the police reports and listening to Suzie's own testimony.

"My ex-husband is a powerful man," Suzie continued softly. "Not like powerful because of being rich, and being able to buy off whatever you need, but powerful in a much worse way. He believes he's right and you can't convince him otherwise. But he's not all bad. He really loves people and wants to do things right, too. He apologizes for his mistakes and..."

Suddenly fearing that Suzie had agreed to the meeting solely so she could sing her husband's praises to Emma—to get her to "leave it alone"—Emma went on full alert.

Could Bill be putting her up to this?

Needing to know what the woman was thinking, but reminding herself not to get intense, she tried to school only compassion into her features. Not assessment. She didn't want to make Suzie feel like it was the two professionals against her.

"So...are you telling me now that the things you told me before—about Bill hitting you, about him beating you up the day you lost your baby, rather than you falling as you both told the doctor when he took you in— none of that was true?"

For a moment Suzie straightened. "That was true," she said. "I've never lied to you." She lowered her head again. "That day...my baby... I knew I had to at least try... I told you the truth because of my baby, not because I really thought that you could do anything about him. My baby deserved to have the truth known."

"You could keep quiet for yourself, but not for your child," Sara said and Suzie nodded.

"So what about now?" Emma asked, in control of her emotions now, honing in. "Is he hurting you again, Suzie?"

Her hair hanging to her lap, she shook her head. Emma looked to Sara over the bent head, and Sara gave a little negative shake of the head. Advising her not to push?

But if they only had this one chance.

"Then why are you here?" Emma asked the question raging most in her mind at the moment.

Suzie looked over at her. "You asked to speak with me."

It was a compliment to her. She filed that away. "I meant, why are you in counseling at the Stand?"

"I'm afraid."

"Of Bill?"

Suzie nodded.

"He's hitting you again, isn't he?"

Head bowed, she shook her head again. As though

the man's power over her was so great, she just couldn't admit his crimes. Not after what had happened before.

"How did you get those bruises?" Emma was referring to the most recent injury, the one reported to the team the week prior, which, among other things, had left Suzie with a bruise on her chin. It was yellowed now, but still visible if you knew what you were looking for.

"I fell." Suzie's face was hidden by her hair.

She could push. But not as hard as Bill was already doing, she surmised.

"Can you do something for me?" Emma just went with her instincts. She could trust them.

Raising her head, Suzie looked at her.

"I have a question, something that's been bothering me. From the past."

Suzie nodded.

"When I asked you who Bill thought the father of your baby might be if it wasn't him, you never answered me. Why?"

Eyes filling with tears, Suzie said, "Because it was so wrong. So crazy. And ugly. I…I didn't want…the guy…to know. He'd be so hurt by Bill's accusations…"

"Who was he?"

"He was just a nice guy! Younger than me by seven years. His mother had just died and his stepfather was working all the time."

"How did you meet him?"

"He was in our neighborhood—the old one before the divorce. I moved after Bill went to prison, after he broke in."

"So why did Bill think that you'd…that this kid and you had…"

Suzie shook her head, tears falling in earnest now.

"I talked to him," she said. "I should never have talked to him. I saw him outside and I said hello. He asked if he could mow our grass, and I said sure. Bill was working so hard at the shop and we were busy at work and I didn't have time. He needed the money. And it gave him something constructive to do." The woman talked about a couple of times the boy had talked to her. How he'd come to her a time or two when he was having a rough time.

"You liked him." Sara handed over a tissue box and Suzie took two.

"Of course I liked him!" she said, wiping her eyes and nose. "He was a sweet kid. Bill and I were trying to have a family and he'd just lost his mother. I liked that I could help him, even a little bit. It made me feel good about myself. But not in a guy-girl kind of way! I was seven years older than him! What Bill said…not only would it have made me a criminal, but it would have changed his life forever, too. Ruined it probably because his stepfather would have kicked him out."

"Did you ever tell the kid what Bill thought?"

"Of course not. And I didn't tell anyone else, either. I knew Bill wouldn't. It just made him look bad, thinking something sick like that. And anyway, by the time we were going to trial, we already had the DNA and Bill knew the truth."

"Can I know the boy's name?"

Suzie stared at her then, almost pleadingly. "I'd rather not say." Her words were strong. Clear. "He's got a life now, I'm sure. Maybe in college. I'm not going to be responsible for messing up his life. He was an innocent kid."

But if he could corroborate Bill's abuse…it could be

the missing piece Emma needed. To convince Jayden. And the court. If they could get a warrant for Bill's phone records…anything.

"Did he ever see Bill hurt you?"

"No. Bill always made sure that was just between me and him."

"And what about the bruises? Did he ever ask about them?"

Suzie shook her head. "Bill didn't hit me in the face often. And the one time he did, I stayed inside until the bruise faded, and then covered it with a little bit of makeup, like when I went to work."

She remembered that. Bill hadn't hit Suzie in the face until toward the end, when his abuse had escalated.

As it had been doing for the past three months. Since Bill had been released from prison. She had enough evidence to know that Bill Heber was hurting his wife. But so much of it was circumstantial…she needed something solid to get the man back behind bars. For good.

The one thing she wasn't going to do was berate this poor woman. Scooting over, she took Suzie's hand. Not a usual move for her—instigating any physical contact other than a handshake with any of her victims—but she did it. "I know you didn't fall, Suzie."

"Yes, I did." The woman didn't pull her hand away.

Emma found that significant. Wondered if Sara did, too.

"Please, Ms. Martin, just leave it alone."

Leave it alone. The expression stunned her. Scared her, too. But words came to her.

"I'll leave you alone if you promise me one thing."

"What?"

"Promise me that you'll stay in touch with Sara.

Whether group counseling, or just joining a craft group or something here at the Stand. You come here, at least twice a week, and you won't hear from me again."

Suzie held her gaze for a long moment, her lashes still wet from her recently shed tears. "I come here and you won't try to see me again? Or get someone else to ask me questions?"

Suzie had told her everything she was going to. Or felt she could. Emma nodded.

"Okay." The other woman smiled. When her face relaxed, Emma could see a hint of the beauty she must have been before worry and fear, grief and abuse, had misshaped her nose, and driven so many lines around her mouth and eyes.

"Okay." With a quick goodbye to Sara, Emma left Suzie alone with the woman who could help her to heal.

She'd leave Suzie alone. No way she was walking away from the rest of it. She had a job to do.

Chapter 18

Sorry, can't make it. Something came up at work. Rain check?

Jayden read the text for the fourth time since it had come in more than an hour before. He still hadn't answered.

Of course, if Emma wanted to come over, he'd welcome her. But what were they doing here? If it was just sex, as they'd agreed, he wouldn't be feeling disappointed when she put work first, would he?

And if he was starting to want more from her than just sex, he had to stop.

So, was he pretending sex was all it was? And professional admiration and respect, of course.

Or was he just let down because he'd been looking forward to another night of passion?

For the brief time he'd been protecting her, after their first night of sex, he hadn't had to ask himself any tough questions. He'd had a purpose for spending so much time with her. Now that she had the police watching her house, he didn't have that out.

There'd been no further threats. Luke was back in custody. Chances were she was out of danger anyway.

The evening stretching before him shouldn't present any kind of challenge. He dealt with them at the end of every single day.

He typed out a response to her text: Sure. But didn't hit Send. If he ignored her completely, it could look like he was upset that she'd canceled. Or seem rude, like she didn't matter enough to deserve a response.

Was he seriously sitting there spending time on such a ridiculous issue?

Hitting Send, he clicked on his contacts, zipping through to find Harold Wallace's number. If his client was free, maybe they could go together to see his son. The boy was waiting a court appearance and Jayden wanted him to know he had people pulling for him. He wanted the boy to know that while what he'd done was grotesquely wrong, Jayden would help him right that wrong as much as he could, as long as the boy knew that he still had to pay for what he did. And that his future actions would have to reflect that.

They wouldn't know, until they all appeared before the juvenile court judge, exactly what kind of future the boy could expect to have. Or how little or much effect Jayden could have on that.

He was on his way to pick up Harold when his phone rang. Clicking the hands-free button on his steering wheel, he glanced at the dash display.

Emma.

"Hey, did you get it worked out?" he asked, referring to whatever business had come up that evening, preventing her from meeting his cat.

He'd not only gone searching for the thing, he'd coaxed it out from under his bed with his last can of tuna.

"I had a call from Sara at The Lemonade Stand. She said Suzie was there and willing to talk to me."

His gut sank. Could be Suzie was finally ready to admit that it wasn't Bill who was hurting her. To admit who was. But he didn't think so. Not by the tone in Emma's voice.

"I thought she'd skipped her last counseling session," Jayden said. "That she was done going. Has she been abused again?"

That question was most important. Above all, they wanted Suzie safe.

"No. She's fine. Physically. But she's not okay, Jayden. The woman is so afraid of her ex-husband, she can hardly hold up her head."

Bill wasn't going to catch his break. He could feel it coming.

"Is she naming him as her abuser?" he asked.

"No."

"But she told you who's been hurting her?"

"No. She's sticking to her story that she fell."

"Maybe it's time that I talk to Bill," he said. "Tell him the truth about Suzie's current situation."

"I don't know…" Emma hesitated. "If he admits what he's done, he can get help. The court will go easier on him… But he still continues to deny—"

"If it's not him, he might have some idea who's doing

it." Jayden hadn't wanted Bill to know about the abuse, believing it was in Bill's best interests that he not know. "I just can't guarantee that he won't try to find the guy himself," he said. "I'll continue to keep a strong eye on him, of course, but once he knows she's being abused, chances are—"

"No." Emma's voice was strong, sure, as she interrupted him. Filling his car with such a presence of her, he could almost believe she was sitting there with him.

Because she was getting that much inside his head?

"If he knows Suzie talked to me…" She started and stopped. "Just no, Jayden, please. The more I think about it, I think talking to him would be the last thing you should do. If he thinks you're still believing in him, he's less likely to feel threatened. By me, or Suzie. I thought a truck was following me again this morning. It was only for a block or two, and I'm sure I'm overreacting, but, please…don't escalate Bill's tension. Not right now."

"Luke's back in custody. That should have taken care of that threat," he had to point out.

"You still think Bill didn't do it? Either make the threat at my house or hurt Suzie?"

"I don't believe he did, no. But I'm watching him as though he did, you have my word on that."

"That woman is petrified of him," she stressed.

"A fact for which he takes full accountability and is paying for every day, will pay for for the rest of his life. Bill knows his jealousy was out of hand, that he created an unhealthy amount of stress for her. He knows he lost the love his life, her, because of it. He's not going to bother Suzie. To the contrary, he just wants her to be happy. You didn't put him in jail for the rest of his life, Emma, but he's there anyway. In his own personal jail."

"I heard something tonight and I feel as though I need to tell you—" she wavered "—but I don't know if I can trust you not to tell him."

Wow. That slammed him. Probably more than it should have done. "Bottom line, we're on the same side," he reminded her. "If you tell me not to tell him, I won't. I'm his champion, his counselor, but I'm also, in a sense, his jailer. I do my job—both sides—with equal fervor." It was the one given in his life. That work. It wouldn't change.

"In the transcript from four years ago, when I asked Suzie who Bill thought had fathered her child, she didn't answer. Tonight she did."

He was curious, too. "And?"

"It was a teenage neighbor kid. Bill came home and caught her talking to him a time or two. He'd just lost his mother and was having troubles with his stepfather. They never had sex. She paid him to cut their grass. It was sweet. She said it made her feel good about herself to be able to help him."

"Why didn't she say all of this then?" he asked.

"She didn't want him to know that her husband was making sick accusations about him."

"It could have helped her case, could have showed Bill's state of mind." He knew the man had been in a bad way. He hadn't known how bad.

The whole thing was sad beyond belief, for everyone involved.

"She was afraid even the accusations could ruin the kid's life. Afraid that if it got out and Bill got defensive, he might convince someone the accusations were true. She said that even the accusations would probably have had his stepfather kicking him out. They were on really tenuous ground."

Jayden needed to talk to Bill. To know why Bill had left out this piece of information. But he'd given Emma his word. He wouldn't do it.

But that didn't make him any less desirous of the answer to his question. Why had Bill left out such a vital piece of information?

Could be, since the information hadn't come out in court, since it had never come out of Suzie's mouth until that night, that Bill had chosen not to dig his hole any deeper, by bringing it up.

Kind of like Jayden not telling anyone about Emory. He would never forget. He paid every single day. Would always pay. Not talking didn't mean he was trying to hide from his truth. It meant it went too deep, hit too hard, to expose it to anyone but himself.

And maybe Bill had been trying to spare the kid, too. Most particularly after DNA came back showing the lie to his fears. And how deeply in trouble his paranoia had gotten him.

"Suzie believes that Bill's all-powerful," Emma continued. "That he has the ability to make people believe, say and do what he wants."

"If that were true, she wouldn't have testified against him."

"Suzie didn't do that for herself. She did it for her baby. Just like she kept quiet about the kid for his sake."

Jayden got where she was going. He just had no idea how to turn her around on this one. He hoped to God some facts turned up soon. Or that counseling loosened Suzie's tongue some more.

This Heber case had to end. He turned a corner in

the darkness, a block from Harold's girlfriend's house, and parked.

"I'm telling you, Jayden, she's scared to death of him. Sara saw it, too."

"Maybe that's because she hasn't seen him to know that he's changed." Or had she?

"Is it too late for me to stop by?" Her question was hesitant. And he didn't think because of the hour. It wasn't that late.

"I'm on my way to meet a client," he told her, not adding who or why. He could have done. She knew the circumstances behind his being shot the previous week. Had been careful of his ribs every time they'd been together.

"Okay, I still haven't been home from work." Did she sound relieved? He couldn't be sure. Wasn't particularly pleased if she had been.

Things were getting awkward. That wasn't supposed to happen.

"Jayden?"

"Yeah?"

"I think we should put a time frame on our sexual responsibility. You know, getting it out of our systems and moving on."

Sexual responsibility. He liked how it sounded.

"Agreed. You have one in mind?"

"Yes. I'm thinking maybe another week."

His crotch gave a minor leap. It wasn't ending. And yet, it would.

He was good with that…right?

Emma stopped at Jayden's on her way home from a late meeting on Tuesday night. She'd beat a motion to suppress in court that morning, pertaining to her up-coming trial, and was feeling great. They didn't talk about work. They really spoke very little.

And when she started to doze off, she got up and left. It was all very satisfying—beyond satisfying physically—and kind and decent. And, as she drove away, it all left her feeling a little flat, too.

She hadn't seen the cat. Had no idea what Jayden had had for dinner or how his day had gone. Hadn't told him about the judge allowing her to use the evidence the defense had wanted thrown out.

Maybe it was the beginning of the end…this sense of letdown. Setting the end date could have triggered a feeling of sadness.

When he'd kissed her goodbye, it had taken all she'd had not to climb right back into bed with him. She was hot now, just thinking about it. Tingling with need.

Unbelievable, considering he'd met that need three times in the past two hours. Three times.

Turning out of his neighborhood and toward her own, she enjoyed the lack of traffic on the July weeknight. Most California towns would be thriving with tourists, filling the sidewalks, driving the streets, but Santa Raquel had mostly private beaches. And very little overnight lodging. They got a few day visitors during the summer and sometimes—

A truck pulled up alongside her as she turned onto the two-lane coastal road that was the shortest route to her little gated section of town. Had she been so preoccupied in thought she'd turned in front of it? She hadn't even seen his lights. Slowing immediately, Emma gave room for him to pull in front of her. Clearly he had the right of way. He hadn't come from behind her, so he had to have already been on the road.

Another reason they should put streetlights on the coastal road. At least the section that ran through town. It came up every couple of years at council meetings and residents, overall, wanted to preserve the quiet sanctity of the ocean. But up on the cliff like it was, also made it dangerous…

The truck didn't move from her side. Didn't pull ahead.

Or behind.

What the…? Heart slamming in her chest, she realized what was happening. As if in slow motion. The truck wasn't budging from beside her as she drove on the dark road. She slowed. The truck slowed. She sped up, the truck sped up. Inching closer and closer to her. The driver was going to send her over the cliff.

Or try to.

She pictured the road, the curves, the areas that weren't as steep. Those with houses below.

He wasn't just going to ram her.

She knew it was a he now, though she couldn't make out anything other than a baseball cap. And broad shoulders.

She knew who it was, too, without even seeing his face.

Bill Heber must have found out she'd talked to Suzie the night before.

Emma kept herself steady on the road. Putting herself in his mind. Thinking like him. It was the only way to beat him.

And to keep her own panic from getting her killed. She was the one person he hadn't been able to deceive or to threaten into submission. If he hadn't pled to the breaking and entering, thinking his explanation that he'd only been retrieving his own things would have gotten him off with no jail time, he'd probably have won that one, too.

He'd have to make her car going over the edge look like an accident. The best way to do that was to catch her on a curve. And she knew which one. About a quarter mile ahead. The thoughts came clearly...blocking everything else. She had only herself to rely on. Both hands on the wheel, she couldn't pick up her phone, but pushed the button on her steering wheel and said, "Call 9-1-1." The trembling in her voice shocked her, but she couldn't dwell on it. Couldn't allow the distraction.

Heard the ringing. And slowed her car. She had to get a description of the truck. It was a two-door. She couldn't tell what color. Not white or light. The truck slowed, too, clearly out to get her, though the driver never glanced her way. Didn't give her a chance to ID him. And with him staying right beside her, she couldn't get a make, model or license plate.

"Hello, what's your emergency?"

Damn it! Find an identifying something!

"I'm Prosecutor Emma Martin. I'm being run off—"

The truck lurched toward her. Before the curve. She saw it coming. Knew—

A flash of excruciating pain. And then...

Nothing.

Chapter 19

Jayden got the call as soon the ambulance left the scene. Chantel was there and wanted his location app information on Bill Heber. Officers were already on their way to Bill's house, to bring him in for questioning, but Chantel didn't expect them to find him there. Jayden, having already stepped into his waiting jeans and thrown on his shirt while they spoke, slipped into shoes and was grabbing his keys. He had to get to the hospital. Had to get to Emma. He couldn't lose her like this. Yeah, she was going to move on from his life, but she'd still be around. They'd run into each other now and then. He could always pick up a phone and call her. He couldn't consider a world without her in it. No more loss.

And not because of him.

Pray, God, he wasn't responsible for this. He was

the one who should be fighting for his life or losing his life, not her.

No one knew if Emma was going to make it. Chantel only said it looked bad.

Her parents, as next of kin, had been called in Florida.

Telling Chantel to hold on, he quickly called up the app. Bill's phone registered at an address he recognized. "It says he's at his group session," he said. "He goes two evenings a week." He gave Chantel the location as he was getting into his car. And then hung up and called Bill.

The man answered almost immediately. He wouldn't have if he'd been in session. Was Bill working him? Was he really so off on this one that he'd fallen under a perp's manipulation? Was Bill's whole life a scam?

If Emma didn't pull through…

"Where are you?" Jayden asked, focusing on his area of control.

"Just leaving group."

"You been there all night?"

"Since seven."

"You know I can verify that."

"What's going on?" The man's tone sounded more resigned than defensive.

"The police are looking for you in connection with an accident that happened in Santa Raquel tonight. Go with them. Cooperate fully, and if your alibi checks out, you'll be home in time for bed." He had done his job.

But Emma was hurt. *It's bad.* Chantel's words replayed. *It's bad.*

"One other thing, Bill."

"Yeah?"

"You ever know of a high school kid in your old neighborhood? Maybe he cut your grass or something."

"Nope. Most of them were little. Elementary school. A couple of sisters in high school. And an older dude halfway down the street, lived alone. You can check me up on that, too," he said. Jayden could hear the click-click of a turn signal. "I'm still in touch with a couple of the guys. My shop did work on their cars and I called 'em when I was back to work. I called a bunch of my old clients. Nothing said I couldn't and I needed the business."

"I'll need their names," Jayden said.

"Yeah. What the…?" A slew of curse words followed. "There are cop cars in front of my place. I'm not driving into that."

"Yes you are. Are you on your street?"

"I'm one street over."

"Slow down and hold on. Do not hang up."

Not waiting for a response, Jayden made a couple of quick calls, got patched into the lead officer on the scene at Bill's place and let him know that he'd talked his client in. He also warned them that Bill had an alibi. If anyone roughed him up, they could face departmental or even legal challenge. Then he switched back over to Bill.

"Okay, drive normally and head home," he said.

"I got any choice in that matter?" the man asked.

"Not really. Not a smart one." Jayden wasn't at his best. He was almost at the hospital. "I just spoke with the officer in charge. He'll take you to the station, verify your alibi, and you'll be free to go."

"So much for second chances, huh?"

"You're living it, buddy. I just made the call for you. The rest is up to you."

"This accident…was it Suzie?" There was no bravado in the man's voice at all now.

"No."

"I'm here," Bill said.

Jayden stayed on the line long enough to hear Bill cooperating with officers and then hung up. He'd just pulled into the hospital parking lot.

It's bad.

Heading into the hospital, he could hardly breathe. Or hold panic at bay. If Emma didn't make it…

Jayden wasn't a praying man, but as he waited for the elevator, after reading the text from Chantel, telling him what floor she was on, where to meet her, he asked every power in existence to keep Emma alive. She was a warm, wonderful, bright and vivacious woman who gave far more to the world than Jayden could ever hope to do.

The lights were bright. Too bright. Giving everything a stark white hue that wasn't pleasant. Darkness was better. Underneath her, everything was hard. Flat. A board.

Blinking briefly in between the dark peace seemed necessary, but was painful.

Faces hovered over her. Around her. Intent. Focused. Busy.

Voices mumbled. Something beeped. Her arm hurt.

And her head. Someone touched it. She winced and that hurt, too.

"She's awake."

Whatever was touching her head didn't even pause.

"Emma? I'm Janelle. I'm a nurse. We need you to lie completely still, okay? We're almost through here and you're going to be just fine."

Keeping her eyes closed, she was happy to comply. She preferred darkness, anyway.

The next time Emma opened her eyes, she was still in the same small space, with the same bright lights, but there was only one face there. Beside her, not directly above.

She recognized it. And felt immediate relief.

"Jayden." Her back didn't hurt as much. The board felt…softer. She no longer craved the darkness.

"Yeah," he said. It was only when she felt the pressure of his fingers squeezing hers that she realized he was holding them. "I'm right here."

She could see that.

"How long have I been here?"

"A couple of hours. They gave you something to help you rest."

She wanted to rest and to move, too. But was afraid to. Flash memories of pain splashed in and out. Mostly her head. She had feeling in all of her parts. She'd already assured herself of that much. But she had to move. To know for sure she could.

Because her feet didn't hurt, she started with them.

"I'm in bed," she said aloud.

"Yeah." Jayden's expression didn't look anything like it usually did when he was watching her in bed. "You were upstairs for testing, but you're back in the ER. You were in an accident."

Right. The truck. And the cliff. She pushed away the mental pictures popping in and out. Just for a moment.

"I was on a board."

"They were afraid you might have neck or spinal injuries."

Emma wanted to move her legs immediately. To move everything. Get out of bed and go home. Except that she didn't want to move her head. It felt...not like her own. "Do I?" she asked.

"Nope. Everything came back clear." His lips softened a bit at that one. Almost smiled.

"My head hurts."

"You've got a bad gash, just below your hairline on the left side. And you're concussed."

She lifted a hand to her forehead, knocked into a bandage. "I can't feel anything there."

"They numbed it to put in the stitches. Seventeen of them."

Glancing down at his shirt pocket, he pulled out his phone, held it up to her. "It's your parents," he told her. "They've been calling every half hour. They're on standby for a flight out."

"No. They don't need to come," she said. "Seriously, I don't want them to come." She wasn't sure what she wanted, but to be coddled by her parents, having them worrying about every move she made...

She only had a week of sex left with Jayden. That fact was absolutely clear in her befuddled mind. This was their week.

"You talk to them." He handed her the phone.

Jayden had given her parents his number. They'd obviously been conversing. Something felt completely right about that.

She had no problem assuring her mom and dad that she was all right. And then spent the next five minutes struggling to get them to understand that they didn't need to hop on plane. She would be fine, as the doctor had told them both.

"But when you're released, you shouldn't be home alone, not with a head injury." Her mother just wouldn't let up. Her head hurt. Her throat was dry. But her thoughts were clearing, in spite of her brief attempt to hold them at bay.

"I won't be alone, Mom," she said. She had police watching her home, right? Or was that over now? Was Bill in custody?

She looked at Jayden. He nodded. It took her a second to realize he didn't know she'd been wondering about Bill's arrest.

The evening came tumbling back with speed. And clarity. To a point. There were some foggy areas. And some complete blankness, too.

"No…a friend will be staying with me." She glanced at him again. He nodded again.

It made sense. If they didn't have Bill yet, she was still in danger. Jayden had said he'd protect her. She remembered that clearly from the week before.

She remembered a lot more, too. Mostly everything.

When Jayden took the phone and assured her parents that the department would make certain that Emma didn't go home alone, and that someone would let them know if anything changed, Emma closed her eyes.

And smiled.

"What did you tell my parents about us?" Emma's question came after several minutes of silence while she seemingly dozed. She kept fading in and out, but the doctor had said some of that was due to the pain medication they'd given her.

Jayden had just slipped his phone back into his pocket when the question came. Her voice was getting stronger by the moment.

Emma still had spots of dried blood on her temple. And a spot to the left of her nose. Her normally flyaway curls were plastered to her forehead. They'd cut off the clothes she'd been wearing, in their haste to check her for possible injuries.

Assuming she made it through the next twenty-four hours without an unexpected glitch, she was going to be just fine. Thank all the powers that be.

"I told them that I'm a parole officer and we've been working on a case together."

"So…when I just told them a friend would be staying with me, they didn't know I meant you."

"There's no reason why they should." He'd wanted them to know she was special to him the first time he'd spoken to them. The sensation came and went, depending on the moment.

She turned her head to stare up at the ceiling. "How long do I have to lie here?"

"They're moving you to a room, just for tonight. Assuming everything goes as they expect, you'll be free to leave tomorrow. You're incredibly lucky…"

She could have died…

His stomach felt again the insidious twist of fear that had attacked him on and off since Chantel's call.

"Do you remember anything about the accident?" he asked. Someone would be in to take her report officially, but he had to know. Had to do something.

Work was his panacea. His life. It was all he could

do. A life had been lost because of him. He didn't deserve to go create one of his own when he'd cost another.

She told him about the truck. About trying to find any kind of identifier. About the baseball cap and broad shoulders. All things she'd told the dispatcher on the phone.

"It was no accident," she finished. "He forced me over that cliff…"

He so easily could have. And she'd have been dead.

"You swerved to the left, Em," he told her, pushing back against another wave of emotion. "When he started to come over, you gunned it and swerved to the left, in front of him. You plowed into a row of shrubbery."

And the sunglasses she'd had on top of her head—having put them there when she'd picked them up from the counter when she'd left his house—had slid down just enough that the force of the airbag had rammed them into her head.

There'd been a lot of blood. She'd been unconscious.

"It was Bill," she told him.

"He had an alibi." He wasn't going to lie to her about it. Knew that he'd probably never convince her the man wasn't after her. "He was picked up pulling into his driveway before they even got you to the hospital, but has already been released. He was at group all evening and several people there have verified the information."

"They could be lying. They're all ex-cons, rememb—" She stopped suddenly, a memory surfacing from her earlier meeting with Suzie Heber. "When I was leaving the Stand, Suzie asked me to please 'leave it alone.' Those exact words."

He knew Chantel's team had been through all of

Emma's current case files, anything that someone might want her to "leave alone." They were calling a couple of people in for questioning about their whereabouts, both on the night her back door had been vandalized and for that evening, as well, and he told her so.

She nodded. Frowned at him. He didn't want anything worrying her. Didn't want her bothered.

"What?" he asked.

"Is it wrong for me to be glad you're here?"

"I don't know."

"You think you should go? I can get one of the girls to come stay with me if I need help when I get out of here. Marta would do it."

"I'm not going anywhere." That wasn't debatable, as far as he was concerned. "Whether it's Bill or some other maniac, right now you're in danger. And speaking of which, I should probably have the numbers for your friends. The accident's going to be on the news. A prosecutor being targeted, twice in one week... I had a call from Chantel and they're going to be asking for the public's help in finding this guy."

He'd keep it about business, no matter how much he struggled with needing more.

"Thank you." She didn't smile. Didn't reach out a hand to him. But the look in her eye sent another bout of emotion surging through him.

"I'm just glad you're okay," he told her. Praying that's that all it was. That he wasn't starting to need more from their association than he could have. And that she wasn't, either.

He didn't say that, though.

He also didn't tell her that Bill said there was no teenage boy in his old neighborhood. In the morning he'd be checking with the two names the man had given him, Bill's former neighbors and current clients, to see what they had to say.

And he was going to be checking in with Bill way more than the man would like.

But for the most part, he was sticking to the prosecutor like glue.

Just until the danger had passed.

Chapter 20

Jayden stayed at the hospital until Emma was settled in her room for the night. A couple of her law school friends were on their way in and he didn't want to run into them—didn't want to just be a work associate, couldn't be anything else. Officers were stationed at her door. A precaution and maybe overkill, but he didn't think so. And was glad that Chantel was taking the situation as seriously as she was.

No doubt about it, if not for Emma's quick thinking in gunning her car and pulling left, she'd have been over that cliff and gone.

He tried all night long, as he tossed and turned, to get over that thought. Her coming so close to death: stark fear shot through him yet again. It kept happening. Over and over. He'd finally fall asleep, only to wake up with a stab of fear. By morning he was pissed.

Mostly with himself.

If all her morning tests went well and everything else remained stable and responsive throughout the day, she'd be ready for him to take her home late that afternoon. He was stopping by her place to pick up some clothes.

"Marta and Stef offered to stay with me," she told him when he called from his car just after seven to see how her night had gone. He'd just come from Bill's old neighborhood, catching his neighbors before they left for work, and heard from both men that neither of them could remember a teenage boy living in their neighborhood, or even staying over the summer. "They offered to pick up clothes and things, too."

So she was telling him he wasn't needed? He, after all, wasn't even a friend.

He was a cop whose offender might possibly have tried to kill a prosecutor. He didn't think so. Bill's alibi was strong.

But something wasn't adding up. Clearly someone was hurting Suzie. Doctor's reports didn't lie about such things. But he didn't think she was being completely honest, either.

Out of fear? Or something else?

Emma had texted before she'd gone to sleep the night before, as he'd requested before he left, to give him the results of the MRI. The findings corroborated the preliminary brain scan: other than the concussion, she was fine.

There was no reason he had to get her clothes, but he wanted to. Wanted to help her in ways that he'd never imagined. "I'm staying with you," he told her. He wasn't going to change his mind, even if she had a houseful of friends getting her clothes. "Or another trained officer is. That's Chantel's edict, not mine. It's either that or move you to a safe house."

"I'm not going to stop working," she told him, sounding like the woman he knew—and was hesitant to admit, even to himself, he cared for. "Whatever it is I'm supposed to leave alone—and I know it's Suzie's case—I'm not doing it. Bullying is wrong."

So was her possibly dying at the age of thirty-two at the hands of a maniac.

"No one's going to stop looking for whoever is behind the threats, Emma. But it would make a lot of us feel better to know you're safe."

"I thought we had that handled with you staying with me."

Well, yes, they did. So she wasn't reneging. Doing a quick look-back on the conversation, he could find no place where she'd said she was changing her mind.

Nope, he'd conjured that one up on his own. Due to the damned fear that had been attacking him like a plague. Fear that she meant too much to him.

Fear that he couldn't do anything about it.

Fear that he was going to hurt her somehow.

"And your friends and the clothes?" he asked.

"I told them I had that covered."

Oh. Seemed like the sun had just come out from behind a cloud. Maybe it had.

Glancing toward the sky as he drove, he didn't see a single cloud. Hadn't noticed any that morning, either. But he still felt like smiling.

"They think I'm seeing someone."

She dropped the bomb on him right when he was

starting to feel better. And yet…he didn't feel himself exploding. He just felt…still okay.

"What did you tell them?"

"Nothing, which is why they think that. What was I going to say? I'm in a sexually responsible situation?" She paused. "Frankly, I'm just as good with them drawing their own conclusions for now. It'll keep them off my back for a while. They mean well. And I love them dearly. But if I want to be single for the rest of my life and raise a family that way, then that's my business."

He agreed. Completely. Was glad to hear her say the words aloud—confirmation that they were both still on the same page. A little bit of disappointment was to be expected. In his world, with the choices he'd made for himself, it was a given.

"But, Jayden? Just so you know…if I ever was going to change my mind about the single part, which I haven't, it would be with you."

She disconnected before he could get words past the constriction in his throat.

Emma was on edge, filled with too much energy to be comfortable lying around after less than a day at home. She'd begun working from bed while she'd still been in the hospital, having a coworker submit an emergency motion to put off her trial a week, and going over other hearings that had to be postponed, or turned over to someone else.

Once she got home, she took her computer to bed with her—other than at night when Jayden climbed in beside her. Just to sleep, he announced. No sex for at least another forty-eight hours. His wishes, not doctor's orders.

She'd wanted to ask for a postponement of the previously agreed upon date for the end of their fling, but didn't.

It seemed like her accident, as horrible as it had been, might have had a great gift hiding in there, too. When she'd woken in her hospital room to see Jayden there, sitting alone with her, holding her hand...

He'd let go after that one squeeze, but he'd been there. Holding her hand.

Like she mattered to him.

And she'd known, opening her eyes and seeing him, that she'd felt better just seeing his face.

What it all meant, she didn't know. Didn't even want to guess. Or hope. She just wanted to go with the flow. Maybe it was Ms. Shadow rearing her head, but it didn't feel that way to Emma. Over the past couple of days— since Jayden had left Sunday morning—she'd been free from her war with her lesser self.

Could be she was changing. Healing from the past. Learning who she was. Finding peace with her place in the world.

Could be, though, she was off on the wild side, falling in love with the wrong guy, and would end up face-planted in a well of self-disgust again.

This time really seemed different, though. She wasn't frantic. Or refusing to listen to the "mother" voice inside her.

She'd give it a few days. See what happened. And how she felt.

In the meantime, she'd called Chantel, asked about the teenage boy who'd lived in Suzie's old neighborhood four years before.

The detective called back Thursday afternoon. Emma was showered, in shorts and a cropped black shirt at her

219 Tara Taylor Quinn

desk, feeling fine, other than a bit of pulling at the incision site on her forehead. Her hair covered the cut, which she was told to leave unbandaged now. Other than the stitches, and residual moments of panic when she relived that night on the road two days before, she was pretty much fully recovered. She'd even driven to the grocery store for some veggies for lunch.

"My guys talked to seven different households in that neighborhood, all of whom had been there for more than four years, and not one of them was aware of a teenage boy living in the neighborhood back then," Chantel said.

Getting up from her desk, Emma walked to the window, looked out at her pool. She hadn't been out to it since the night a trespasser had entered her yard and vandalized her sliding-glass door. Her pool guy had been there...

He had a key to the back gate. Could he have been the one who'd—

No. There was absolutely nothing he'd need her to "leave alone." And he was as short as she was.

There'd been no teenage boy in Suzie's neighborhood?

"I don't get it." She broke the silence that had fallen on the line. "Suzie didn't feed me that information. She'd have never mentioned the kid before I specifically asked the question."

"Did her answer seem hesitant?" Chantel asked. "Like she was making it up as she went along? Maybe to throw you off someone else?"

Because what if there *was* someone else? Someone who knew of Bill's crimes and was trying to frame him?

"No," she said, disappointed that they didn't have their answer. Emma interviewed and questioned people every single day. Witnesses, defendants, even expert witnesses and police officers. She was pretty good at figuring out when someone was lying to her...

"She gave instances, like she was reliving them," she told Chantel. "She'd smile, one time she almost started to cry, as she talked about the kid. And what Bill would have done to him, an innocent boy."

"What does Jayden have to say about it?"

"Nothing. I asked him not to question Bill about it, to protect Suzie. I sure don't want him going after her because she talked to me..."

"My guys tell me that Jayden was in the neighborhood Tuesday morning. He talked to at least a couple of the families we talked to."

Everything within Emma froze. Jayden Powell had had no reason to be in that neighborhood. His job was to keep an eye on Bill Heber. Period. So what had he been doing, talking to Heber's old neighbors? After she'd told him about the kid? He was a wild man. A man who didn't follow protocol unless it suited him. He did what he believed he needed to do to get the job done, no matter the ramifications to himself.

He was a man who lived for his work. Lived his work. To give offenders second chances.

Just how much would he do to protect Bill's? He'd admitted the case was personal to him.

Had she let Shadow blind her to the truth? Was Jayden going to protect Bill at all cost?

Back at her desk, she forced herself to focus. "What did he ask them?"

"Just what we did...about any teenager who might have been in the neighborhood. It sounds like he only hit up a couple of houses and left, like he was on the street no more than five minutes or so."

Chantel didn't sound at all worried. To the contrary, her tone held…admiration. Could Jayden have been in the neighborhood to find dirt on Bill? To corroborate Suzie's story in the only way he could, since Emma had made him promise not to talk to Bill himself?

Emma just wished, since the information about the kid had come from her, that Jayden had told her about his plans. That he'd included her.

He was under no professional obligation to do so.

But that didn't stop her from being disappointed that he hadn't.

Jayden stopped to pick up dinner from his favorite beachside bistro on the way home Thursday evening. Other than the huge fact that they were no closer to finding out who'd tried to run Emma off the road Tuesday night, he'd had a fairly decent week. The parole board had upheld his recommendation that Luke Lincoln's parole be revoked. For the time being, the offender was sitting in a jail cell and his wife and daughter had returned home to resume their lives.

Harold Wallace and his son had had some good news, too. The boy was being charged as a juvenile with battery of an officer, not attempted murder, and while he'd be serving time in detention, his sentence would much less than it might have been. And Harold and his girlfriend, who were planning to get married within a couple of weeks, would have visitation rights.

And Jayden's self-mandated, forty-eight hours of no sex with Emma, just to be sure there were no adverse reactions to her head injury, was up…if she felt the same way. He waved to the officer who'd been watching her home while Jayden was at work, and let himself into the house with the key she'd given him.

He only had the key until she was no longer a target. Still, it felt damned good, using it. As long as he was making her happy by doing so. It couldn't be about him. He couldn't lose sight of his mission. Or he'd lose the ability to see any good in himself. Any honor in his life. He'd made himself a promise—his life was not to enjoy. His life would only be used to serve others. How could he reach out for fullness when he'd been responsible for preventing someone else from experiencing any more life?

There'd been no forward movement on Emma's case. Chantel and everyone else involved had reached major frustration levels. Emma hadn't been able to put any identifiers on the truck and, even with the incident being broadcast on the local news, no one had seen the accident. They'd found skid marks on the road. Knew the truck had newer tires on it, but make and model—it could have been any of more than a thousand trucks in the city of Santa Raquel alone.

The sex between him and Emma was mind-blowing that night. He took more care to be gentle, to rein himself in, even when Emma tried to get him to play harder. And yet, when they climaxed, looking into each other's eyes, he could have sworn their bodies left the bed for a second. Nuts, he knew. But there it was.

Friday night was more of the same. Their coupling was maybe not as quiet, yet when they reached their peaks, the waves came again and again, prolonging the ecstasy so long, emotions crept in with the physical bliss to escalate the satisfaction in a way he'd never before known.

Normally they went right to sleep afterward. After the out-of-body experience he'd just had, he wasn't ready for sleep, but was loath to say anything to Emma. Was she finding their time together as odd as he was? As powerful?

Instead of waning, his passion just seemed to be procreating.

The idea brought a wave of panic. Passion drained from his system. It was an understood rule of life. Something he counted on.

"I have to ask you something." Her words didn't ease his discomfort any.

"Of course," he said, bracing himself.

"Why didn't you tell me you followed up on what I told you Suzie said about the kid in the neighborhood?"

He wanted the answer to be obvious. Something like, because he'd been under no professional obligation to do so.

"How do you know I did?" He was disappointed in the lameness of his question as he lay there on his back in the dark. He and Emma didn't cuddle when they slept.

"I told Chantel about it and when her guys went to question everyone in the neighborhood, you'd already been there."

"I only talked to a couple of guys." Like that made any difference? Or in any way spoke to her original question? Why hadn't he told her?

"I know. I've actually known for a couple of days."

Turning his head, he tried to read her expression in the darkness. "And you're only bringing it up now?"

"It's been bugging me. I tried to let it go, but I think I really need to know."

Need to know. He was lying in quicksand. More dangerous than quicksand because while it might swallow him up, it wasn't going to kill him. No, he'd be left lying there with no way to save himself from making another grave mistake—breaking the promise he'd made to himself in a deal that allowed him to live with what he'd once been.

"I didn't tell you because I didn't want you to think that I was overstepping my position."

"Even though you did."

"It was the night of the accident," he said, trying to figure it all out. "I had new information where Bill was concerned, if what Suzie had just told you was true. You'd almost been killed. I had to know if I was wrong and Bill was involved."

"He is involved, Jayden. I'm sure of it." She took a breath. "I know the evidence is mostly still just circumstantial, but it's strongly circumstantial. And if we could get Suzie's testimony... She wanted to talk to me...she had more to say when she was sitting there facing me again. She just didn't have the courage to say it."

"There *was* no teenage boy in the neighborhood," he told her. "Chantel's people talked to a lot more people than I did, and I'm sure she told you as much."

"I think there was a boy, just not on their street. We're honing in on just that one street. Maybe he lived on the next block over. Or behind them. The way Suzie talked about him—the specifics and emotion involved—I'm sure there was a young man. And that she's protecting him."

He wasn't so sure, though he understood her perspective. He didn't like that they couldn't find any other obvious suspects for targeting Emma, but something was not adding up in her scenario.

"What if Suzie's been lying to you all along?"

Emma sat straight up in bed. "She's the victim here, Jayden, and now you're trying to make her out to be a liar? We've seen the X-rays, read the expert testimony, in addition to her own. The case is about who hit her, remember?"

Stepping into the shorts and T-shirt she'd put on first thing in the morning, she headed for the door.

He hadn't meant, in any way, to say that Suzie wasn't the victim. Only that she wasn't being straight with them about the circumstances of her abuse. Because she was scared to death, probably. He wasn't so much faulting her as he was trying to get to the whole truth so they could make the right arrest and protect not only Suzie but Emma, too.

He didn't get up and go tell her so. He got up, grabbed a blanket and pillow off the spare bed and went out to the couch instead.

She was pissed at him.

Maybe that was for the best.

Chapter 21

It only took Emma a couple of minutes, and a cooler mind, to calm down.

Shaking her head, she leaned against the kitchen counter, arms crossed over her middle, and listened as Jayden moved out to the couch. She didn't blame him. She was letting emotion get in the way of work.

He'd made the absolute right choice to go hard after Bill, to use whatever information he had to find some proof that would allow them to put Bill's sorry ass in jail. He did what she'd have done. What she'd have *wanted* him to do.

He hadn't told her because he hadn't wanted her to know he'd stepped out of line?

She straightened. Wait a minute.

So…she'd been letting emotions, personal emotions,

cloud her judgment when she'd been hurt that he hadn't told her what he'd done.

But he'd not told her...for the exact same reason! He'd been letting personal emotions cloud *his* judgment.

They both were developing feelings and letting those emotions interfere!

She stood there alone, absorbing her discovery. What in hell did they do now?

They had to at least talk about it. That much was clear.

To discuss options. Probabilities.

Whether or not there were any possibilities for their fling to turn into something else.

It was way too soon to tell anything for sure, of course. But should they at least discuss opening some doors? As long as they were both putting everything on the table, keeping their eyes wide open?

Was there a way to have a long-term situation?

Or possibly even a family, down the road, *without* the marriage? Or even living together?

Maybe she could still inseminate as planned, raise her child, and he'd be like an "uncle" who visited often. Could she do that?

Or was that more of the "too wild" thinking that got her into trouble?

Was it possible—could she even open the door to the possibility—that she'd been rash in her decision to never have another long-term partnership?

Or was Ms. Shadow in control? Messing with her head. Trying to convince her she could have all these things. Just like Ms. Shadow had led her to the back of Keith's bike all those years ago.

The only answer she had at the moment was that

she couldn't leave Jayden lying on the couch. Couldn't leave them both hanging there with her stomping out leading to awkwardness in the morning. It was exactly the kind of thing they were trying to avoid.

She owed him an apology.

"Jayden?" Forgoing lights, she sat on the end of the couch, her hip against the balled-up blanket. He'd pulled on his jeans and was lying there flat on his back.

"Yeah?"

"I'm sorry. I overstepped."

"You're fine. It was a valid question."

"Not really. Not with what we signed up for."

"Maybe that was unrealistic."

So he was seeing that, too. The relief was heady. Not nearly as much as being in his arms, but in a really cool way, just the same.

Scooting so that her hip pressed against his feet, she put her hand on the blanket covering them. Liking the cozy feel of them.

"Maybe we should talk about that." Darkness gave her courage. Or, could she hope, the side of herself that she normally tamped down was finally finding a way to live in the world with her without hurting her or others?

"I'm listening."

He was open to having a conversation, then? The whole idea was new to her, at least to her conscious self. The accident, the scare of it mainly, had changed her. Opened her eyes to the vibrancy of life.

Waking to see him there…the way that had felt…she couldn't deny what that had shown her.

"Maybe this…thing…isn't just sexual. Maybe we really like each other, too." She tried out the words, for her own sake as much as his. They were charting new territory together. That's how relationships worked.

Not that they were necessarily going to have one, but...

"There's that distinct possibility." There was no humor in his tone. Or sarcasm, either. Still...

"You don't sound happy about that."

"It creates all kinds of difficulties."

Like her getting upset and leaving the bed because he hadn't told her something. Because she'd been hurt.

"Acknowledging the complications of a situation helps minimize them," she said.

He didn't reply.

"Do you want to stop seeing each other? Other than if necessary for work?"

"You're being targeted, Em. I'm not going any-where."

Right. Because of the job. She was hugely grateful for that. And for the police patrol, too. But sooner or later that was going to have to end. It was not like the city could afford to be her bodyguard forever.

"Do you want us to stop...everything personal?" If that was his choice, then...

God, don't let it be his choice.

"Do you?"

"No."

"Then let's leave it at that."

"At what?"

He put an arm over his eyes. Then sat up. She missed the warmth of his feet against her.

"We continue to have a personal side to our relations and see where it goes."

As in…see if it took them into a partnership that might not end? She had to know but was afraid to ask.

Didn't want to push him. Or herself, either.

"We've worked well together, this past week and a half," she said, thinking about all that they'd been through. Disagreeing about Bill. Her accident. Dinners and the greatest sex she'd ever had. He'd been a companion through much of it. Professional and otherwise.

"I like having you around," she admitted.

His sideways glance at her contained a grin. Her body started to flame again. "I like being around," he told her.

"So if we both keep liking it…say, for a long time, we're agreeing to let that happen?"

He looked her way again. Nodded.

"And if, at some point, we want more, like to become a family of some sort? What then? I'm not talking about you fathering my child, or even being a dad, but more like an uncle…"

Still turned her way in the darkness, he leaned back and slightly away from her. "It's not going to happen, Em. The family part. I'm never going to marry or be any kind of a father figure to any children. It's a choice I've made. I thought you understood that."

He didn't speak with ease. She could hear the intensity behind his words. And the pain.

Reaching a hand up to his face, she broke all their rules at once. "Why?" Pushing. Wanting. Needing. She wasn't sure what she'd want their bond to look like in the future. Wasn't sure she'd ever trust life and love enough to marry again. But she knew she needed to know if there was a chance. "I need to know why, Jayden."

He remained silent, let her touch him, but didn't touch back.

"I want this—us—more than anything I can remember," she said, unable to just give up. "We fit each other…" At least for now. Committed to their work like they were…anyone else would be hurt by the job coming first, but not Jayden. And not her. They understood the need. The drive.

"I just need to know why, Jayden. Please?"

When he shook his head, the disappointment was so crushing, she couldn't get up at first. Her hand slid from his face, but she sat there, struggling. Not knowing what to do.

Afraid she was going to cry. And that was something she'd promised herself she'd never do again. Not over a man…

"I killed a boy."

Emma had no idea what she'd been expecting, but it most definitely had not been that. Unmoving on the couch, she stared at the man with whom she was afraid she was falling in love. And his face was filled with a pain more severe than anything she'd ever known.

Jayden had never expected to hear those words, in his voice, outside his own head. Wasn't even sure he'd said them aloud at first, as he sat there trying to make out Emma's expression in the darkness.

"He was my friend. Or rather, a kid that worshipped me that I took for granted." He wasn't going to spare himself. Especially not with her.

Things were getting far too emotionally dangerous, threatening his life as it needed to be.

She wanted to open the door to signing on with him. Because she didn't completely know him.

That was why he had to tell her.

"What happened?" She hadn't pulled back. If anything, she'd leaned closer.

"I grew up an only child who could do no wrong, in a wealthy home with parents who adored me. I was entitled, self-centered, and sure I'd get my own way, whatever way I chose that to be. I worked hard, but things came easy to me, too. I was a B student because I didn't need the A and didn't want to spend time studying. I wanted to play sports, any and all of them. I chose football, was the quarterback of my high school team all four years, made state, and then chose not to play in college. Too many other things that I wanted to tackle."

"Did you do drugs?" she asked.

"No." His father wouldn't have tolerated that. "But I could put away some beers. And I used a fake ID and went to a strip club for my sixteenth birthday." He was giving her the stuff that mattered. The misdeeds that defined him.

"Did you ever get arrested?"

"No." That would have changed things with his Dad, too.

"It sounds like you were a normal guy with a great life. You were lucky, yeah, to be born to good parents with financial security, but you didn't squander the opportunity. You made the most of it."

He'd done what he'd wanted to do. Period. Just turned out that what he'd wanted to do had served him well.

Leaning forward, he put his elbows on his knees, looked at the floor. "There was this kid, Emory Smith. He was in my high school, a couple of years behind me.

He used to tag around after me whenever he could. Like an adoring puppy. I liked being so great that I had fans.

"Emory tried out for football his sophomore year. He wasn't real big, or all that tough, but he was in great shape, had determination and dedication, and a leg that wouldn't quit. He played first string kicker my last year. And then his last two years after I left. Helped take the team to state again the year after I graduated."

Emory had studied, too. Had straight A's. And worked twenty hours a week at some fast-food joint.

"My freshman year of college at the University of Southern California, I pledged the most prestigious frat on campus. I quickly rose up the ranks. And I learned how to drink. *Really* drink. Anything. Anywhere. As much as anyone wanted to give me. I wasn't playing football, but I was still working out, playing intramural sports, having a great time. I thought life was great. A game that was never going to end."

There would always be an end. That's what he needed her to understand.

"Emory used to come down to campus to hang out," he continued. "He kept saying that he couldn't wait to graduate and get to Southern Cal. I knew he had better things waiting for him, but I didn't say so. I just kept telling him, 'Yeah, kid, you do that.' He got a scholarship to Harvard, for Christ's sake. He was going to change the world. I never figured he'd give all that up. I thought he was just talking, you know, like kids do. That whole Southern Cal thing, I never took is seriously."

"What happened?" Her question came again. Softly. Almost as though she knew he needed to be led over the bridge that wasn't going to let him turn back.

Or go forward, either, as she'd soon find out.

"He followed me to Southern Cal." He told her the god-awful truth. "He'd been scouted by the team, got a scholarship there, too, and started in the very first game of the season. Damn near set a field goal record. He'd wanted me to come to one of his games, but I was done with that. I didn't want to be out on the field badly enough to do the work required. And if I couldn't be out on the field, I didn't want to be there. College football isn't like high school. Physically, maybe they're similar, but in high school, to most of the guys, it's a game. In college, it's work. With the goal of making it a career."

"You were smart to see that. And make the appropriate choice for you."

He'd been all about a good time. Living life. Doing pretty much whatever the hell he'd wanted to do. He was a golden boy.

"Did you do well academically?" she queried.

"Yeah." He'd done what little he'd had to do to meet his father's minimum requirement of B's across the board.

Eyes adjusting to the near darkness, with only the moon to light his view, Jayden could still pretty much make out every nuance in Emma's face. She focused on him, as though prepared for whatever was to come.

As if she already knew death waited at the end. Which of course, she did. He'd told her he'd killed a boy.

"Even after I ditched his first game, Emory was still hanging on me, so I thought I'd do him a solid and sponsor him for the frat. He could meet up with some of the coolest guys at school, guys who were his own age. I figured I was giving him the best days of his life. Four years of them."

"You were being kind." The words were firecrackers. Soft, almost whisper-like firecrackers.

"In order to get into the frat, pledges had to pass some...tests."

"Hazing," Emma said.

He shrugged. He'd gone through it. Hadn't felt hazed. It had all been a big game to him. A challenge. He'd never felt better the night he'd been the first to make it back to the frat house. He'd been appointed freshman liaison to the fraternity's campus board for how well he'd done that night.

"Pledges are taken out by their sponsors, dumped in a particularly dense part of some woods with more alcohol than they could ever drink, a tracking device and nothing else. No compass. No phone. Their only challenge was to make it back. Their upperclassman sponsors tracked them and if, in a specified amount of time, they weren't headed in the right direction, they were picked up. Dropped off at campus. And let go."

His chin sinking to his chest, Jayden tightened up. His lungs. His muscles. Everything about him grew tight. Uneasy.

"I can see what's coming," Emma said, still attempting to rescue him from himself. There was nothing she could to change his story. "You were Emory's sponsor, so you had to be the one to go pick him up when he didn't make it back."

He looked at her. So far, she had it right.

"When he knew he'd been dumped by you...after all those years of idolizing you, of giving up Harvard to be close to you, he committed suicide, didn't he?"

Wouldn't have made him feel any less guilty if he had. But...

"No." He continued, "When I dropped Emory off, I gave him the same edge I'd been given when I was a pledge. I told him about a cliff not far from where we were, practically led him to it. I told him if he jumped, he could swim across the lake and be within a hundred yards of the house. A couple of the other guys were giving their pledges the same advice. We'd already decided to let the three of them in… The other two made it back. They had to search the lake for Emory's body."

A look of horror passed over her face. It was a vision he was never going to forget. Because it was a replica of the same look he saw in his mirror every single morning.

Chapter 22

Emma ached all over. Ached to take Jayden in her arms and ease his pain. Ached for him. With him. He hadn't killed anyone. But he'd unknowingly sent a young man to his death.

No way that wouldn't have changed him forever.

Processing in the way she knew, she asked, "Were there any charges pressed?"

In today's world there might have been, but back then...

"No. No one forced him to jump off that cliff. And he didn't tell anyone he wasn't a strong swimmer. Two other guys, who'd both had more to drink than he had, made it back. Emory didn't even have enough alcohol in his system to be considered legally drunk. And our folks could all afford to get us the best lawyers." He said the last word with bitterness.

"Your parents got you a high-powered lawyer?"

"They tried. I fired him. I was an adult and within my rights to do so. I planned to use a public defender. Maybe I thought it would look better. I don't know what I thought. As it turned out, we hadn't needed lawyers. The fraternity was disbanded, though."

"What about Emory's family? His parents? Did they come after you?"

"Not that I was ever made aware. I've always figured they probably tried. They would have to have wanted to. I apparently had more control over their son than they did…all their years of teaching, of guiding…and I, in my obliviousness, undid it all. I knew how much value he put in what I said. I should have been more responsible to that."

Maybe. But he'd been a kid, too. Not a parent.

"You've never talked to them?" she asked. "Even at the funeral?"

"I didn't go. I didn't want to cause them any more pain…"

"And since?"

"The same."

"You deal with people who have things to be sorry for every day of your life, Jayden. What's one of the first things they're told to do if they want to get right with themselves and their world?"

"Make amends." He glanced away and then back. "No way I can bring him back," he said. "I can't help this one. Except, by living in such a way that I don't cause them further pain or bitterness. Like having a family of my own when they'll never have the grand-children Emory could have given them."

What he said made logical sense. But it didn't sit

right with Emma's heart. Her own choices didn't sit all that great with her heart most of the time, either. Not in an emotional sense. Ms. Shadow tended to have more control in that area.

"It still seems like…you're deciding for them how they feel. What they need. Maybe you should at least try to see them. Maybe they'd welcome a chance to yell at you, if nothing else. It might help them. And if they don't want to see you, they'll mostly likely just refuse the gesture." He had to at least try. It seemed so clear to her.

He didn't respond.

Other than his own self-loathing, Jayden showed little emotion at all. She understood. That kind of pain didn't let itself out. Didn't let you know even a moment's relief.

"When my baby died, I wished they'd throw me in jail," she said, though this wasn't about her. She just had no coping skills to share with him on this one. Sometimes the pain was so deep, the best you could do was sit in it with someone.

He glanced over at her then and the look in his eyes… she didn't really get it. They glistened. And weren't completely dead.

"Instead we're left to pay a silent price for the rest of our lives." He nodded as he held her gaze.

She got it then. The thing between them. It was a whole lot more than a fling. Way beyond business. They were like souls, meeting in the only place they ever could.

Aloneness.

They could hang out. Talk. Have sex. She could

maybe even raise a child. But ultimate union? Their personal prisons weren't ever going to allow that.

She scooted over to him. Wrapped her arms around his neck and buried her head in his chest. They might not have it all, but they had something.

When his arms finally wrapped around her, too, squeezing tight, she was thankful they no longer had to be solitary in their confinements.

Standing in the shower the next morning, Jayden tried to wash off everything that was different about him and return to the person he knew. He'd left Emma's house before she was even out of bed. Purposely. Though he'd joined her back in bed the evening before, he'd lain awake most of the night.

Was he helping her, a woman grieving for the child she'd lost when she'd been still partially a child herself, a woman who had a sizable collection of past relationship hurts? Or was he just serving himself?

Did it matter if he was getting what he wanted in being with Emma, as long as he didn't have a family with her?

Walking away from her, once they'd caught whoever was behind the threats, didn't seem right. And yet... finding his own personal happiness...not right, either. He'd promised himself he wouldn't waltz out and have what he'd stolen from Emory.

There were some things that couldn't change.

His father had taught him that.

Stopping with his head under the spray, he straightened, pulling himself out of the water completely as that last thought occurred to him. His father...who never changed. Sometimes that was a good thing.

And Jayden had witnessed times when, while it wasn't necessarily bad, it seemed…sad somehow. Like never tasting new foods. Such a small thing. But almost seemed…wasteful…somehow, to have perfectly good taste buds in your mouth and not let them have an experience…

Shutting off the water, he grabbed his towel. Dried off as he always did. Top down. Feet last. And thought about Emma's suggestion that he try to see the Smiths.

He wanted to hate the idea. To know in his gut that it was wrong. He'd been over the question in every way he could ask and answer it during the long night hours.

And feared that it was himself he was sparing by staying away from Emory's parents all these years. How could he face them, knowing what he'd done?

Because, like Emma had said, if the Smiths didn't want to see him, they didn't need him to protect them from it happening. They'd simply say no.

It would be different if they'd ever told him to stay away from them. Then he'd be doing so for their sakes. Out of respect.

So…was it himself he was protecting?

And so thinking, how could he not at least offer to see them?

It was Saturday. A day he'd taken off because of the week they'd had. He'd planned to surf. Work out. Buy cat food.

Maybe try to get a look at the thing. And figure out what to call it. It was eating the food he left every morning. Leaving messes for him to clean.

Officers would be on Emma's house until he returned to her house that evening. Or someone would catch a lucky break and they'd find the guy trying to shut her up. For all he knew, she'd be going into the office. She often did on Saturdays. And since she'd been working from home all week, she'd probably want to get caught up on things while the office was quiet.

That's what he would choose to do if it were him: go to his office.

Putting on dark shorts and a casual pullover shirt, he slipped on a pair of dock shoes and grabbed his keys. The gym was open all day. He could go to the beach in the afternoon and at least get in some swimming. Maybe, that morning, he'd drive down to see his folks. To talk to his dad about trying new foods.

On his way, he made a call. Asked Leon, his sometime partner, for a favor. And when Leon got back to him with a number, he instructed his hands-free dialing assistant to make the call.

Emory's mother started to cry when he identified himself to her. Told him he was welcome to come by anytime. And within the hour, he was sitting in her living room, holding a glass of tea he didn't want.

She'd moved since he'd known them. Into a much smaller place. Emory had had a younger sister, he recalled, who was now married with a couple of kids and living just a couple of blocks away.

Mrs. Smith—Ms. *White*, now that she was divorced—lived alone.

Another nail in his coffin.

The death of a child was one of the major causes for divorce, Jayden knew from his many hours of counseling studies.

"I'm just so sorry," he blurted out in the middle of their catching-up politeness. "I wish it could have been me, not him, Ms. White. I swear to you, not a day goes by that I don't think of him. Every morning, I know my goal is to live in a way that would honor my having known him."

He didn't say Emory's name. Found himself oddly out of sorts. Emotional. Almost weak with it.

Tears filled her eyes. She straightened, smiling. Didn't seem weak at all.

"He adored you, Jayden. All he ever wanted was to be like you, and the sad truth was, it wasn't ever going to happen. He'd always been a small boy, small-boned. He could build his strength, but he was never going to have broad shoulders. Or a body that could tackle other men."

"I shouldn't have encouraged him."

"To the contrary—you were the one who saved him."

He shook his head. Hadn't she been told the truth of what had happened? Could that be possible?

"You did." She continued, "He never had any friends. Never fit in. He told me once, in junior high, that he felt like a freak. I think that's why he originally insisted on trying out for football. And then he met you. The quarterback. A star. You noticed him. And rather than crush his dream, you showed him a way he could be part of the team. He became a kicker, and his whole life changed. He loved high school. He dated. Went out. Had friends. You gave that to him."

At what cost? he wondered. He'd taken so much more.

"He'll never give you grandchildren."

"No, he won't. But I already have grandchildren. I babysit for them five days a week. Some people don't get that lucky."

Jayden didn't buy it. She was just being nice. He shouldn't have come.

"Emory died doing what he wanted to do more than anything else in the world," she said softly, tearing up again. "He died becoming a brother to you."

His vision blurred slightly. He blinked.

"And Mr. Smith…does he feel the same way?" he asked. Man-to-man, would Emory's father let the bitterness fly? Give Jayden the lashing he deserved?

"He's still embittered. Angry."

Rightfully so. If it would do the man any good to berate Jayden in person, he'd stop by there, too. If she'd give him an address.

"My ex-husband blames himself for pushing Emory so hard. Wanting him to be a man. He was part of the reason Emory chose football—to find his manhood. His father had played. When Emory played his first high school game, you'd have thought his father had won the lottery. And when he got a scholarship, it's all my ex-husband could talk about. He was being a dad. Trying to have relationship with his son.

"If Emory had chosen to go to Harvard, my ex-husband would have bragged about that, too. But he doesn't see it that way." She sighed softly. "He thinks he drove Emory to be something he was not. That he pushed him into choosing to prove himself yet again by jumping off that cliff. He cut me off first, certain that I blamed him. No amount of telling him different, no amount of counseling, could get through to him. When our daughter got married, he withdrew even more. He hasn't even met his second grandchild…"

Jayden ended up spending half a day with Emory's mother. He took her out to lunch. Told her about his career. About using every day he had left on earth to honor life. To put others first. To make up for the selfish ass he'd been.

He didn't put it in quite those words, but he needed her to know. Her son's life had mattered. So much so, that Jayden's was completely shaped by it.

On his way out of town he tried to see Emory's father, too.

The man was polite, respectful, but didn't want to meet.

Jayden understood completely. There were days he struggled to look himself in the mirror, too, but maybe it would be a little easier, going forward. He'd failed Emory, but he'd helped him, too, even if it had been unknowingly. And he hadn't been solely responsible for the boy's pushing himself too hard as Jayden had previously somehow thought.

Maybe, he'd reach out to Mr. Smith again. However often it took, until he and the man could find some kind of way to forgive each other—and then themselves.

Emma was at her desk at work, organizing the coming week and trying to get everything done quickly so that the deputy standing outside her door could move on to other pursuits. Because it was Saturday, the courts regular security detail was absent, but she couldn't be in the building without protection.

Maybe overkill. Maybe not.

At least when the officers were sitting outside her house, they were there on a first-come, first-serve basis when it came to extra pay. That was city. The court was county detail.

She almost ignored her cell when it rang, figuring she could return the call from home. But when she looked and saw it was Jayden, she picked up. As far as she knew, he was working.

Or doing whatever he did when he wasn't.

Maybe someday she'd know what he did for fun—or even do it with him sometimes.

"I've been thinking about that teenager Suzie told you about," he said. "I agree with you that there's got to be something in it. When you were relaying what she told you, in such detail…she had to have been talking about something real. Or she's a consummate liar. If she's lying, she's covering for someone else. If not, we need to find the kid. He'd be twenty-one or -two by now. He might be able to tell us something about her that we don't know."

Or about Bill. More likely about Bill.

"Okay."

"I just wanted you to know that I'm heading back to talk to the neighbors again. Just to see if there's anything at all they can tell us…"

He couldn't do so as a parole officer. But there was no law against a guy talking to someone who was willing to talk. Private detectives did it all the time.

But the real news was not that he was working outside his normal boundaries. She suspected Jayden did stuff like that all the time. It was the risk-taker in him. The guy who didn't just fly by what was expected of him. But rather by what he expected of himself.

The real news was that he'd called to let her know he was going back.

There'd been no professional reason for him to have done so.

And she wasn't sure if she should allow herself to make something of that. She wanted to so badly believe there was something more than physical fire between them, even if it was highly unconventional.

But in the past anytime she'd trusted her "wants," listened to the Ms. Shadow side of her, others had been hurt. And she had been, too.

Still, she couldn't close the door to the possibility. She and Jayden were special. No matter which side of her she asked.

Chapter 23

Jayden got nothing. Neither of the guys who lived in Bill's old neighborhood and used him as their mechanic knew anything about a teenager who'd maybe mowed Bill's grass four years ago or been friendly with the family in any way. Neither of them had ever seen any man at Suzie's house other than Bill.

He knew what Emma would say. They were Bill's clients. They could be lying for him, if he was giving them a good deal on their classic auto work—or just because they were friends and maybe thought what happened between a husband and wife was their business. Not Jayden's.

Jayden didn't think Bill was the man who'd abused Suzie. He just didn't.

But then he never would have thought Ms. White would invite him to please come see her again—but she had as she'd hugged him goodbye. As often as he'd like. He'd never ever foreseen that his presence could bring her a piece of her son back. Or bring her peace of any kind.

He wasn't off his personal hook. If he'd had half an awareness about himself back then, he should have figured that Emory couldn't swim across that lake. He was the one who'd suggested the kid be a kicker because he knew he'd be made into meat out on the football field otherwise—because he was small. Emory could kick like no one Jayden had ever seen, but that hadn't meant he had stamina or upper body strength.

Figuring he'd head back to his place and change and then tackle the ocean for a while, he was headed in that direction when his car dash signaled a call from Chantel.

"Powell," he answered immediately.

"It's Bill Heber." Chantel didn't explain. Didn't need to. "We finally got the warrant for any surveillance cameras outside stores that sell lipstick between Santa Raquel and Bill's place. It was a long shot, but we've spent the week following every long shot we had. They were all we had."

"You've got him on tape? Buying lipstick?" Jayden found that hard to believe. Wanted the culprit found and punished, but he wanted it done right.

He wanted the right man.

Arresting someone would make everyone feel better, the department, the courts, could relax. But only if the guy they arrested was the one who'd made the threats. Bill had been in group Tuesday night when Emma had been forced off the road. His thoughts flew...

"We've got him on camera leaving a drugstore not

far from his work," Chantel reported. "A clerk there made a positive ID. She remembered him because the one tube of lipstick was all he bought. She told us what kind and it was a match to what the lab had come up with. He paid cash. Officers are on their way to pick him up now."

A lot of work for a tube of lipstick, he thought. And a battery charge. But Suzie—a woman who refused to help law enforcement and the justice system keep her safe—wasn't the only reason why everyone in the system was working overtime on this one. When Bill had threatened a prosecutor, he'd upped his ante considerably.

Pulling over, he called up the location app on his phone. "He's at work," he told her, feeling sick. To his stomach—and at heart. He'd promised himself he wouldn't fail again, not in a big way. And he'd failed Emma. A woman who...

"Yeah, I already called to verify that," Chantel, continuing their conversation, interrupted his thoughts. But not the weight, settling heavier and heavier on him.

"Let me know when you have him in custody."

"Will do. You want to let Emma know or should I?"

Jayden was the one staying with her at night. "I will, and thanks, Detective."

"I'm just sorry it didn't turn out differently. I know you were really pulling for this one."

"You going to try to get him on the abuse, too?"

"Yep."

"You mind if Emma and I head over to Suzie's to let her know an arrest has been made?" He was thinking of Emma. "I think she'd like to talk to her before anyone else gets to her, to try to get a statement out of her now that Bill's been caught with hard evidence of harassment at least. When she talked to her on Monday, Emma said she thought Suzie wanted to tell her more than she had."

Emma could have called the detective herself, but since he already had Chantel on the line...

"If Emma wants to go, I'm all for it. If not, let me know and I'll send someone over to notify Suzie when we've got him in custody."

Not normal protocol—but not a lot about this case was normal. On any level.

Someone was in the outer office. Emma heard her deputy talking, and then recognized the answering male voice with a familiar slide of warmth in her belly.

Jayden was there?

Rising, straightening her Lycra, calf-length brown skirt and white top, she ran a hand through her curls. They'd opened the door to becoming something.

Everything mattered more now.

Would he greet her with a kiss? It was after hours. They were virtually alone. Couples did that...

It took her a full thirty seconds to wonder why he'd come to her work at all. Why he hadn't called beforehand. She was already reaching for her satchel before he'd even told her why he was there.

He'd explained what had happened by the time they were in his car and Chantel called to say that Bill was officially in custody. And that they'd found a dark blue baseball cap in his truck. His tire tracks didn't match the tires found at Tuesday night's scene, but he had an entire garage of vehicles he could have had access to. He evidently wasn't dumb enough to use his own.

"Thank God," Emma said after they told the detective they were on their way to Suzie's and hung up. "I can't believe it's over!" She was free! Safe! Suzie was safe!

And, she realized, there was no reason that Jayden had to spend the night with her that night. He'd probably welcome a night in his own home. With his own things. Getting up to take a shower, without having to drive home first.

She wanted to ask him if he wanted to get dinner or something, to celebrate. And it occurred to her that maybe he'd had second thoughts about their talk the night before.

Then she saw Jayden's expressionless face.

"What's wrong?"

"I just hope they've got the right man," he finally said. "I can't explain him buying lipstick. I didn't get a chance to speak with him, obviously, but…"

"It's okay if you were wrong," she told him. "The man's a fool for not appreciating the chance you were giving him."

He shook his head. "It doesn't add up to me. The note on your door, I can almost see that one. But trying to drive you off the road? And beating up on his wife the second he gets out of jail? The times he got upset with her in the past—and he admits to doing so, just not hitting her—all stemmed from rational scenarios he'd built in his head. Just showing up at her house out of the blue and beating up on her…it doesn't fit him. And driving you off the road…it's irrational. He's not."

Emma listened to him. Wanted to be able to help him. But couldn't.

"I'm sorry." She'd been right on this one. She was

good at her job. Had studied the case far longer than Jayden had. Was a professional doing her job. But she was sorry that the guy he'd been standing up for had turned out to be manipulating him. "I know you thought he was different," she offered when he said nothing.

As a professional, she could make the rest of the ride across town in perfectly acceptable silence. As Jayden's...whatever she was going to be...she was finding the silence difficult.

"I hope to God, if you're right and Bill did this, that Suzie will talk to you as you expected she wanted to do on Monday night. That she'll give specifics. Something that points irrevocably to Bill."

She hoped so, too.

He needed the women safe: both Emma *and* Suzie. If Bill was their man, Jayden would do whatever he could to get the man back in prison as fast as possible. He could have Bill's parole revoked, which would send him back while he awaited trial on all of the new charges.

Jayden's problem wasn't in being wrong... He wasn't real thrilled that Emma seemingly didn't pick up on his feelings. But then, when a guy didn't give anything of himself to anyone, how could he expect them to magically know him? Know what he'd do? Or how he'd feel?

He'd figured his solitary life would preclude such considerations. But now...

Everything was confused. Confusing *him.*

"I went to see Emory's mom today."

Emma had been instrumental in the visit. It seemed okay to fill her in.

"And?"

He told her about the woman's surprising pleasure

in seeing him. And then about Emory's father's self-imposed exile. All afternoon Jayden had been kind of seeing himself in that story—wondering if maybe he was wasting a life, and dishonoring Emory by doing so, hurting loved ones who still needed him, as Tom Smith was doing.

Or if he was falling hard for the prosecutor and was grasping at straws as a way to justify breaking his word to himself.

"Everyone makes mistakes," Emma said when he'd been half holding his breath to see if she also saw similarities between him and Mr. Smith. "Maybe the real challenge is not in being perfect, but in learning to forgive yourself when you aren't."

She was looking out the window, not at him. Speaking for herself? For him? Just speaking? Throwing out a platitude? Or wondering on her own behalf? Didn't seem to matter. He felt like she'd just slapped another defining moment on him. Another possible perspective change for his brain to process.

And wasn't sure he was ready for that.

Maybe he was a lot more like his father than he'd thought.

Or maybe he was just afraid to give himself a real second chance.

Emma couldn't believe she was finally going to get the second chance to help Suzie Heber. To free her from the fiend who'd married a sweet young woman and made her life a living hell. Heading up the walk to Suzie's front door, she stepped slightly in front of Jayden. Leading the way.

Suzie knew her.

She was feeling proprietary. She was trying not to focus on the fact that he'd pretty well given her a warning back there in the car. Telling her about Emory's father, who couldn't live any kind of full life, couldn't engage in an intimate relationship, or be a part of a family. Not even when the daughter and grandkids involved were his own.

It seemed obvious to her that Jayden had found a man who was in the same place he was. Who'd been damaged in the same way. He was telling her there was no hope for the two of them.

She didn't want to accept any of it.

Knocking on the front door even before Jayden was fully beside her, she pasted a smile on her face in case Suzie glanced through the peephole before pulling open the door.

She was the bearer of good news, not there to badger or pressure a victim into coming forward.

The smile was completely earnest when she heard the door start to open, and then Emma could feel it fade when she saw Suzie standing there. The woman kind of blinked, oddly, but when Emma asked if they could come in, she only paused for a second before nodding and then quickly stepped back.

"He's in the bath—" Suzie was whispering. Emma thought she'd heard the words right, but couldn't be sure. She glanced back at Jayden, to see his reaction, and saw him reaching for his gun.

"Drop it now or she dies."

Emma's gaze swung back around to see a man she'd never seen before, pointing a gun directly at her head. She heard Jayden's gun drop to the floor.

"I'm sorry," Suzie said tremulously. It was unclear

who she was talking to, Emma or the man holding the gun. The woman was holding her arm in front of her, with her hand. Emma realized, too late, that it had an odd twist to it. Had to be broken.

"Just calm down here." Jayden stepped in front of Emma, holding his arms out wide and angling himself to cover Suzie, too. "You don't want to do this," he said. "Lower the gun and let's talk. See if we can take care of this right here. Right now. No one gets hurt. It just ends."

"It doesn't end," the man said, pointing the gun directly at Jayden's chest. The guy was taller than Jayden. Six-one or so. His beard made it hard to determine his age. His hair was unremarkable. But the baseball cap on the coffee table—it was dark blue.

Jayden's phone rang.

"Don't answer it," the man said. They all listened until the ringing stopped.

Heart pounding, Emma stared at the man. Petrified. Jayden wasn't wearing his vest. If…

"I'm a prosecutor," she said. "I can make a deal with you, assuming you give me a chance, a reason, to be able to do so."

"I know who you are," the man said, moving his gun toward Jayden's shoulder almost directly in front of her head. "If you'd been able to convict the bastard the first time around, none of this would have happened. Now. All three of you. Move. Slowly. Right here." He pointed to the couch with his free hand, without taking his gaze off of them. "Side by side. Sit," he instructed.

Emma moved first. No way she was going to take a chance on irritating the guy to the point he pulled that trigger. She'd rather be dead herself than lose Jayden.

Or Suzie.

She sat in the middle of the couch. Jayden dropped down on her left, pushing his thigh into hers. Suzie was on her right. Not touching her.

"Please, Kyle," Suzie begged, not crying but sounding like she was fighting tears. "You know I love you. Deep down, you know."

"It's all messed up now," he said. "If she'd done her job right the first time, he'd never have gotten out. But no, she screwed that one up. And then, when it's all going to finally be okay, she goes and sticks her nose in things again..."

"It wasn't okay," Emma said, not sure why she wasn't keeping her mouth shut. She just knew she couldn't stop fighting until he stopped her. "I just got involved two weeks ago and someone beat up on Suzie three months ago."

Jayden's nudge was almost imperceptible. Was he telling her to stop? Or that she was on the right track?

"Kyle," he said, "how old are you?"

"Shut up!" The man roared, swung the gun within a couple of inches of Jayden's head. Close enough that Emma could see his hand shaking.

And she figured out who he was. The kid they'd all been looking for. Suzie hadn't lied about his existence. But it seemed she might have been lying about her relationship with him. And about his age, too. This was no sixteen- or eighteen-year-old kid. He was easily in his twenties.

Maybe Bill had been right to question the paternity of his child.

Her entire soul was shaking. She tried to find Ms. Shadow, to hide behind her, but came up empty.

"I know you didn't hurt Suzie four years ago," Emma said, just talking. She was going to fall apart if she just sat. She couldn't think. Couldn't figure out a plan. She was scared to death. "I know what Bill did to her," she continued. "It's why I went for the murder charge. I made a mistake there, though. If I'd gone for battery, I'd have won."

Kyle, whoever he was, was standing right in front of them, moving the gun back and forth between the three of them. There was no doubt in her mind that if any of them made any kind of move that he construed to be an attempt to help themselves or to get away, he'd shoot that gun. He was ready.

"But I can win this time," she told him. "Bill's in custody. That's what we came here to tell Suzie. That she was safe."

"You're lying," he said, spraying spittle at their feet. The gun jerked a little as he moved it from one to the other of them.

"I'm not lying. I can't prove it to you without making a phone call, but I can guarantee you that if you turn on the television, it'll be all over the news soon enough. And we've got evidence this time to get a conviction. Hard evidence. They found video surveillance of him buying the lipstick he used to vandalize my back door. Threatening an officer of the court, that's serious stuff, there." Her court voice wasn't in that room. She could hear herself trembling in every word, knew he could hear it, too.

Kyle pointed his gun at Suzie. "Go on," he said. "Turn on the TV. And then come stand with me."

This was it. Their chance. Emma realized one second was all they might get. Him distracted, covering Suzie and them, too.

She wanted to make a run for it. If Kyle turned on her, shot her, Jayden would be able to save Suzie. And himself.

All she had to do was to run in the direction opposite from Suzie.

But her limbs wouldn't move. She was frozen to the couch.

Fairly certain that she was going to die there.

Chapter 24

Jayden's gun lay on the floor where he'd dropped it. At least ten feet away. Chances of him getting there before Kyle shot one of the women, or him and then the women, were pretty slim.

He had to get Kyle to come closer to him. To create a chance to grab the younger man, to take his gun.

Suzie had turned on the television and was standing next to Kyle. He'd wrapped his free arm around her neck, holding her close to him.

"Let's just go, Kyle," she said softly, looking up at him. "Just me and you. We can go out the back door and get away from here. Go where nobody will ever bother us again."

Kyle glanced at her for a second, almost as though he was considering the option.

"You're the kid from the neighborhood," Emma said from beside him. "Isn't he, Suzie?" she asked.

Jayden had figured as much, as well. Was more focusing on being poised to cover her body with his if he saw any hint of movement in that trigger finger. Something told him the guy wasn't going to kill Suzie. He loved her.

And he was emotionally unstable, too. The odd way Suzie was holding her arm, had propped it on her wrist when she'd had to use her good hand to hold the TV remote, was evidence of the young man's propensity for violence.

Suzie didn't say a word.

"What's she talking about?" Kyle pulled his arm tight around Suzie's neck. "You got someone else now, too?"

"You know I don't, Kyle," Suzie said, staring up at him. Jayden wasn't a great expert on relationships but it looked to him like the woman really loved the guy.

"Then who's this neighborhood kid?"

He was looking at Jayden when he asked the question, but the way he pulled against Suzie again made it clear who he was talking to.

"You," she said. "I told them I met you in our old neighborhood. They don't know…"

Know what?

Emma's leg pressed against Jayden's. Maybe she knew. Maybe she was just scared. He had to get her out of there. To make certain that she had a chance to have her baby.

She'd lost one already. She wasn't going to lose a chance to have another…

"What don't we know?" Jayden asked quietly. There was no point in threatening Kyle. Their best hope was to get him to relax enough that he'd come closer. If nothing else, they had to do all they could to diffuse his panic as much as possible. He was like a bomb; any little change could set him off.

"You really don't know?" He was looking at Emma, a sneer on his face. Like he had one over on her.

"I didn't tell anyone, Kyle," Suzie said. "Not then, and not now. I told you so. I told you I'd protect you and I always have…"

He looked at Suzie then, as though what she'd said really mattered to him, and Jayden leaped. He didn't think. Didn't plan. Just leaped off the couch and toward that gun, knowing that he'd either get to it in time, or feel its spray mutilate his insides.

Either way, he was giving Emma and Suzie a chance to run.

Emma heard the shot ring out before she realized what Jayden was doing. He moved. Blood spattered. Horror filled every sinew of her body.

And she saw Kyle drop to the floor with Jayden going down on top of him.

"Kyle!" Suzie screamed, blood on her clothes, her chin.

Emma rushed toward the bodies as Suzie dropped to her knees beside them. It took Emma a second to realize that Kyle was free of Jayden. That Jayden was kneeling over the fallen young man, his fingers at Kyle's throat. And that officers were piling in through the front door like someone was throwing a surprise party.

Her gaze landed on the floor where Jayden's knee rested beside Kyle's hand. His gun was still tangled up in his fingers, and it took her a second to realize that it had fallen to the floor, too. Kyle still had his gun?

Nothing made sense for a second.

Jayden was alive. Moving. And reaching for her. He slid his hands around her waist and they stood up together. "You okay?" Jayden asked, his voice strong. Sure.

She didn't know what she was. Before she could find words, Chantel was there, standing beside the two of them, while a female officer led a hysterical Suzie outside and officers surrounded the body on the floor.

"You two okay?"

Not trusting her voice, Emma nodded. Jayden was fine. Alive. Standing next to her. His shoulder, clear down to his wrist, touching hers.

"I'm fine," Jayden said aloud.

"I thought you'd been shot!" The words sounded strangled as Emma finally got them out. She needed a small dark place to go hide so she could curl up in a ball and cry.

"For a second there, I thought so, too." Jayden sounded relieved, but dead serious. "What...how did you...?"

"We were outside," Chantel said. "When we got here, saw him with Suzie in a neck hold and you two at gunpoint, we surrounded the place, and everyone had orders, if anyone saw a shot, he or she was to take it. Period. When he dropped his guard to look at Suzie..." She shrugged. "I can tell you I about swallowed my heart when I saw Jayden jump on the chance, too..."

He'd just jumped right up there, willing to get himself killed...not knowing the police were outside...

Like he didn't value his life enough to...

"If they hadn't been outside, you might have been killed." Emma got those words out loud and clear.

"But you and Suzie would have had a chance to run for help."

Chantel nodded. "You deserve a medal for that one, Powell," she said.

A medal, hell. What he'd earned was Emma's fury.

Emma was clearly pissed. Anger was a common response to extreme fear. That was what Jayden told himself as they walked outside to give their statements.

"How did you guys get here so fast?" Emma asked, walking more with Chantel than with him as they exited the house.

"Fate," the blond detective said, leading them to an unmarked car with doors opened. "Or people doing their jobs and it all coming together at exactly the right time," she added, looking back at the house. "One of the neighbors you saw today, you told him Suzie had been hurt again…"

"Camden Harris. I was impressing upon him that it was urgent he tell me anything he knew that could help us or he could possibly find himself an accomplice to charges he didn't want to face. He didn't budge." Jayden was at Emma's side again. Where he planned to stay. For a while at least. Until he could convince himself that she was really safe. Alive and *safe.*

"Not with you, but you got to him. That call I got when I was on the phone with you…it was him. Camden Harris." They'd reached the unmarked car. Emma sat sideways on the back seat, her feet on the ground. Jayden stood beside her, his leg touching hers, while Chantel shielded them from a news car that had pulled up. "He said you gave him my number and that he had information. Turns out he knew a lot more than he was saying. He'd kept quiet because he didn't want to jeopardize his marriage…"

"His marriage?" Emma asked, standing again.

"He'd seen Suzie with bruises in the past," Chantel said, nodding. "He called out to her once, asked her if she was okay. He knew Bill, liked him. She told him he wasn't hurting her and he believed her. Or tried to. Sometimes people let themselves be convinced. He knew Bill had a tendency to be overprotective, that he was jealous of anyone looking at his wife. Bill had even asked him a time or two if he'd ever seen anyone over at his house. Asked him to keep an eye on the place. But at the same time, Bill was a decent guy. Fair businessman. Gave jobs to guys down on their luck. Helped out in the neighborhood anytime there was a problem. Fast-forward to a week when Camden's wife was out of town and Suzie and Bill had another fight. He went over after Bill took off and one thing led to another…"

"*Harris* was the one she slept with?" Jayden asked. Bill had had legitimate reason for his jealousy. He'd said more than once that a man knows these things. Jayden had just put it down to the man's insanity where his wife was concerned. Nothing would excuse the hell Bill put Susie through, however.

"It only happened that once," Chantel said. "But that's why the neighbor never said anything to anyone about what happened later. He truly loves his wife and he was afraid if he ever said anything, the fact that he slept with Suzie might come out. While he was over there that night, she got a phone call. It was Kyle. Bill's son."

"What!" Emma screeched while Jayden's jaw dropped.

"His son?"

"Illegitimate," Chantel confirmed, "but yes. He'd lost his mother. His stepfather didn't want him around, and he'd come to Bill for help. But Bill didn't want a teenage boy around his twenty-four-year-old wife and told him he couldn't stay. So Suzie helped him behind Bill's back. After Bill was sent to prison, she let Kyle move in with her and eventually they became a couple."

Jayden felt like he was on some other planet. "There's nothing in Bill's records about having a son."

"He didn't believe an ex-girlfriend when she told him she was pregnant and the baby was his. She moved on, married, and raised the boy with her new husband. He just found out Bill was his father when his mother died."

Damn. Jayden was guessing Bill still didn't consider the boy his own, which was why he hadn't told Jayden about him.

But…

"So did Camden Harris confirm that Bill *was* hitting Suzie four years ago? Or not? He'd let a guy go on beating up his wife just so that he didn't have to tell his own wife he'd screwed around on her?"

"Suzie never admitted it to him. He figured, without her testimony, there was no way he could prove it…"

"Detective?" The female officer who'd led Suzie out walked up.

"Yes?" Chantel faced her.

"I just thought you'd want to know." The uniformed woman included Jayden and Emma in her look. "She gave us a full confession…said she'd testify to all of it. She's got proof that Bill hit her and killed their baby.

Kyle was at their house at the time. He got roughed up pretty bad, too, trying to help her. But he got video on his cell phone of at least part of it…"

That, if Suzie had shared with them, would have been what Emma had needed to win her conviction. But then Suzie would have exposed Kyle…

"She was already half in love with the kid, though she wasn't acting on it," the officer said. "Bill guessed that she had feelings for Kyle, but other than that one time with Harris, she wasn't unfaithful to her husband. She and Kyle didn't start anything until after she divorced Bill and Kyle had turned nineteen."

Jayden had heard enough. He'd been had. Emma had been right. He'd refused to turn his back on Bill, had insisted on being there for the guy…because he hadn't been there for Emory?

Or just because the older man had been that good at seeming sincere? He'd really believed Bill had changed. That the man had been honoring his second chance.

Not sure to do with that, Jayden had never felt more lost. Emma could have died because he'd been wrong… "And when Bill got out from prison, and found out they were still together, he started in again," Emma said. The conclusion was obvious.

"No." Chantel's words yanked Jayden's steely gaze straight to her. He couldn't look away. "Bill left them alone. Except that he started sending Suzie cash every week. Turns out the apple didn't fall far from the tree, even though they hardly knew each other. She didn't tell Kyle about the money. Said she knew he wouldn't want them to have it, but they needed it so badly. Of course, he found out and couldn't stand that Suzie was taking money from his father, her ex-husband, and he got it in his head that she still loved Bill. He was as jealous of his dad as his dad was of him. The night he found out about the money was the first time he hit her."

Wait. "So Bill hasn't been near Suzie since he got out?"

"She says she hasn't seen him since he went to prison."

He'd been right about Bill.

Dear God, he'd been right. Weak with relief, and sad, too, Jayden stood there, allowing himself to give himself a little credit.

"But the lipstick...?" Emma said, frowning.

"Bill admitted that he left that threat on your back door," Chantel said as a flash from a news crew's camera went off, not far from them.

Jayden stepped closer to Emma, keeping her out of sight, as officers moved in the yard, and police cars, many with their lights still flashing, continued to block the road.

"When Jayden started questioning him," Chantel continued, "he thought you were gunning for him. After I got off the phone with the neighbor, I went in and told him what I knew. He let me know that he was protected by double jeopardy for whatever happened four years ago, at which time I told him that if we tied him to the current crimes, and we could, you could use the past to make his sentence more severe. I wasn't sure you could—" she looked at Emma "—but at that point I didn't care a whole lot about telling him the truth. That's when he told me that all he'd done was write that note on your back door. He didn't know Suzie was being beat up again. He was really shook up when he heard that."

Because he'd really changed? Because the second chance mattered? Or because he thought he was the only one allowed to punish *his* woman? The whole thing left Jayden feeling like he needed to puke.

"So the truck running me off the road...?"

"That was Kyle." The female officer—Jayden couldn't make out her name badge—spoke up. "He'd gotten home before Suzie on Monday night and was threatening to beat some sense into her if she didn't tell him where she'd been. She told him that she'd talked to you—" the officer nodded at Emma "—about Bill, thinking that that would appease him, but he knew how you'd gone after his dad and was certain that you were now gunning for him..."

"So...wait a minute," Emma said. "None of this explains how you all came to be outside when—"

"Bill swore to us that he hadn't seen his ex-wife since he got out and said that if anyone was hurting Suzie, it was Kyle. Said the kid had a vile temper. I'm guessing he inherited his father's temper," Chantel told them, "and depending on how much he witnessed between Suzie and Bill, or how much Suzie told him, he learned it at the hands of his father. He wasn't violent with her until Bill was released and Kyle found out about the money. Bill is the one who told us Kyle and Suzie lived together. We knew the two of you were heading over to tell Suzie that Bill was locked up. I tried to call to warn you. When you didn't pick up, I brought a backup team just to be safe. When we first arrived, Kyle had the three of you on the couch. Protocol said we had to call in a hostage team to try to talk him down, but before the team got here, he had Suzie by the neck. I made the call to shoot at first opportunity..."

Emma shook her head. Frowning.

"But the baseball caps..."

"Suzie works at a printing shop," Chantel said. "They do promotional items for businesses."

"Like hats," Emma said.

Chantel nodded. "She'd given Bill one of the hats. Said he looked sexy in it. I can only assume she thought his son looked sexy in one, too."

"They both loved her," Emma said right about the time Jayden was ready to lose his lunch. "And sadly, she probably loved them, too."

"I think you're right about that," the female officer said. And then, looking at Chantel, she said, "They've read her her rights, and have her in the back of the car. You want us to book her?"

Chantel looked at Emma, who shook her head. "She had a one-night affair with a neighbor. There's no crime in that…" Emma was saying.

"She withheld evidence…talking to you as she did Monday night. Not telling you the truth about Kyle…" Chantel interrupted.

Chantel seemed to think that her words might change Emma's mind, but Jayden knew better. No one was perfect. But Suzie was the victim here.

It wasn't pretty. In fact, the whole thing was damned ugly.

But Emma was going to try to give her a second chance at life.

Chapter 25

She was reeling. Ready to fall over. And still standing. Maybe because it let her lean against Jayden. To stay connected to him. Emma focused on his warmth as he used the key she'd given him to open her front door. They'd pick up her car in the morning.

At that moment, just getting inside her gated community where there were no flashing lights and no more questions, from police or press, had been the priority.

Jayden had to shower. His clothes were blood-spattered. She followed him into her bedroom, watched as he dropped the bag he'd grabbed during a brief stop at his place, at the end of her bed.

In all the nights they'd spent together, he'd never brought any personal items into her home before. She'd given him a spare toothbrush—one she'd received free from the dentist—and that had been the extent of his ablutions in her home.

He hadn't asked her if she'd wanted him to stay over. She hadn't said she did. He'd just said, as they'd left the scene, that he had to stop by his place, and she'd nodded. Waited in the car. And seen him come out with the bag.

"I thought you were dead." She'd told herself to leave it alone. Leave *him* alone. Parts of her didn't listen. Because all of her needed him. Really needed him.

"I'm fine." His words didn't take away the sting.

"You might not have been if Chantel and her team hadn't been outside."

"It was a risk I had to take."

Yeah, that pissed her off.

He stripped off his shirt. Walked toward her bathroom. "No, you didn't," she said, following him. From one vantage point, outside, she could see herself following him, all shrewlike. From another—*in*side—she couldn't stop herself.

"You could have stayed on that couch. Let the news come on and show him that Bill really was in custody. That could have calmed him enough for us, or Suzie, to get him to drop the gun."

Undoing the button on his shorts, he gave her a nod. "It could have. I had to take the surest way to save your life."

"You have no respect for your own."

With his shorts undone, but still hanging off his hips, he dropped his hands. Eyes narrowed, he looked at her. "Come again?"

"You were willing to throw your life away, like it doesn't even matter," she told him. And then took a couple of steps closer. "Well, I have to tell you, it matters to me. And I'm sure to your parents and to a whole lot of other people, too. You might find it worthless, but it's got value. A lot of it."

Okay, she was coming unglued.

He didn't grin. She had to give him credit for that. But he cocked his head, and that was just about as bad.

"You can go ahead and think you're another Tom Smith, Jayden. You can find justification for shutting out life as some sort of penance, but I've got to tell you, you're just taking the coward's way out. Running from the tough stuff. And hurting the people who love you, too, which is even more of waste."

"I am, am I?"

"Yes." She'd been right about Bill Heber four years before. And she was right about this, too.

"And you can speak for the people who love me, why? You've spoken to them?" He took a step closer to her, not menacing at all. More like he was toying with her. Or challenging her.

She didn't like either option.

"One of them." So there. He thought he knew it all, and…

She stared at him. Emotionally exhausted. Not sure how much fight she had left in her.

He took a step back. Smart man.

"I don't think I'm Mr. Smith, by the way," Jayden told her. "Listening to Emory's mother…she divorced him because he pretty much forced her to, but it's clear she still loves him. That she needs him. And his daughter, and her kids…it's like he's robbing Peter to pay Paul, as my mother would say. And another one from her— two wrongs don't make a right."

"I think I'd like your mother."

"I'm sure she'd like you, too."

Was he ever going to take those shorts off? Get in the shower, so they could go to bed? Couldn't he see she was rocking on her feet?

"We've known each other…how long?" she asked him. Because she was thinking the answer.

"I don't know. Two years. Three maybe."

Three and a half, and she was counting. She'd been lead on a case, opposing parole, and he'd been at the hearing, giving his report on preliminary housing interviews and recommendations. He'd recommended the woman for parole.

She'd won. The woman had hung herself in her cell six months later.

She'd been right. Professionally. Facts had surfaced after the woman's death that had substantiated that.

But he'd been right, too. Knowing that the woman valued a second chance so much she'd taken her life when that chance had been denied her.

"What's it matter how long we've known each other?" he asked, curious.

"It doesn't."

Or did it?

"I was wrong to lash out at you earlier today, about… you know, not being perfect. Insinuating that you were failing the real challenge—learning to forgive yourself," she said.

"Okay."

"I was upset, thinking you were giving yourself permission to not have a life, with Emory's father as your justification."

"And it would have mattered to you so much…if I was like him?"

"I don't know." She shrugged. Picked a piece of lint off the carpet. Adjusted one of the pillows on the bed.

Wondered what was in his bag. Did he normally sleep in pajamas? Had he brought them over?

"What you said about the real challenge being learning to forgive yourself…" he said, moving to the end of the bed. "You might have been right about that."

She glanced at him. "You think so?"

"Do you?"

"I know I need to be a little better about it, myself," she said. Poor Ms. Shadow Side. Emma had shunned a part of herself, a valid, real, worthy part, because she couldn't handle the excruciating pain life had brought her. She'd been running away from herself. "I didn't want my baby to die, Jayden. I already loved it so much…"

She was crying. She couldn't believe it. Tears streamed out of her eyes and down her face. She'd almost lost Jayden that night.

Lost him before she'd even had him. Except as a play toy.

He nodded. "I know."

"How could you know? You weren't there. You didn't even know me then."

"But I know you now."

He wasn't touching her. The bed practically separated them, with her at the side and him at the end. And yet…she'd never felt so intimately connected to him.

"I know you now, too." Her throat started to dry up.

Jutting his chin, he nodded again then said, "You looked like you wanted to let Suzie go tonight."

"She made mistakes. Maybe some big ones. But she was the victim. Not the criminal. She didn't tell me that he was the one hitting her when I spoke to her Monday night, but she could have argued that she wasn't under obligation to testify against her spouse."

"She's not his spouse."

"I think she is," Emma told him. "I noticed that she had a wedding ring on a chain around her neck. I think we're going to find out that they were married."

Sometimes life was hard. Too hard. Like when you got on a motorcycle to please the man you thought you loved and your baby died. Or you tried to give a guy the life he thought he wanted and he died instead.

And sometimes life blessed you, too. Didn't it?

"I found out something tonight," she said, thinking about courage. About reasons to live. To get up every day. To fight for justice.

"What's that?"

"I don't want to know what my life would be like without you in it."

Yep, she got another nod. She could almost have predicted that one.

"You going to take your shower?" she asked.

He didn't nod. At least he did her that favor, saved her from one more of those infuriating nods. Stripping off his shorts, and then his briefs, he strode naked to her shower, turned on the water, and stepped inside.

Good thing, too.

He didn't see the tears, or hear the sobs, that burst from her as she undressed, turned out the bedroom light and crawled into bed.

Jayden took a long shower. He washed away the blood of the man who'd been shot that night. And maybe a bit of the blood that he'd had on his conscience for more than a decade. He'd done Emory Smith a huge disservice.

And maybe he'd given the boy his greatest desire in life, too.

Who knew why some died young and others lived past the times their minds even knew who they were?

Jayden sure as hell didn't.

He'd been wrong about Bill Heber—the man really *had* killed his own child in his wife's body. And he'd been right, too—Bill had honored his second chance.

And loved his wife—albeit in a sick way that was unacceptable.

Jayden stayed under the spray after all but the bathroom light went out. Until the water ran cold. And then, reaching for one of the two towels he'd seen on a rack, he dried himself off. Top to bottom. Feet last.

A guy needed some things he could rely on. Some things that didn't change.

But if he was going to be true to himself, to keep his word and honor life—both that had been and that which was left—he had to know when change was necessary and when it wasn't. He had to have the courage to face that change. Or to turn away from it.

No matter how much it hurt, he had to make a choice.

Hanging his towel, he turned out the light. Padded across the carpet, pulled down the covers and slid beneath them.

Emma didn't move. After several nights in bed with her, he'd grown to recognize the sound of her breathing as she slept. He didn't hear it.

She might still be awake.

Hands shaking, he slid up against her back, pressed his chin over her shoulder and whispered in her ear. "I don't ever want to know what life is like without you in it."

She didn't turn. Didn't seem to move at all.

"I don't know what the future brings," he told her. "I don't know what mistakes I might make. I don't know if I'll ever be an asshole again. But I know I'll make mistakes. And be selfish sometimes… I can promise to always put your happiness before my own. I might not do it." He had to stop. Emotion clogged his throat. He could feel every breath she took. And took them with her. Calming. Wanting to sleep.

Just lie there with her and sleep.

"I'm not always going to agree with you." Her words entered the air on a whisper.

"I'm going to be right sometimes," he told her.

"I don't want to know what my life would be like without you in it." She was crying again as she repeated her earlier words.

He turned her over, blinking away a moisture that astounded him. Scared him, even. No one had ever meant to him what she did.

In such a short time.

Or over time.

Maybe he'd been heading in her direction from that first case three years before. Maybe he'd needed more time to heal. Or to pay.

"I don't want to live without you," he told her, looking her straight in the eye in the darkness. He kissed her then.

Slowly. Softly. He was hard. But not needy. Not really even wanting all that much at the moment.

"I want to have a baby, though."

He'd known, of course. She wasn't going to be complete without knowing what it felt like to have her baby grow to fruition inside her.

"I'm not sure I can be a good father." But he knew a man who'd been a darn good example. And might be willing to be a teacher, too.

"See, that's where having two of us trying to have a relationship kind of works, because I *am* sure you can become a good father." Emma's words knocked him off course again.

And onto this new road, once more.

"You're a good father every single time you give one of your clients a second chance," she told him. "You have faith in them. You look after them. You counsel them. You save them from themselves sometimes. And, when necessary, you discipline them. Even when it means holding them accountable for their mistakes. Even when it hurts you to do so."

Had his father ever held him accountable? Jayden couldn't be sure. He'd known there were lines he couldn't cross. So he hadn't really tried.

His father had given him space in which to fly. And maybe kept him tethered on some invisible parental line, too.

But he was a man now. Not a boy. Or a teenager. Or a college kid. He was a grown man. It was time for him to find out if he had what it took to fly without protection.

"I don't want to know what it would be like to spend another night alone in my house with you alone in yours," he said.

She was crying again. He could feel the sobs in her body against his.

"I love you, Emma Martin."

"I love you, too."

The words cascaded around him. Through him. Settling in.

"So...you think we can always remember those we've lost, but forgive ourselves?" He had to ask.

"I do."

"You up for sharing this place with a feral, no-named cat, who you probably won't ever see?" Made sense that they'd live at her place, not his. Hers was ten times as nice.

And gated. Didn't mean harm couldn't come to her there...but there was less chance of it.

"The way I picture it, the cat's going to have a name as soon as I see it and figure out if it's male or female. And, within a month, he or she will be sleeping on the end of our bed."

Yeah, she would see it that way.

And she'd probably be right.

"You think you'll be up for sharing this place with a baby we might make at some point?" she countered.

It would take him some time. He didn't kid himself about that. But for her...and for the child he so badly wanted to have with her...

"You think you can figure a way to get that cat out from under my bed and over here?"

"You going to help me?"

He'd said he didn't want to spend another night in his home with her in hers, so... "Of course."

"Then yes, I can get the cat out."

"And I can share this space with whatever family we make together, canine, feline, human...who knows... maybe even some more fish."

He wasn't thinking it would be easy. Wasn't sure

how good he'd actually be at it, but he'd do it. And give it his all.

Because one thing Jayden knew about himself that just didn't change…

He was a man of his word.

* * * * *

*If you enjoyed this great romance,
keep an eye out for other books in the
Where Secrets are Safe miniseries,
available now from Harlequin!*

WE HOPE YOU ENJOYED
THIS BOOK FROM

HARLEQUIN
ROMANTIC
SUSPENSE

Danger. Passion. Drama.

These heart-racing page-turners will keep you guessing to the very end. Experience the thrill of unexpected plot twists and irresistible chemistry.

4 NEW BOOKS AVAILABLE EVERY MONTH!

#2095 COLTON 911: FAMILY DEFENDER
Colton 911: Grand Rapids • by Tara Taylor Quinn
After a one-night stand with Riley Colton, Charlize Kent is
pregnant. She may be reluctant to have her baby's father in
her life, but with someone threatening her little family, she
knows she needs Riley's help to keep their baby safe.

#2096 EXPOSING COLTON SECRETS
The Coltons of Kansas • by Marie Ferrarella
When Gwen Harrison's controlling boyfriend hires
PI Brooks Colton to "check up on her," she makes the most
of it and recruits him to help find her missing mother. But
when a body is found on a Colton Contrustion demolition
site, the stakes on this cold case get exponentially higher!

#2097 IN THE RANCHER'S PROTECTION
The McCall Adventure Ranch • by Beth Cornelison
Carrie French is escaping an abusive husband when she
seeks refuge at the Double M Ranch—and forms a friendship
with ranch hand Luke Wright. When they end up stranded in
the Rocky Mountains, Carrie's past threatens their future—
and Luke must ensure they make it out alive.

#2098 RESCUE FROM DARKNESS
by Bonnie Vanak
Belle North, a doctor, must team up with the suspicious and
emotionally wounded Kyle Anderson to find the child missing
from a clinic funded by her family, without losing her heart in
the process. But danger awaits both of them, for the person
who kidnapped Anna will stop at nothing to keep her from
being found.

SPECIAL EXCERPT FROM

HHARLEQUIN
ROMANTIC SUSPENSE

Carrie French is escaping an abusive husband when she seeks refuge at the Double M Ranch—and forms a friendship with ranch hand Luke Wright. When they end up stranded in the Rocky Mountains, Carrie's past threatens their future—and Luke must ensure they make it out alive.

Read on for a sneak preview of
In the Rancher's Protection,
the next book in The McCall Adventure Ranch series by Beth Cornelison.

What could she tell him? Her situation was horrid. Frightening. Desperate. And that was why she had to keep Luke out of it. She had to protect him from the ugliness that her life had become and the danger Joseph posed.

But he was standing there, all devastatingly handsome, earnest and worried about her. She had to tell him something. The lies she'd told friends for years to hide the truth tasted all the more sour as they formed on her tongue, so she discarded them for one that was more palatable.

"A few years back I made some…poor choices," she began slowly, picking her words carefully. "And I'm trying to correct those mistakes. Until I get my life back on track, my finances are going to be tight. But I can't make the fresh start I need if I accept money from you or anyone else. I need to do this by myself. To be truly independent and self-sufficient."

"Poor choices, huh?" A hum rumbled from his throat, and he twisted his lips. "We all make those at some point in our lives, don't we?"

With his gaze still locked on her, he inched his palms from her shoulders to her neck, and his thumbs now reached the bottom edge of her chin. His work-roughened hands were paradoxically gentle. The skimming strokes of his calloused fingers against her skin pooled a honeyed lethargy inside her. Reason told her to pull away, but some competing force inside her rooted her to the spot to bask in the tenderness she'd had far too little of in her adult life.

Luke is the kind of man you should be with, the kind of man you deserve.

Don't miss
In the Rancher's Protection *by Beth Cornelison,*
available July 2020 wherever
Harlequin Romantic Suspense
books and ebooks are sold.

Harlequin.com

Get 4 FREE REWARDS!

We'll send you 2 FREE Books plus 2 FREE Mystery Gifts.

Harlequin Romantic Suspense books are heart-racing page-turners with unexpected plot twists and irresistible chemistry that will keep you guessing to the very end.

FREE Value Over **$20**

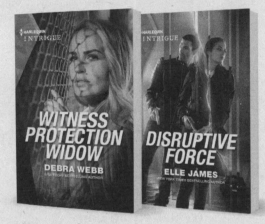

Love *Harlequin romance?*

DISCOVER.

Be the first to find out about promotions, news and exclusive content!

 Facebook.com/HarlequinBooks

Twitter.com/HarlequinBooks

 Instagram.com/HarlequinBooks

Pinterest.com/HarlequinBooks

ReaderService.com

EXPLORE.

Sign up for the Harlequin e-newsletter and download a free book from any series at **TryHarlequin.com**

CONNECT.

Join our Harlequin community to share your thoughts and connect with other romance readers!
Facebook.com/groups/HarlequinConnection